"Hellfire, I never could stand seeing a woman cry!"

With one swift, sure movement Jace's mouth captured Clara's. She felt her knees go weak. She had wanted Jace to kiss her, she realized, from the first moment she'd looked at him.

With a little whimper, she melted into his heat. Instinctively she rose on tiptoe, straining upward to find him.

"Oh, damn it, don't, Clara…" Jace groaned in feeble protest. Then his big hands groped for her through the nightgown and lifted her high and hard against him…

* * *

The Horseman's Bride
Harlequin® Historical #983—March 2010

the Horseman's Bride

ELIZABETH LANE

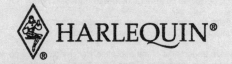

HARLEQUIN®

TORONTO • NEW YORK • LONDON
AMSTERDAM • PARIS • SYDNEY • HAMBURG
STOCKHOLM • ATHENS • TOKYO • MILAN • MADRID
PRAGUE • WARSAW • BUDAPEST • AUCKLAND

ISBN-13: 978-0-373-29583-8

THE HORSEMAN'S BRIDE

Copyright © 2010 by Elizabeth Lane

To Scott, Tiffany, Adam, Alec and Olivia.
Thank you for blessing my life.

Chapter One

~~~
Dutchman's Creek, Colorado
June 7, 1919
~~~

Clara Seavers closed the paddock gate and looped the chain over the wooden post. The morning air was crisp, the sky as blue as a jay's wing above the snowcapped Rockies. It was a perfect day for a ride.

Swinging into the saddle, she urged the two-year-old gelding to a trot. Foxfire, as she'd named the leggy chestnut colt, had been foaled on the Seavers Ranch. Clara had broken him herself. He could run like the wind, but he was skittish and full of ginger. Keeping him under control required constant attention, which was why Clara allowed no one other than herself to ride him.

This morning the colt was responding well. With a press of her boot heels, Clara opened him up to a canter. She could feel the power in the solid body, feel the young horse's impatience to break away and gallop full out across the open pastureland. Only her discipline held him back.

For as long as she could remember, Clara had wanted to breed and train fine horses. She'd passed up her parents' offer of college to stay on the ranch and pursue her dream. Now, at nineteen, she could see that dream coming true. Foxfire was the first of several colts and fillies with champion quarter horse bloodlines. In time, she vowed, the Seavers Ranch would be as well-known for prize horses as it was for cattle.

Gazing across the distant fields, she could see her grandma Gustavson's farm. Days had passed since Clara's last visit to her grandmother. It was high time she paid her another call.

For years Clara's parents had begged the old woman to move into their spacious family ranch house. But Mary Gustavson was as iron willed as her Viking forebearers. She was determined to live out her days on the land she'd homesteaded with her husband, Soren, in the two-story log house where they'd raised seven children.

So far Mary had done all right. For a woman in her seventies, her health was fair, and the rental of pastureland to the Seavers family gave her enough money to live on. She did her own chores and borrowed the ranch hands for occasional heavy work. But seventy-two was too old to be living alone. The family worried increasingly that something would go wrong and no one would be there to help her.

Clara pushed Foxfire to a lope, feeling the joyful stretch of the colt's body between her knees. There was an old barbed-wire fence between the ranch land and her grandmother's property. But the wires were down in several places where the cattle had butted against the posts. It would, as always, be easy to jump the horse through.

They came up fast on the fence, with Clara leaning forward in the saddle. She was urging her mount to a jump when she caught sight of the gleaming new barbed wire at the level of the colt's chest.

Some fool had fixed the fence!

With an unladylike curse, she wrenched the reins to one side. They managed to avoid the fence, but the pressure on his bit-tender mouth sent Foxfire into a frenzy. He reared and stumbled sideways. Thrown from the saddle, Clara slammed to the ground. For a terrifying instant the colt teetered above her, hoofs flailing. Then he regained his balance, wheeled and galloped away.

Clara lay gasping on her back. Cautiously she moved her arms and legs. Nothing felt broken, but the hard landing had knocked the wind out of her. She took a moment to gather her wits. First she needed to catch her breath. Then she would have to get up and catch her horse. After that she intended to hunt down the addle-pated so-and-so who'd replaced the sagging wire and give him a piece of her mind.

"Are you all right?" The voice that spoke was distinctly male, with a gravelly undertone. The face that loomed into sight above her was square-boned with a long, stubbled jaw. Tawny curls, plastered with sweat and dust, tumbled over blazing blue eyes.

It flashed through her mind that her virtue could be in serious danger. But the stranger leaning over her didn't look lustful. He looked concerned—and furious.

Clara struggled to speak but the fall had left her breathless. It was all she could do to return his scowl.

"What in hell's name did you think you were doing?" he growled. "You damn near ran that horse straight into the wire. You could've cut its chest to pieces and broken your own fool neck in the bargain."

Summoning her strength, Clara rose up on her elbows and found her voice. "What right do you have to question me?" she retorted. "Who are you and what are you doing on Seavers land?"

His gaze flickered over the straining buttons of her plaid shirt before returning to her face. His boots, Clara noticed, were expensively made. Most likely the rough-looking fellow had stolen them.

"Begging your pardon." His voice was razor edged. "Until you fell off your horse, I was on the *other* side of the fence—Mrs. Gustavson's fence, if I'm to believe her, and I do. She's hired me to make some repairs."

Fueled by annoyance, Clara scrambled to her feet. One hand brushed the damp earth off the seat of her denim jeans. "Mary Gustavson is my grandmother, and this fence has been down for as long as I can remember. I ride this way when I come to visit her. Whose idea was it to put the wire up?"

"Mine." His jaw was unshaven, his clothes faded and dusty. He looked like a trail bum, but his tone was imperious. "She told me to look around and fix whatever needed fixing. I assumed that included the fence."

Clara glared up at him. He towered a full head above her five-foot-four-inch height. "You must've seen me coming," she said. "Why didn't you shout and warn me?"

"How was I to know you were going to run the damned horse into the fence?"

His mention of the horse reminded her. Glancing past the stranger's broad shoulder she saw Foxfire grazing in the far distance. The skittish colt had experienced a scare. He was going to be the very devil to round up.

"Well, no thanks to you, my horse has bolted. It's going to take a lot of walking to catch him so you'll have to excuse me." She turned to walk away, but his voice stopped her.

"I've got a horse. Allow me to help you—on my own time, not your grandmother's."

It was a decent offer. But his condescending manner made Clara want to slap his face. The man looked like a tramp. But he talked like someone who was used to giving orders. What gave him the right to boss her around?

"I'll thank you for the loan of your horse," she said. "Aside from that, I won't need your help."

His scathing eyes took her measure. He shook his head. "My horse is a stallion. I doubt you could handle him. Stay here and I'll catch your colt myself."

Clara stood her ground. "Foxfire's been spooked. You won't get within fifty paces of him."

"And you can?"

"I broke and trained him. He knows my voice. And I've been riding since I was old enough to walk. I can handle any horse, including your stallion."

Again he shook his head. "I watched you damn near break your silly neck once. I'm not going to stand here and watch you do it again, especially not on my horse. If you want to come along, you can ride behind me."

Without another word he turned and strode away. Only then did Clara catch sight of his horse, grazing on the far side of a big cottonwood tree. It raised its head at the man's approach. Clara's breath caught in her throat.

The rangy bay would have dwarfed most of the cow ponies on the ranch. Its body was flawlessly proportioned, the chest broad and muscular, the head like sculpted bronze. Clara was a good judge of horseflesh. She had never seen a more magnificent animal.

The stranger was halfway to the horse by now. "Wait!" Clara sprinted after him. "Wait, I'm coming with you!"

At close range the stallion was even more impressive. Perfect lines, flaring nostrils. A Thoroughbred, almost certainly. No doubt the man had stolen it. In all good conscience, she should report him to the town marshal. But right now that was the furthest thing from Clara's mind.

A stallion among stallions!

And two of her best mares were coming into season. She was not about to let this horse get away.

The man probably needed money—why else would

he be working for her grandmother? Maybe he would sell her the stallion for a fair price. But did she want the risk of buying a stolen horse? Maybe she could borrow the splendid creature long enough to service her mares.

She waited while the stranger mounted, then gripped his proffered arm. His taut muscles lifted her without effort as she swung up behind him.

Unaccustomed to the extra weight on its haunches, the stallion snorted and danced. Clara had to grip the stranger's waist to keep from sliding off. Beneath the worn chambray shirt, his body was rock hard. He smelled of sweat and sagebrush, with a subtle whiff of her grandmother's lye soap lingering behind his ears. A warm tingle of awareness crept through Clara's body.

She gave herself a mental slap. What did she know about this man? He could be a shyster or a criminal on the run, or worse.

What had possessed a sensible woman like Mary Gustavson to hire him? For all she knew, the scruffy fellow could be planning to slit her throat in the night and steal everything in the house.

Who was this stranger? What was his business?

For her grandmother's sake, she needed to find out. And for her own sake, she'd be keeping a close eye on him—and his stallion.

Jace Denby took the stallion at an easy trot. He didn't want to startle the colt—nor did he want the stallion to rear and dump Miss Clara Seavers on her pretty little ass. He knew who she was, of course. Mary

Gustavson had talked about her granddaughter all through supper last night. When he'd seen the girl flying across the pasture on a chestnut colt that matched the hue of her unruly curls, he'd recognized her at once.

And the instant she'd opened her full-blown rosebud mouth he'd known she was a spoiled brat. Just the kind of female he wanted nothing to do with. Especially since she was so damnably attractive. He couldn't afford the distraction of a pretty young thing accustomed to getting her own way. She'd flirt, wheedle and pout to win him. Then, when he broke her heart, she'd be out for his blood. For him, that could be highly dangerous.

If he had any sense he'd dump Miss Clara Seavers off in the grass and ride for the hills.

She clung to his back, the pressure of her firm breasts burning through his shirt. He hadn't been within touching distance of a woman in months, and this intimate contact wasn't doing him any good. The heat in his groin was fast becoming a bonfire, igniting thoughts of stripping away her light flannel shirt and cradling those breasts in his palms, stroking them until the nipples rose and hardened and her breath came in little gasps of need...

Hellfire, just the idea of it made him harder than a hickory stick. Jace swore under his breath. As a man on the run, it was imperative that he keep his mind above his belt line where it belonged. The last thing he needed was a saucy little hellion like this one pressing her tits against his back.

"You can call me Tanner," he said, using the alias

he'd given Mary Gustavson. "And you, if I'm not mistaken, would be Miss Clara Seavers."

She was silent for a moment. Her knees nested against the backs of his legs, fitting as snugly as the rest of her would fit him, given the chance…

Damn!

"What else did my grandmother tell you?" she asked.

"That you could ride anything on four legs and dance until the band went home."

A lusty little laugh rippled through her body. Jace felt it as much as heard it. "I take it you didn't believe her. Otherwise I'd be sitting where you are."

"No comment." Jace's gaze swept over the pasture, the silky summer grass, the distant foothills dotted with scrub and blooming wildflowers, the soaring peaks of the Rockies and the endless sky above them. Over the past few months he'd learned to savor every day of freedom as if it might be his last. Today was no exception.

"I know a fine animal when I see one," she said. "What's your stallion's name?"

"Doesn't have one."

"Why on earth not? A horse as grand as this one deserves a name, at least."

"Why?" Jace was playing her now, parrying to keep her at a distance. "Does a horse care whether he has a name or not?"

"No. But maybe I do." In the silence that followed, Jace could imagine her ripe lips pursed in a willful pout.

He forced a chuckle. "So you name him. Go ahead."

Again she fell into a pause. The stallion trotted beneath them, its gait like flowing silk. "Galahad," she said. "I'll name him Galahad, after the knight in the King Arthur tales."

"Fine. Galahad's as good a name as any."

"May I ask how you came by him?"

"You're wondering whether I stole him, aren't you?"

"Did you?" she demanded.

"I borrowed him. He belongs to my sister." That much was true, at least. Never mind that she wouldn't believe him. He didn't give a damn about her good opinion. He only planned on staying until he earned enough to move on. Maybe he could make it to California before the cold weather set in. Or maybe Mexico. A man could get lost in Mexico.

"So how do you come to be working for my grandmother?" Her voice dripped suspicion.

"I came by the ranch a couple of days ago looking for work. She was kind enough to hire me and feed me in the bargain. She's one fine lady, Mrs. Gustavson."

"That she is. And my family would kill anybody who tried to take advantage of her, or harm her in any way."

"I take it that's a warning."

"You can take it any way you like." Her arms tightened around him as the horse jumped a shallow ditch. The chestnut colt had raised its head and was watching their approach. Jace slowed the stallion to a walk.

Galahad. At least Clara had chosen a sensible name.

Hollis Rumford, his sister Ruby's late, unlamented husband, had probably called the horse Archduke Puffington of Rumfordshire or something equally silly. Hollis had cared more about his damned horses than he'd cared about his wife and daughters. The last Jace had seen of the bastard, he'd been lying in a pool of blood with three bullet holes in his chest. Jace's only regret was that the shots hadn't hit lower.

Jace hadn't planned on keeping the stallion. But he'd come to realize that traveling on horseback through open country was safer than going by rail or road. And, for all his resolve to remain unattached, he'd developed a fondness for the big bay. As long as Galahad understood who was boss, he was amiable company. The fact that he could outrun any horse west of the Mississippi gave Jace even more reason to keep him.

"Stop." Clara's fingers pressed Jace's ribs. The chestnut colt watched them warily, poised to bolt at the slightest perceived threat. Jace halted the stallion, holding steady as she shifted behind him. "Stay here," she hissed, easing to the ground.

Jace watched her walk away. Despite his teasing, he had to admit she had a horsewoman's grace, an easy way of moving like the sway of long grass in the wind. Her mud-streaked denims—made for a boy, most likely—clung to her hips in a most unboyish way, outlining her firm little buttocks. Her hair fluttered down her back in a glorious tangle of mahogany curls.

Clara had an hourglass figure, her womanly curves offset by a tiny waist. Jace couldn't help comparing her with Eileen Summers, the governor's niece he'd been courting back in Missouri. Eileen was as lean as a saluki, her champagne hair flawlessly sculpted, her usual silken gown skimming her elegant bones. In her slim, white fingers, she'd held the key to a world of power and influence—a world that, for Jace, had vanished with his sister's frantic telephone call. He'd had no chance to tell Eileen what had happened and why he had to leave. But that was likely for the best.

He had no doubt that word had spread like wildfire after he'd left. And the very proper Miss Summers wouldn't have wanted anything to do with an accused murderer on the run.

"Easy, boy…" Clara walked toward the nervous colt, the tall grass swishing against her legs. One hand held the small apple she carried for such emergencies. The stranger sat his horse, his cool gaze following her every movement.

Tanner. Was that his first name or his last name? No matter, it probably wasn't his name at all. He had the look and manner of a man with something to hide. She would need to have a serious talk with her grandmother. Mary Gustavson was far too trusting.

Maybe she should talk with her father as well. Judd Seavers would probably run the stranger off the place with a shotgun. But then the stallion would be gone. She would lose the chance to add his splendid bloodline to next spring's foals.

Her father had enough on his mind. She wouldn't trouble him about the stranger. Not yet, at least.

"Easy..." She held out her hand with the apple on the flat of her palm. Foxfire pricked up his ears. His nostrils twitched. He took a tentative step toward her, thrusting his muzzle toward the treat. "That's it. Good boy!" As the colt munched the apple, Clara caught the bridle with her free hand. Moving cautiously, she eased herself back into the saddle.

The man who called himself Tanner was grinning at her. "Right fine job of horse-catching, Miss Clara," he drawled. "Couldn't have done it better myself."

"You needn't patronize me, Mr. Tanner. There's not that much to catching a horse that *I've* trained." Clara turned the colt back toward the last open section of fence. "Why not build a gate here? We come this way all the time to visit my grandmother. If we can't get through, we'll have to go by way of the road. It's three times the distance."

"Not a bad suggestion. But I'll need to get the boss's approval and see what's in the shed that I can use." He pulled his horse alongside hers. "Meanwhile, as long as we're going the same way, I hope you won't mind my company."

Clara bit back a caustic retort. Tanner's high-handed manner made her bristle. But she'd made up her mind to learn more about the stranger. Here was her chance. She slowed the colt to a walk.

"You seem to know plenty about me," she said. "But I don't know anything about you. Where did you come from?"

Tanner's narrowed eyes swept the grassy pastureland, looking everywhere but at her. In the silence, a meadowlark called from its perch atop a fence post.

"I grew up in Missouri," he said at last. "But whatever kept me there is long gone. Drifting's become a way of life for me. Can't say as I mind it."

"No family?"

He shook his head. "None that I've kept track of. My parents died years ago. The rest moved on."

What about your sister? The one you said lent you the stallion?

The question burned on the tip of Clara's tongue. She bit it back. Confronting Tanner would only put him on guard. Let him go on feeding her lies. He'd already confirmed her suspicions that he was holding something back. Give him enough rope and he was bound to hang himself.

All she needed was a little patience.

But he wasn't making it easy for her.

Why did the man have to be so tall and broad-shouldered? Why did he have to have a chiseled face and eyes like twin blue flames? Right now those eyes looked as if they could burn right through her clothes. Any town boy who looked at her like that would be asking to get his face slapped.

The man was dangerous, she reminded herself. He could be a fugitive, even a murderer. She'd be a fool to let him get too close.

"You don't sound like a trail bum, Mr. Tanner," she said. "You speak like a man who's had some education."

"Any man who can read has the means to educate himself. And it's just Tanner, not Mr. Tanner."

"But do you have a profession? A trade?"

"If I did, would I be out here mending fences?" He gave her a sharp glance. "Would you care to tell me why you're being so nosy?"

Clara met his blazing eyes, resisting the impulse to look away. "I'm very protective of my grandmother," she said. "She's an old woman, and she's much too trusting."

"But I take it you're not so...trusting." He was playing with her now, brazenly confident that he could twist her around his finger. Damn his lying hide! He'd probably charmed her grandmother the same way.

If it weren't for the stallion, she'd run him off the property with a bullwhip!

"Let's just say I'm not a fool," she snapped.

"I can see you're not. And neither is your grandmother. She doesn't keep that loaded shotgun by the door for nothing. If she thought I had any intention of harming her, I'd be picking buckshot out of my rear."

"We'll see about that!" Out of patience, she kneed the colt to a gallop. Tanner didn't try to follow her, but as she shot across the pasture, Clara became aware of a sound behind her. Even without looking back, she knew what it was.

The wretched man was laughing at her!

Jace watched her ride away, her delicious little rump bouncing in the saddle. Miss Clara Seavers was one sweet little spitfire. He'd enjoyed teasing her, but now it was time to back off and leave her alone. The last thing he needed was that bundle of trouble poking into his past.

Mrs. Mary Gustavson was a fine woman. He would miss her conversation and her cooking. But as soon as he finished the work she needed done it would be time to move on. There would be other towns, other farms, other pretty girls to tease. As long as there was a price on his head, nothing was forever. Not for him. It was keep moving or face his death at the end of a rope.

At least his sister Ruby and her two little girls would be all right.

Hollis Rumford had been considered a fine catch when she'd married him ten years ago. Heir to a farm equipment company, he'd been as charming as he was handsome. But his infidelity, drunkenness and abuse had made Ruby's life a living hell. Jace had seen the ugly bruises. He had dried his sister's tears. Lord help him, he wasn't the least bit sorry Hollis was dead. But he would always be sorry he hadn't acted sooner. Maybe if he'd taken Ruby and her daughters away from that monster, he'd still have his old life—his friends, his fine apartment in Springfield, his work as a field geologist and engineer and a future in politics that might have taken him all the way to the Missouri Statehouse or the U.S. Congress. Marriage to Eileen Summers, the governor's niece, would have opened many doors. Now those doors were closed to him forever.

But he hadn't acted in vain, Jace reminded himself.

Now Ruby would be a respectable widow with a fine house and plenty of money. After a proper mourning period, she'd be free to find a new husband—a decent man, God willing, who'd treat her well and be a good father to her girls.

That had to be worth something, didn't it?

Clara found her grandmother seated on the porch in her old cane rocker, her hands busy peeling a bucket of potatoes from the root cellar.

"Hello, dear." Mary Gustavson was tall and raw-boned, her thick white hair swept back from her wrinkled face. Blessed with strong features and corn-flower-blue eyes, she looked like an older version of her daughter Hannah, Clara's mother.

"Good morning, Grandma." Clara swung off her horse, looped the reins over the hitching rail and bounded up the steps to give the old woman a hug. Mary had raised seven children, buried a husband and baby and worked the farm alone for the past nineteen years. Loss and hard times had burnished her spirit to a serene glow that radiated from her face. Clara and her younger siblings, Daniel and Katy, adored her.

"I was just thinking about you, and here you are." Even after decades in America, Mary spoke with a lilting Norwegian accent. "Sit down and visit with me awhile."

"Wait, I'll help you with those potatoes." Clara hurried into the house and returned with an extra paring knife. Sitting on the edge of the porch, she picked up a potato. As she sliced off thin strips of peel, she wondered how best to bring up the subject of her grandmother's new hired man.

"So how is your family?" Mary asked. "Are they all well?"

Clara nodded. "Daniel's got a girlfriend in town. He's pestering Papa to let him drive the car so he can take her for a ride."

Mary chuckled. "I can hardly believe it! It seems like yesterday he was pulling on my apron strings."

"My pesky little brother is sixteen. I can hardly believe it myself. And Katy, at the wise old age of thirteen, says she's never going to let a boy kiss her for as long as she lives."

"Oh, my! That will change in a year or two."

Clara cut up the peeled potato, dropped it in the kettle and picked up another one. "Not too soon, I hope. Sometimes I think she has the right idea."

"And what about you?"

Clara glanced up into Mary's narrowed, knowing eyes. She knew that expression well. Her grandmother had always sensed when something was troubling her. What was she seeing now? Bright eyes? A hot, flushed face?

"I take it you've met my new hired man," Mary said.

Chapter Two

Clara felt the heat rise in her face. If she could feel it, she knew her grandmother could see it. "He's fixed the pasture fence," she said. "I very nearly rode Foxfire into the new barbed wire. Whose idea was it to fix that fence anyway? The wire's been down for years."

"It was Tanner's. But when he brought it up, I thought it was a good idea. I'm getting too old to chase your family's calves out of my garden."

"Oh, dear! Why didn't you say something, Grandma? If we'd known about the calves, my dad would've fixed that fence a long time ago."

Mary shrugged. "Judd is a busy man. I didn't want to bother him about such a little thing. But never mind, it will be fixed now."

"I suggested to Tanner that he put in a gate. That way we can still cut across the pastures when we come to visit you."

"Oh? And what did he say to that?"

"He said he'd have to ask the boss."

"He did, did he?" Mary chuckled as she picked up another potato. "I must say, I like a man who knows his place."

Clara sighed. This wasn't going at all well. "Grandma, what possessed you to hire him? He's a drifter, and you don't know anything about him. He could be a criminal, waiting for a chance to rob you."

"Oh? And what would he steal?" Mary's hands worked deftly as she talked. "The little money I have is safe in the bank. If the man needed food, he'd be welcome to all he could carry. As for the rest, look around you, child. What do I have that's worth taking? My clothes? My pots and pans? My garden tools?" Her eyes twinkled. "My virtue, heaven forbid? Look at me. I'm an old woman. And whatever else Tanner may be, he's a gentleman."

Clara resisted the urge to grind her teeth. The look she'd seen in Tanner's cobalt eyes was *not* the look of a gentleman. "What makes you say that?" she asked.

"I offered to let him sleep upstairs, in the boys' old room. He insisted on laying out his bedroll in the hay shed. Didn't want folks to gossip, he said."

Clara groaned inwardly. As if anyone would gossip about her grandmother letting hired help sleep upstairs! Tanner's excuse had been designed to flatter her and win her confidence. He probably slept outside in case he needed to make a fast getaway. She was becoming less and less inclined to trust the man.

"Why didn't you tell us you needed help?" she

asked. "We could've sent a couple of the ranch hands over to do the work. My father would have paid them."

"I know, dear." Mary quartered a peeled potato and dropped the pieces into the cooking pot. "But you know I don't like accepting charity, even from my own family. Tanner needed work, and I…" A smile creased her cheek. "To tell you the truth, I liked the young man right off. And I enjoy his company over supper at night. It's nice having somebody to talk to."

Clara forced herself to take a long breath before she spoke. "How long does he plan to be here?"

"We haven't talked about it. But once he's made a little money, I expect he'll move on. He doesn't strike me as the sort of man to take root in one place." Mary glanced into the pot. "I believe that's enough potatoes for now. Give me a minute to put them on the stove, dear. Then we can go on with our visit."

She pushed forward to rise from her rocker, but Clara had already picked up the pot. She stood, laying her knife on the porch rail. "I'll do it, Grandma. You stay and rest."

Swinging through the screen door, she strode into the kitchen. The interior of the house was shabby but comfortable. Mary could have bought new dishes and furniture, but the chipped plates, scarred table and mis-matched chairs held precious memories of her husband and children. As Mary was fond of saying, the pieces were old friends and they served her well enough.

In the kitchen, Clara covered the potatoes with water, added a pinch of salt and set the pot on the big black stove to boil. Her grandmother would be waiting out-side, but the quiet house held her in its calm embrace, urging her to linger. Savoring the stillness, she wan-dered into the parlor, where framed photographs of Mary's family covered most of one wall.

Clara knew them well. Here was Reverend Ephraim Gustavson, her mother's younger brother who'd gone off to Africa to be a missionary. And here, on the left was a ten-year-old photograph of her own family—her mother, Hannah, and her handsome, serious father, Judd, with their three children. The two younger ones, Daniel and Katy, were almost as fair as their mother. In their midst, Clara looked like a gypsy changeling. But then, her paternal grandfather had been dark. He'd died long before Clara was born, but she'd seen his picture. Tom Seavers had looked a lot like his younger son Quint—Clara's adored favorite uncle.

Here was Uncle Quint in the photograph taken on his wedding day. He was devilishly handsome with dark chestnut hair, twinkling brown eyes and dimples that matched Clara's. His bride, Aunt Annie, was Mary's second daughter. More delicate than her sister Hannah, she had dark blond hair, intelligent gray eyes and a prac-tical disposition that balanced her husband's impulsive ways.

Clara worshipped her aunt and uncle and looked forward to their rare visits. Never blessed with children, they lived a glamorous life in San Francisco and had traveled all over the world. They always came to the ranch laden with exotic gifts and thrilling stories. On their last visit they'd brought Clara a bolt of white Indian silk, exquisitely embroidered in silver thread. "For your wedding, dear, whenever that might be," Aunt Annie had told her.

Clara's mother had put the treasured fabric away for safekeeping, but every now and then Clara would lift the bolt from the cedar chest, touch the silk with her fingertips and wonder if it would ever be used. Many of the girls she'd known from school were already married. But she'd always been more interested in horses than in boys. The idea of pledging herself to a man for the rest of her life had always seemed as far-fetched as walking on the moon. Not that she wasn't popular. At the town dances, she never lacked for partners. But none of the local boys, even the ones she'd allowed to kiss her, had piqued her interest. They were nice enough, but not one of them had offered a challenge to her way of thinking. In fact, they hadn't challenged her at all. They had no curiosity, no desire to test the limits of their small, safe lives. On the other hand, a certain blue-eyed hired man…

The sound of muted voices from the front porch yanked her attention back to the present. At first she thought Tanner had come back to talk with Mary. But she was halfway out the door when she realized that the speaker wasn't Tanner. By then it was too late to reach for Mary's shotgun.

At the foot of the porch, two grubby-looking men sat bareback astride a drooping piebald horse. The man in front held a cocked .22 rifle, aimed straight at Mary.

And Tanner was nowhere in sight.

"Go back inside, Clara." Mary's voice was low and taut.

"Come on out here, sweetie." The man in front grinned beneath his greasy bowler hat, showing gummy, tobacco-stained teeth. "Let's have a look at you."

Clara walked past Mary as far as the porch railing. She could almost feel the two men eyeing her. She could sense their dirty thoughts, like hands crawling over her body. Her nerves were screaming, but she knew better than to show fear. She kept her head up, her gaze direct.

"That's a good girl," the man in the bowler chuckled. "How about unbuttoning that shirt and giving us a show?" When Clara hesitated, his voice lowered to a growl. "Do it, girlie, or the old lady gets it right between the eyes."

Hands trembling, Clara fumbled with her shirt buttons. The .22 was a small-caliber weapon, mostly good for rabbits and vermin. Hard-core murderers would likely be carrying a more powerful gun. Still, at close range a well-aimed shot could be deadly. She couldn't take chances with her grandmother's life.

"Come on, honey, we ain't got all day. Let's see them titties."

Clara's fingers had unbuttoned the shirt past the top of her light summer union suit. The thin fabric left little to the imagination, but she had no choice except to keep going. Fear clawed at her gut. The men wouldn't be satisfied with seeing her breasts, she knew. It would be all too easy for one of them to drag her down and rape her while his partner held the gun on Mary.

And then what? Would they murder both women to hide their crime, or maybe just for the pleasure of it? Perhaps the gun was only for show, and they did their real killing with knives or ropes.

Where was Tanner when they needed him?

Her fingers had reached her belt line. The shirt gaped open to the waist. The man with the gun was leering at her. "The underwear, too, missy. Go on, don't be bashful!"

Clara groped for a shoulder strap. She was dimly aware of the second man, his long legs wrapping the horse's flanks. He had pale hair and the dull-eyed look of a beast. His tongue licked his full, red lips in anticipation. Her stomach clenched.

"Stop this!" Mary's voice shook. "Go inside the house. Take whatever you need, but leave my granddaughter alone! She's an innocent girl!"

"Save your breath, lady. You ain't the one giving orders. We'll have our fun with honey pie, here, and take anything we want. And since I get first pick, I'll be taking this smart little red pony you got tied to the hitching rail. He should make right sweet ridin'. Almost as sweet as—"

"No!" Driven by a blast of rage, Clara sprang between the gunman and her grandmother. One hand snatched up the knife she'd left on the porch railing. Brandishing the blade, she defied the gunman. "Don't you touch my horse!" she hissed. "If you come near him or my grandmother, so help me, I'll cut you to bloody ribbons!"

The man's jaw dropped. For an instant his greasy face reflected shock. Then he grinned. "Why, you feisty little bitch! I'll show you a thing or—"

"Drop the gun, you bastard!" Tanner's voice rang with cold authority as he stepped from behind the toolshed. "Drop it and reach for the sky, both of you!"

Tanner had spoken from behind the two men. Now he moved forward to where they could see the .38 revolver in his hand. The .22 thudded to the ground as four hands went up.

"We was only funnin', mister," the gunman whined. "We never meant to hurt the ladies."

"Sure you didn't." Tanner pulled back the pistol's hammer. "The knives, too. Nice and slow. Don't make any sudden moves and give me an excuse to pull this trigger. I'd shoot you in a heartbeat."

Rooted to the spot, Clara watched the men draw their hunting knives and toss them to the gravel. Mary had risen and slipped into the house. She emerged with the shotgun cocked and aimed at the two desperados.

"I've got your back, Tanner," she said. "Say the word and I'll blow them to kingdom come."

"I knew I could count on you." Tanner's grin flashed. Then for the first time, he seemed to notice Clara. "When you get yourself together, Miss Clara, maybe you could get down here and gather up their weapons."

Cheeks blazing, Clara put down the paring knife and fumbled with her buttons. She must have looked like a fool, standing there with her chest exposed, brandishing that pathetic little blade. Behind that sneer, Tanner was probably laughing his head off.

"What should we do with these two buzzards, Mary? Do you want me to shoot them for you?"

Tanner seemed to be playing with the two men, trying to make them squirm.

"That's tempting," Mary replied. "But I suppose the right thing would be to lock them in the granary and telephone for the marshal."

Clara had come down off the porch, close enough for her to see the twitch of a muscle in Tanner's cheek as he hesitated. What if he didn't want Mary to call in the law? What if he was worried about being seen?

Still pondering, she moved to the far side of the horse and bent to pick up the gun and the two knives. That was when she saw the flicker of movement. The dull-eyed man who sat in the rear had slipped a thin-bladed knife out of his boot.

"No!" she screamed, but it was too late. The man's supple hand moved with the speed of a striking rattle-snake. The knife sliced the air, sinking hilt-deep into Tanner's right shoulder.

A curse exploded between Tanner's lips. His gun hand sagged. The man in front yanked the reins and the piebald reared and wheeled, its hoof grazing Clara's head. Clara reeled backward, lost her balance and went down rolling to avoid being trampled.

The shotgun roared behind the fleeing outlaws. But Mary had fired high. The blast went over their heads as the horse thundered down the drive toward the main road with the two men clinging to its back.

Still dazed, Clara struggled to her feet. Mary had collapsed in the rocker with the shotgun across her knees. Tanner had lowered the pistol. His face was ashen. His torn sleeve oozed crimson where the knife handle jutted out of his shoulder.

Clara could feel a throbbing lump at her hairline where the iron shoe had grazed her skull. A wet trickle threaded its way down her temple.

Mary laid the shotgun on the porch and rose shakily to her feet. "We'll need some wrappings," she said. "I'll get something we can tear into strips. Meanwhile, Clara, you'd better help this fellow to the porch before he takes a header. Don't try to take the knife out until we've got something to stop the blood."

"I'll be all right." Tanner spoke through clenched teeth, swaying a little as he staggered toward the steps. Clara darted to his side and braced herself against his left arm. His body was warm and damp, the muscles rock hard through the worn chambray shirt. She felt the contact as a shimmering current of heat.

Mary paused at the door. "I suppose we should call the marshal. He'll want to pick up their weapons and question us about what happened."

Clara felt Tanner's body tighten against her, felt his hesitation. "Why bother?" he asked. "In the time it takes the marshal to get here, those ruffians could be halfway to the next county."

"But what if they try to rob somebody else?"

"They're unarmed, Mary. And they know we can identify them. Trust me, all they'll want to do is hightail it out of here, as far away as they can get."

Beside him, Clara studied the chiseled profile, the narrowed eyes and tense jaw. Where she stood against his side, she could feel the pounding of his heart. If her grandmother called the marshal, she sensed Tanner would slip away and be gone—along with his beautiful stallion, and a wound that could be fatal if left untreated.

He had just rescued them, possibly saving their lives. Would it be so wrong to keep him here a little longer?

"Tanner's right, Grandma," she said. "Once those men are outside the marshal's jurisdiction, there's nothing he can do. Why waste his time?"

His eyes flashed toward her, caught her gaze and held it. In those fathomless blue depths she read gratitude, suspicion and a world of questions.

Mary sighed. "Oh, that makes sense, I suppose. But I hate the thought of that awful pair getting away. I'd have aimed lower but I didn't want to hit that poor horse." She opened the screen door and hurried into the house.

Clara supported Tanner as they covered the short distance toward the porch. "You don't need to hold me up," he muttered. "My legs are fine."

"Don't be so proud!" she scolded him. "You're in shock. You look as if you could pass out any second, and you're about to drop that pistol." She took the heavy .38, which was barely dangling from his fingers. "Here, sit on the steps. I'll get you something to drink."

"I'm guessing there's no whiskey." He sank onto the middle step with a grunt of pain. His left hand clutched his right arm, the fingers tight below the wound.

"My grandmother does keep a little—strictly for medicinal purposes. Will you be all right while I get it?"

"Just get the blasted whiskey!"

"Hang on." She dashed into the house, letting the screen door slam shut behind her.

Only after she'd gone did Jace give vent to the pain that pooled like molten lead around the knife in his shoulder. A string of obscenities purpled the air. If nothing else, the muttered oaths braced his courage. The wound itself didn't appear that serious, but if that blade was as filthy as the bastard who'd thrown it, he could be in danger of blood poisoning.

The girl had surprised him, standing there like a defiant little cat pitted against a pair of mongrel curs. He'd been in the woodshed looking for gate timbers when the two ruffians appeared. It had taken him precious minutes to circle around and retrieve the pistol he'd hidden in his bedroll. He'd returned to find her with her shirt gaping open as she threatened two armed criminals with that silly little paring knife.

His mouth had gone dry at the sight of her.

He'd be smart to banish the image from his mind, Jace lectured himself. Clara Seavers was a lady. Her courage and fighting spirit merited his respect. But the memory of her standing there on the porch, her proud little breasts straining against the wispy fabric that covered them, would fuel his erotic dreams for nights to come.

Damn!

He shifted his weight on the step. The movement shot pain all the way down to his fingertips. Biting back a moan, he focused his gaze on the circling flight of a red-tailed hawk. Beyond the pasture, where the road stretched into open country, the two intruders had long since vanished from sight.

What would have happened if he hadn't been here? The thought sent a dark chill down his spine. He found himself wanting to catch up with the miscreants and rip them limb from limb. If either of them had so much as laid a hand on her...

Jace shook his head, silently cursing his own helplessness. He should be counting his blessings that the idiots *had* gotten away. If he and Mary had been able to hold them, the marshal would have been called in, and he'd have found himself dragged to jail along with them. Even now, he had to wonder if the men, if apprehended, would be able to identify him. Now would be the smart time to climb on his horse and ride away. But he was in no condition to go anywhere.

Why had Clara backed his argument against calling the marshal? Was she just talking common sense, or had those big sarsaparilla eyes seen through his facade to the fugitive he was? And if she suspected the truth, why had she helped him? Was it some kind of trick, meant to lull him into a false sense of security?

Were the women calling in the law even as he waited?

Jace's hands had clenched into fists. Slowly he forced his fingers to relax, forced his mind away from the searing pain in his shoulder. Damn it, where was that whiskey? His ears strained for the patter of Clara's light footsteps crossing the floor. He remembered the cool touch of her fingers, the pressure of her body against his side. He could feel himself swaying, getting light-headed. The pain was intoxicating. Maybe he should just grab the knife, yank it out and try to get to his horse. His hand crept toward knife handle.

"No!"

She was here now, rushing across the porch with Mary on her heels. As the screen door slammed shut, she dropped to her knees beside him. One hand clutched a pillow. The other clasped a bottle of cheap whiskey. "Give me that," he growled, reaching to twist it out of her hand.

"No." She moved the bottle aside. "There's only a little bit left, and we'll need it to disinfect the wound."

"Hell's bells, what happened to the rest? Have you been imbibing, Mary?"

The older woman's mouth twitched. "I'll have you know I've had that same bottle for six years, and it's only been used for medicinal purposes."

"Now, you I'd believe." Jace's head was swimming. He fought to stay alert. For all he knew, he could pass out and wake up in handcuffs, on his way to jail.

"Be still and lie down." Clara maneuvered him onto the pillow. "You can talk after we get this knife out of you and dress the wound."

Jace lay with his head cushioned, trying to imagine her bending over him under very different circumstances. His fantasy didn't help much. The blade was buried a good six inches in his shoulder. This already hurt like hell. And it was just going to get worse.

"Here, bite on this." Mary was pushing something between his teeth. It felt like a table knife wrapped in layers of cloth.

"Just get it over with," he muttered around the obstruction in his mouth.

"Ready?" Clara knelt beside him, the whiskey bottle beside her on the porch. Her nimble fingers ripped away his shirtsleeve, exposing the flesh around the wound. Then her hands closed around the knife. Her eyes narrowed. Her jaw tensed.

"Now!" In one swift move she pulled the blade free. Jace gasped, muttered and passed into darkness.

The knife dropped from Clara's shaking fingers and clattered to the porch. Blood was soaking Tanner's shirt and pooling below his collarbone. It seeped into the towel she was using to stanch the flow. She struggled to ignore her lurching stomach. Blood had always made her feel queasy.

"Let it bleed a little more." Mary would have tended to Tanner herself, but a bad knee made it painful for her to get down beside him. "It's a deep wound, and Lord knows what was on that knife blade. The more dirt washes out, the less the chance of festering. That's the real danger now."

"But there's so much blood. You're sure it's safe?"

"I've seen worse." Mary's mouth tightened, and Clara knew she was remembering the long-ago day when her youngest son had lost an arm in a threshing machine accident. The boy had survived and grown up to be a teacher. Mary had eventually considered the injury a blessing because, when he was of age, it had kept him from going to war.

"Tanner should be fine as long as we can keep the wound clean," she said. "But any sign of infection, and we'll need to get him right to a doctor."

Tanner's eyelids fluttered open. "No doctor," he rasped. "I'll be fine."

"We'll see about that." Mary handed Clara two more clean towels, dropped the wrappings in the rocker and turned to walk inside. "Go ahead and stanch the bleeding, Clara. Then you can disinfect the wound with whiskey. I'll need a few minutes to make a poultice."

Clara wadded one of the towels and held it against the wound, leaning forward to increase the pressure of her hands. His eyes watched her, blinding blue in the shadows of the porch. The ripped shirt showed a glimpse of fair skin with a virile dusting of light brown hair.

"How do you feel?" she asked, unsettled by his nearness.

"Like hell." He managed a grimace. "But thanks for asking."

"You're in good hands with my grandmother. She makes her own poultices with herbs the Indians used in the old days—yarrow, cedar bark, pitch pine and things I can't even name. There's nothing better for wounds."

"Let's hope you're right. I don't take well to being a patient." A grunt of pain escaped his lips as Clara increased the pressure of the towel.

"It may take time to get your strength back," she

said. "You've lost a lot of blood. And by the way, I haven't thanked you for saving us."

"I wasn't sure you needed saving. You seemed to have the situation well in hand with that vicious little paring knife."

A beat of silence ticked past before she realized he was teasing her. "They were going to take Foxfire," she said. "Nobody takes my horse."

His eyes narrowed. "That sounds like a warning."

"Take it any way you like," she said.

"Whatever you might think, I'm not a thief, Clara. Galahad, as you named him, was borrowed—with his owner's permission."

He bit off the end of the last word, as if realizing he'd said too much. Questions flocked into Clara's mind. Where had the stallion come from? Why would anyone lend such a prized animal when an ordinary mount would do? She willed herself to keep silent as she lifted the towel and checked the wound. Showing too much curiosity might put Tanner on alert.

But he'd just given her the perfect opening, Clara reminded herself. She'd be a fool not to seize it.

The bleeding had slowed. Applying a fresh towel to the wound, she cleared her throat. "Speaking of Galahad, I've a favor to ask."

Tanner's left eyebrow quirked in an unspoken question. Clara took it as a signal to plunge ahead.

"I have two fine mares, both of them champion quarter horses. They'll be coming into estrus soon. I'd like to breed them with your stallion."

Tanner's brows met in a scowl. "You're quite the little negotiator, Miss Clara Seavers. First you get a man helpless on his back. Then you ask him for a favor. What would you do if I said no—stick that knife in my shoulder again?"

"Of course not. If it's a question of money, I'd be happy to pay you a reasonable stud fee. How much would you want?"

He winced as she lifted away the towel. "Maybe you ought to ask Galahad."

"Be serious! This is important to me." She picked up the whiskey bottle and twisted out the stopper. The bottle was nearly empty. Less than an inch remained in the bottom. "Brace yourself, this is going to sting."

Before he could argue or stop her, she splashed the whiskey into the open wound. He shuddered, mouthing curses between clenched teeth. Seconds passed before he exhaled and spoke.

"I am being serious. I wouldn't feel right about taking money for Galahad's services, especially from you or your family. But as a gesture of goodwill, why not? If Galahad and I are still around when your mares are ready…" A shadow flickered in the depths of his eyes. "You can borrow him on one condition."

"Name it." She laughed nervously. What was she getting herself into?

"Just this. If I ever need it, promise you'll grant me one request."

Apprehension tightened Clara's throat. Her voice emerged as a whisper. "What sort of request?"

"I won't know until the time comes. But trust me, I'd never do anything to put you in harm's way."

"You sound as if you're asking for my soul."

His laugh was quick and harsh. "And you're looking at me as if I were the devil himself."

"For all I know, you could be."

He laughed again, flinching at the pain in his shoulder. "Would the devil be lying here bleeding on your grandmother's porch, Miss Clara? Galahad's a champion Thoroughbred with a pedigree as old as the *Mayflower.* I can't show you his papers but I can promise he'll sire damned good foals. So what's it to be, yes or no?"

"What if it's no?"

"Then it's no loss to either of us—and no gain."

Clara hesitated. At the age of six, on a visit to her uncle Quint in San Francisco, she'd survived a frightening ordeal at the hands of kidnappers. And while that story had a happy ending, having brought her uncle Quint and aunt Annie together, the experience had left her with an excess of caution. She tended to seek out familiar situations where she felt safe. That need for security had colored her choices, including the decision to stay on the ranch instead of going away to school.

Now she quivered on the edge of what she feared most of all—the unknown. Tanner's stallion could sire a line of superb horses, maybe the finest in Colorado. But to get that line demanded risk—perhaps more risk than she dared take.

The man intrigued her as well—his air of mystery,

the virile energy that drove his body and the secrets that lurked in his eyes, like a flash of darkness in a blue mountain lake.

How could she trust him?

How could she walk away?

Mary's heavy tread echoed across the kitchen floor. Any second now she'd be coming outside. Tanner lay watching, waiting for his answer. His eyes blazed with challenge, measuring her courage, daring her to step off the precipice.

Mary's footsteps were approaching the door. The words trembled on Clara's lips. She drew a sharp breath.

"You have my answer," she said. "It's yes."

Chapter Three

Jace's breath hissed through clenched teeth as Clara laid the steaming poultice on his wound. The heat of the cudlike herbal mass reminded him of the mustard plasters his mother had used on his chest when he was a boy. But the concoction smelled more like a mixture of swamp mud, skunk cabbage and cow manure.

"What the devil's in this stuff, Mary?" he muttered.

The older woman had taken a seat in the nearby rocking chair. "Nothing that would hurt you. When Soren and I settled this land there were no doctors and none of the medicines you can buy now. An old Indian woman—a Ute, as I recall—showed me the plants her people used. I've kept a stock of them on hand ever since."

"Grandma's shown me a few things for doctoring horses. But I'll never be as good as she is." Clara smoothed the edge of the poultice and covered it with a folded square of clean muslin. She had cut away the sleeve and shoulder of Jace's shirt with Mary's scissors. Through the haze of pain he felt the brush of her fingertips on his bare skin. She had small, almost child-like hands, the nails clipped short and the palms lightly callused. They worked with quiet efficiency. Tender, sensible little hands.

Her breath warmed his ear as she leaned close to wrap the dressing in place. Her hair smelled of fresh lavender soap.

"You mean to say your only doctoring experience is with horses?" he teased her.

"Horses and men are pretty much the same." Her eyes flashed toward him. In the shade of the porch, their color was like dark maple syrup flecked with glints of sunshine. For a breath-stopping instant her gaze held his. Then she glanced down again, veiling the look with the black fringe of her lashes.

Jace exhaled the breath he'd been holding in. Lord, didn't the girl realize the effect those eyes could have on a man? She seemed so artless, so damnably innocent.

The lessons he'd like to teach her…

Jace gave himself a mental slap. If he didn't get his mind back above his belt line, he could find himself in serious trouble.

Resting his arm across her knees, Clara wound the wrapping over his shoulder and around his arm, once, then twice more before she split the end and tied the tails in a knot. "There, it's done." She glanced up at her grandmother. "Now what?"

"Now he needs to rest." Mary rose from her chair. "I've got some tea brewing that will ease the pain. Help him inside, Clara. He can stretch out on that spare bed in my sewing room."

"Now wait a minute," Jace protested. "I'll be fine. There's no reason to—"

"I won't have you getting up and keeling over on me," Mary snapped. "The bed's made, and you're going to rest until you're stronger. Come along now while I get the tea."

Jace gave in with a sigh. He respected Mary Gustavson too much to argue. Besides, he felt like hell.

He waited while Clara braced herself beneath his good arm. Her body was warm and curvy against his side. Thankfully, he was in no condition to take advantage of her nearness. His shoulder throbbed, his vision swam in and out of focus and his knees felt like rubber.

"Here we go." She supported him with one arm and used her free hand to open the screen. Jace swore silently. He felt as helpless as a baby. If these two females wanted to turn him over to the law now, he'd have no chance of getting away.

Leaning to balance his weight, she guided him across the floor to the little room that opened off the kitchen. The curtains were drawn, but in the dim light Jace could see the treadle sewing machine in one corner and the patchwork quilt on the narrow bed. Glancing at the door, he was relieved to notice that it had no lock.

Mary followed them into the room holding a blue

china mug between her hands. She thrust it toward Jace as he sat on the edge of the bed. "Drink this before you lie down," she said. "It will help you rest."

The molasses-colored liquid was barely cool enough to drink. Its taste was bitter, but Jace knew better than to argue or to ask what was in it. He emptied the mug in a few swallows, suppressing the urge to gag.

"Give me your feet." Clara worked Jace's boots down over his heels and dropped them on the floor. It occurred to him to wonder whether his socks smelled, but it was only a fleeting thought. By now his eyelids were leaden weights. His body seemed to be sinking into the patchwork coverlet. The instincts that had kept him free for the past four months were screaming in his head, but he had no power to act on them.

Clara leaned over him, her eyes dark smudges in the pale oval of her face. "Rest now," she said. "I'll be back tomorrow with the mares. You should be feeling better by then."

Remember...one favor. Jace struggled to speak, but his lips refused to form words. He only knew that the promise he'd extracted might turn out to be the one chance of saving him, like a hidden ace up a gambler's sleeve.

But now it might already be too late. He was losing his grip, sinking into a black fog.

He kept his eyes on her face until the darkness pulled him under.

Clara took the colt at an easy trot toward home. The sun was at high morning, the sky a blazing blue that promised a hot afternoon. But the weather was the last thing on Clara's mind.

She'd left Tanner asleep on Mary's spare bed, his shoulder dressed and bandaged, his senses drugged by Mary's potent jimsonweed tea. Knocking him out was the only way to make sure he'd stay put. His body was in shock and he'd lost enough blood to make him weak. He needed to stay off his feet, at least until tomorrow.

After he'd slipped away she had lingered a moment, looking down at him. In sleep he'd looked strangely vulnerable—tawny hair tumbling over his forehead, mahogany lashes lying still against his tanned cheeks.

Where the shirt had been cut away, his skin was like warm ivory. A ray of sunlight, falling between the curtains, made a golden pool in the hollow of his throat. He was a beautiful man, Clara thought—as beautiful in his own way as the stallion he rode.

But who was he and what was he hiding?

Resisting the urge to touch him, Clara had unfolded an afghan from the back of a chair and laid it over his sleeping body. Then she'd tiptoed out of the room and closed the door behind her.

Before leaving, she'd unsaddled Galahad and loosed him in the corral with Mary's two geldings. The power of the big stallion had thrilled her. Tomorrow she would bring her two mares to the farm and turn them out together in the same pasture. When they were ready to breed, the stallion would know what to do.

She could only hope Tanner would stay around long enough for it to happen.

She was putting way too much trust in the man, Clara lectured herself. For all she knew, he could disappear some night, taking her mares with him.

But that didn't sound like Tanner. The scenario would be too simple, the crime too easily solved. Tanner had said he wasn't a thief, and she was inclined to believe him. But other secrets lurked behind his intriguing manner. Clearly he wasn't the man he pretended to be.

She passed through the opening in the fence where Tanner had planned to build a gate. Seeing the place again brought home the memory of lying on her back, opening her eyes to the sight of his face. For that one heart-stopping instant, his blue eyes had pierced her, held her, touched her in some deep place. Then he'd spoken angrily, shattering the spell.

What had she agreed to when she'd accepted his bargain? An open promise in exchange for the use of the stallion—she must have been out of her mind! He could ask any favor of her and she'd be honor-bound to grant it.

What would that favor be?

Tanner had stepped in to save her and her grandmother. But that didn't mean he was a good man. For all she knew, he could be plotting something wicked and scheming to make her a part of it. When he'd urged Mary not to call the marshal, she had backed him. But it was her heart, not her head that had made the decision. Tanner was a compellingly attractive man, the stuff of a young girl's dreams and fantasies. But she couldn't allow herself to be naïve about him any longer.

It was possible that she really had made a bargain with the devil.

Across the pasture, the two-story Seavers home rose above a flowering orchard. Painted pale cream, with tall windows and dark green shutters, the spacious house was as stately as it was comfortable. Beyond it, the barn, sheds and stables stretched toward the far paddock. Clara had grown up here, with her parents and her younger brother and sister. There was no place on earth she would rather be than here on the ranch, surrounded by her beloved horses and her family.

Slowing Foxfire to a walk, she pondered how much to tell her parents. Judd and Hannah Seavers were protective of Mary and would welcome any excuse to pluck her off the farm and settle her in their home. But Mary was fiercely independent. She'd insisted that Clara not tell them about the two men who'd come by. Clara had reluctantly agreed. But sooner or later, her parents would have to know about Tanner.

Say too much, and they'd go flying over to Mary's to make sure she was safe.

Say too little, and they'd suspect her of keeping something from them. Either way, there could be trouble.

Clara was still weighing her words as she approached the open pasture gate. The sight of milling men and horses surprised her until she remembered. This was the day her father and the hired cowhands would be driving the cattle to summer pasture in the mountains. It appeared they were about to ride out.

Relief swept over her as she rode into the yard. Her father would be away for at least a week, maybe longer. Hopefully, by the time he returned, the mares would be bred, Tanner would be gone and there'd be no need for questions.

There would still be her mother to get around. But one parent would be easier to manage than two.

Her brother, Daniel, grinned at her as he reined in his skittish horse. He loved going off with the men on the spring cattle drive, and he was in high spirits. Katy sat pouting on the front steps. She had begged her father to let her go along, too. He had given her a firm refusal.

Clara unsaddled Foxfire and turned him out to graze in the paddock. When she returned to the house, her father and mother were saying goodbye on the porch. What a striking couple they made, she thought. Judd Seavers, nearing fifty, was tall and lean, his handsome features leathered by sun and wind. His wife, Hannah, a decade younger, was a classic beauty with thick wheaten hair and a lushly rounded figure. Even after two decades of marriage, they had eyes only for each other.

Katy was still huddled on the top step. Reaching down, Judd ruffled her corn silk hair. "Don't be upset, Katydid," he said, using his pet name for her. "You'll find plenty of adventures around here."

In response, she turned, wrapped her arms around his legs and hugged them hard. Clara stepped up to embrace him next. "Take care of things, girl," he whispered. "You're the one I can always count on."

Guilt stabbed Clara as she kissed his cheek and stepped aside to make way for her mother. Her father was honorable to his very bones. He was depending on her, and here she was plotting behind his back.

She could only hope that her scheme would turn out for the best.

Judd and Hannah's kiss was long and heartfelt. Hannah had sent her husband off and welcomed him home countless times over the past twenty years. But each time they clung together as if the parting would be their last. It was almost as if they were two parts of the same soul, neither of them complete without the other.

Clara was well aware of the six-month interval between the date of their wedding and the date of her own birth. She'd never discussed it with her mother, but it didn't take a mathematician to figure out that Hannah had been a pregnant bride. Clara had come to accept the fact, and refused to let it trouble her. Her parents loved each other. They had raised a close and loving family. The past was, as her grandmother would say, water under the bridge.

Judd released his wife, strode down the steps and mounted his horse. Clara stood on the porch with her mother and sister, watching as the men rode down the long drive and out the gate. Only when the dust had settled behind the horses did the three of them turn and go into the house.

Run!
The word screamed through Jace's mind as he

galloped the stallion across the open fields. By now the police would be arriving at the house. When they discovered his abandoned Packard in the drive and his muddy boot prints on the carpet, they'd be after him like a pack of bloodhounds.

The roads would be blocked. His best chance of a clean getaway depended on catching the midnight train. If he could scramble aboard unseen, leaving the horse to find its way home, he'd be well into Kansas by morning.

By now the westbound freight would be approaching the Wilson's Creek Bridge. When it slowed down for the crossing he'd have one chance to leap aboard—but only if he could get there in time.

The midnight wind was bitter, the moon a pale scimitar veiled by tattered clouds. Behind him, Rumford's grand plantation-style house rose out of the flatland, growing smaller with distance. Jace thought of his comfortable apartment in town—gone, like everything else he owned. If he went back for so much as a toothbrush the police would close in and he would finish his life at the end of a rope. He had no choice except to run and keep running.

The train whistle screamed through the darkness. Jace pressed forward in the saddle, cursing as he lashed the horse with the reins. On the far side of the field, the headlamp glowed like a great yellow eye as the engine raced toward the bridge. A ghostly plume of steam trailed from the stack.

Even then, he knew he wasn't going to make it. But something drove him on. Maybe it was the madness of what had happened tonight—what he'd seen and done and all it implied. Or maybe he was just in shock. The rhythm of hoofbeats pounded through his body. The moon blurred. The wind moaned in his ears.

By the time he neared the bridge, the engine had reached the far side of the creek and picked up speed. Boxcars and flatcars rattled along behind it, going fast, too fast. Could he still do it? Could he fling himself out of the saddle and make the leap? Catch something and hold on?

Would it matter if he died trying?

The whistle shrilled a deafening blast. The stallion screamed, leaping and twisting in terror. Flung out of the saddle, Jace felt himself flying, falling, tumbling toward the rushing wheels...

He woke with a jerk, damning the dream that haunted so many of his nights. The room was dark, the stars glowing faintly through the gauzy curtains. His body felt chilled, his skin paper dry. Only when he tried to sit up and felt pain shoot down his arm did he remember the knife wound and how he'd come by it.

Sinking back onto the pillow, he eased himself to full awareness. He was lying on the bed in Mary's sewing room, where she'd insisted he stay. A lacy crocheted afghan covered his legs. His shirt was cut away and his boots were missing, but otherwise he was fully dressed.

The rank herbal odor of the poultice seeped through the dressing on his shoulder. Whatever Mary had concocted out of those mysterious jars had yet to work its wonders. The soreness was no worse, but he was beginning to chill. Not a good sign.

Damnation, what a time to be laid up!

Too uncomfortable to go back to sleep, he slid his legs off the couch and pushed himself to his feet. The light-headedness was better, but Jace felt disoriented, like a child awakening in a strange room.

Somehow he needed to get out of here.

His boots were nowhere to be found. For all he knew, Mary could have hidden them to keep him from leaving. Stocking footed, he padded to the front door, opened it quietly and stepped out onto the porch.

The gibbous moon rode low in the west but the sky was still dark, the stars still bright. Insect-seeking bats swished through the moonlight. From the brushy hillside beyond the pasture, the plaintive cry of a coyote rose and faded into stillness.

Someone had put the stallion in the corral with Mary's two geldings. He could make out their shifting forms and hear the soft snorting sounds they made as they dozed. He'd be smart to saddle up and leave now— ride off into the peaceful darkness with no one the wiser. He could make his way into the hills, maybe find somewhere to hole up until he felt strong enough to move on.

It was a tempting idea, but not a practical one. He would need his boots, and he didn't want to leave without the .38 Smith & Wesson. He recalled seeing the gun on the porch, but it was no longer there. The knife and the .22 taken from the robbers had been put away as well.

Leaning on the porch rail, Jace stared out into the darkness. Tomorrow would be Wednesday, the day Mary had said she made her weekly trip to town. What were the odds she would see the marshal there and mention the robbery attempt? And what were the odds the marshal would show her his collection of Wanted posters to see if there was anyone who looked familiar?

The posters were out there—in the big towns, at least. Jace had seen one himself. He looked like a dandy in a suit, vest and tie, his hair and mustache immaculately trimmed.

He had since shaved off the mustache and let his hair grow longer. Even so, his picture would be easy enough to recognize. When Mary discovered her new hired man was wanted for murder, all hell was bound to break loose.

He would wait until she'd left for town, Jace resolved. As soon as she was out of sight, he would find his boots and pistol, pack his bedroll, saddle his horse and make tracks. By the time Mary returned, with or without the law, he'd be long gone.

As for the luscious Miss Seavers, she'd be disappointed about the stallion. But even a face as pretty as hers wasn't worth the risk of getting arrested. Clara would just have to find herself another stud.

The cool night wind raised goose bumps on his bare skin. A shiver passed through his body as he turned away from the rail. A few more hours of sleep might be a good idea. He was going to need his strength tomorrow.

The coyote howled again, a lonely, distant sound

like the far-off whistle of a train. The cry echoed in
Jace's ears as he went back inside and closed the door.

By the time Clara finished her breakfast, the sun
had risen above the peaks. She whistled snatches of a
ragtime tune as she tied the two mares into a lead rope
and saddled Tarboy, the steady black gelding she would
ride. If things went as hoped, by this time next year
she'd have two of the finest foals in the county.

The mares, Belle and Jemima, usually came into
estrus at the same time. The changes in their bodies
tended to make them cranky. Jemima became a biter
when she was in season. Belle's specialty was digging
in her hooves and refusing to be led. Today, both of them
were their usual sweet selves, a sign that nature had yet
to take its course.

"Just wait till you see who's waiting for you, ladies,"
Clara chattered as she checked the knots. "If this
handsome fellow doesn't make your hearts flutter—"

"Clara, what in heaven's name are you up to?" Her
mother stood in the doorway of the barn. The stern expression on her face was one Clara knew all too well.

Lying, she knew, would only get her in more trouble.
"I'm on my way to Grandma's," she said. "There's a
man doing some work for her, and he has this beautiful stallion. I'm taking the mares over there and leaving
them to be bred."

"A man? A stranger?" Hannah was instantly on the
alert. "What's he doing there?"

"Just some fixing and mending. He came by last

week looking for work. He seems trustworthy enough, and Grandma seems to like him."

"But a stranger off the road! Why didn't she let us know she needed help?"

"You know how Grandma is. Sometimes she likes to do things on her own."

"Yes, I know. I'd go over there myself, right now, but the seamstress is coming in half an hour to measure Katy for three new dresses. That girl is growing so fast, I can't keep her in clothes." Hannah made a little huffing sound. "After that I'll be driving into town for a meeting of the Women's League. We've already started planning the July Fourth celebration. What's this hired man like?"

"He's a perfect gentleman, Mama. Believe me, you have nothing to worry about." Clara avoided her mother's eyes. Sometimes a daughter had to fudge a little.

"Well, do be careful, dear. You mustn't allow yourself to be alone with the man. That could be dangerous." She turned back toward the house, then paused. "Katy's going with me to visit her friend Alice. I'll expect to see you here when I get home."

"Certainly, Mama. Don't worry about me."

Clara sagged with relief as her mother walked back to the house. Why did her parents have to treat her like a child? She was nineteen and already doing her share of the ranch work. She broke and trained the horses, looked after things in the tack room and helped with the roping, branding and herding when her father was shorthanded. She even knew how to manage the accounts. Yet her mother was still telling her where she could go and what time to be home.

Her parents loved her, Clara reminded herself. They had nearly lost her on that long-ago visit to San Francisco, and they'd never gotten over it. How could she blame them for wanting to keep her safe?

Pushing the thought aside, she mounted Tarboy and rode out of the barn with the mares trailing behind. It was a relief that she didn't need to sneak. Her mother knew where she was going and why. But the hidden secrets were already weaving their web—the two robbers, Tanner's injury, her own suspicions and her compelling attraction to a man who had trouble written all over him.

This morning the sky was overcast, with sooty clouds brooding above the peaks. As Clara took the horses across the pasture, a flock of blackbirds rose from the grass, swirling and sweeping like the folds of a magician's cloak. Their harsh twittering filled her ears as they circled north to settle on a neighbor's freshly plowed field.

Maybe she should share her suspicions with her grandmother, Clara thought. Mary liked and trusted Tanner. She would probably dismiss what she was told. But she needed to be alerted to the holes in Tanner's story. Otherwise he might take advantage of her kindness and the old woman could end up being hurt. If that happened after Clara failed to speak up, she would have no one to blame but herself.

She would talk to Mary as soon as she could get her alone, Clara resolved. She wasn't looking forward to broaching the subject of Tanner, but it had to be done.

Only as she reached the opening in the fence did she remember that today was Wednesday, Mary's marketing day. Mary liked to hitch up her buggy and leave early to get to town, do her errands and visit a few friends. Unless she'd stayed home to look after Tanner, she could already be gone.

And if Mary was gone, Tanner would be there alone.

Clara held the horses to a brisk walk, but her pulse had begun to gallop. The memory of those eyes riveting hers, demanding an unspoken promise, triggered a blaze of heat from the core of her body. She felt the burn in her belly, in her tingling breasts and hot cheeks.

Don't be a fool! she lashed herself. Tanner wasn't like the boys she flirted with at summer dances. He was a man—a secretive and dangerous man. She'd do well to heed her mother's advice and stay away from him.

On the far side of the pasture she could see her grandmother's farm. If Mary wasn't there, Clara resolved, she would deliver the mares to the paddock, turn the stallion in with them and check on Tanner's whereabouts. If she spoke with him at all, it would be the briefest exchange. After that she would take her leave and go home.

On approach, her grandmother's place looked even quieter than usual. Only one horse, Mary's dun gelding, remained in the corral. The other gelding and the stallion were missing.

Perplexed, Clara rode into the farmyard. Mary must have taken the second gelding—she needed just one horse for her old buggy. But where was Galahad? Surely Tanner wouldn't have ridden the stallion into town. If he was sick enough to need a doctor, Mary would have taken him in the buggy.

Dismounting, she hitched Tarboy to a fence post, led the mares into the empty paddock and untied their lead ropes. The feeling that something was wrong nagged at her as she strode across the yard.

As she mounted the porch steps, a new and ghastly possibility struck her. What if the two road bandits had returned? With Tanner drugged and sleeping, they could have overpowered Mary, recovered their weapons, ransacked the house and left with the two horses.

What would she find inside the house? Sick with dread, she opened the door and stepped into the shadows.

The parlor was cool and silent, with nothing out of place. Mary's shotgun was missing, but she often took it with her, tucked under the seat for emergencies. Likewise, the kitchen was in order, the table cleared, the breakfast dishes washed and put away. A glance into Mary's open bedroom revealed a neatly made bed. The door to the room where Tanner had slept was closed.

Heart pounding, Clara opened the door far enough to see into the small sewing room. The rumpled bed was empty. The pungent odor of Mary's poultice lingered in the quiet air.

Tanner was gone.

Chapter Four

Wheeling in her tracks, Clara raced back outside. Maybe the barn would give her some answers. If the buggy was gone, she could be reasonably sure that Mary was on her way to town. And if Tanner's gear was missing…

As the pieces slid into place, her worry turned to a simmering anger. It was the only explanation that made sense. The wretched man had waited until Mary left. Then he'd packed his things and hit the road, taking the stallion with him.

So help her, she would hunt him to the ends of the earth!

The barn door stood ajar. Seething, Clara flung it open and strode inside. The first thing she noticed was the absence of the buggy. The second thing she saw was Galahad, standing in the open space between the door and the stalls. He was bridled and saddled, with Tanner's bedroll lashed into place behind the cantle.

The stallion snorted at her approach. His elegant

head jerked upward, a hint that something was wrong. Moving slowly, Clara held out her hand and spoke in a soothing voice. "It's all right, boy. Nobody's going to hurt you. I'll just—"

The words died in her throat as she caught a glimpse of a plaid shirt and saw the long, still form lying face-down in the straw.

It was Tanner.

For an awful moment she thought he'd been trampled. But as she dropped to a crouch beside him, she saw no sign of hoof marks, bruising or blood. A light touch of her palm on his back confirmed that he was breathing, but his body felt surprisingly warm. The back of his neck was flushed above the soft flannel collar.

She took a moment to lead the stallion to a safe distance, then crouched beside him again. "Tanner!" She shook his uninjured shoulder and heard a feeble groan in response. "Tanner, wake up!" He muttered something she couldn't understand. Maybe the man was delirious.

"Come on! I've got to get you back in the house, and I can't do it without your help!" Working her hands beneath him, she rolled him onto his back. He groaned again. His eyes blinked open. There was a flicker of rec-ognition.

"What the hell..." he muttered.

"You're sick, Tanner. I'm guessing you passed out. You've got to get up." Seizing his hand, she tried to pull him. He shook free of her clasp.

"I can do it," he growled, bracing on his good arm and working his legs beneath his hips. Clara bit back the impulse to rail at him for trying to leave. Tanner would get an earful later on, when she judged he was out of danger.

If he survived.

He staggered to his feet, swaying like a drunkard. His face was flushed, his skin dry. With a puncture wound, fever was the worst of signs.

"Can you walk?" she asked him.

Tanner's jaw tightened. He took two steps. On the third step, his knee buckled and he stumbled forward. Clara caught him, bracing against his side.

"You're getting good at this, Miss Clara," he muttered.

"Just be quiet and move your feet. I'm too upset to listen to your charming blather!"

His body was rock solid against her side. Its heat radiated from the line of contact, sending shimmers along her nerves. With every step the awareness grew stronger. This wasn't good, Clara lectured herself. She'd resolved not to rail at him but her only hope of distraction was fury.

"What were you thinking?" she stormed. "You could've passed out and died on the road! And even if you hadn't, I'd have tracked you down and whipped you within an inch of your worthless life!"

His laugh was raw edged. "Now that I'd like to see. You might look right fetching with a whip in your hand."

"This isn't funny, Tanner. Did my grandmother know you planned on leaving?"

He swayed to one side. Clara had to clasp his ribs with her arms to keep him steady. "Your grandmother is one fine lady," he growled. "But I don't need anybody's permission to go. Not even yours."

"Of all the arrogant, underhanded—" Clara bit back the rest of the sentence. "What about the stallion? I brought my mares over this morning. You said—"

"I said you could use him if I was still here."

"Yes, you did. And then you ran out on me."

"Well, hell, I don't seem to be going anywhere now, do I?"

"Stop joking! You've got a fever. If your wound's infected, you'll need a doctor."

He stiffened against her. "No. No doctor."

"Don't be a fool! You could lose your arm, even your life!"

They had reached the bottom of the porch steps. Tanner's breath rasped with effort as he dragged his feet up each one. "Tell you what, Miss Clara Seavers. If I don't pull through, Galahad's yours. Can't think of a better life for him than Colorado grass and a steady supply of willing ladies."

His voice had begun to slur. Clara eased him through the front door. If he passed out again, there was no way she'd be able to get him into bed. "You'd better not say that," she joked feebly. "I might be tempted to get a gun and shoot you."

"I have no doubt you'd pull the trigger without even

blinking." His voice seemed to float out of his body. His boots stumbled across the floor.

"Just a few more steps. Stay with me, Tanner." By now she was supporting much of his weight. Sweat dripped down her body, soaking through her under-clothes. Thankfully she'd left the door to the sewing room open. Crowding close, they staggered to the foot of the bed.

"Hold on, we— Oh!" Clara gasped as Tanner toppled like a felled tree onto the bed. With no time to pull away, she landed flat on her back with his body on top of her.

She pushed and squirmed, trying to wriggle free. Her frenetic motions produced startling waves of pleasure in her lower body—not what she ought to be feeling at a time like this. Having grown up around ranch animals, she knew about sex, and she knew the nature of the hard ridge inside Tanner's jeans. He was too sick to be dangerous, she told herself. He was just acting on instinct. Her reaction, on the other hand, was much harder to explain. All she knew was that she was rapidly losing control. Whatever was happening, it had to stop. Now.

"Blast it, Tanner, move!" Working her hands free, she hooked his jaw and lifted his head. His eyelids twitched and opened. His first expression was a puzzled scowl. Then his face transformed into a drowsy grin.

"I don't know how this happened, but I'm not a man to refuse an invitation," he murmured, settling himself more firmly between her legs.

"Get…off…me!" She slapped him hard enough to

smart. With a rough chuckle he braced his good arm, raising his body enough for her to roll free. Clara tumbled off the bed and scrambled to her feet. "I can't believe my grandma thought you were a gentleman!" she huffed.

"Don't look at me. You're the one who started this."

"If you weren't so sick I'd slap you again," Clara retorted. "Turn over so I can take your boots off. Then I'll need to look at your wound."

Shifting on the bed, he turned over, stretched out his legs and lay still while Clara worked the boots off his feet. "It looked fine when your grandmother changed the dressing this morning."

"Well, something's going on." Clara tossed the boots under the bed. "How long have you had a fever?"

"Not sure." He was lying back on the pillow now, looking exhausted. "Didn't feel too bad before she left."

"So you thought you'd just saddle up and go."

Tanner managed a feeble shrug. He was drifting away from her again. Working in haste now, Clara attacked the buttons of his clean shirt, peeling back the upper part to reveal the fresh bandage her grandmother had laid in place earlier. Tanner watched her with heavy-lidded eyes as she untied the wrappings and lifted away the dressing. This morning Mary hadn't bothered with the poultice. The wound appeared clean and free of infection.

"How does it look?" His voice slurred slightly.

"Fine on the surface. But that blade went in deep. The germs could have gotten into your bloodstream."

His mouthed response—likely a curse—trailed off as his eyes closed. Clara laid a cautious hand on his forehead. His skin was burning.

Clara replaced the dressing over the wound. If only her grandmother hadn't gone to town! Clara had only a cursory knowledge of Mary's mysterious dried herbs. Some of them were potent cures; but misused, they could be dangerous, even poisonous. Experiment too freely, and she'd be as likely to kill Tanner as to heal him.

Rushing to the kitchen, she put the kettle on to boil, opened the cupboard and began rummaging through the jars, bags and little pots her grandmother kept on the top shelf. Just to be safe, she would use only the herbs she recognized. If she could just manage to keep Tanner stable, Mary could do more for him when she arrived home. For now, she could simply pray that Tanner's body would be strong enough to fight the infection.

Willow bark…everyone knew it was the best thing for fevers. But would an unchecked fever be best for fighting the infection? Deliberating, Clara decided not to take that chance. Tanner's temperature felt dangerously high. At least some willow bark tea might make him more comfortable.

She crumbled the dried bark and tossed it into the boiling water. Then she went back in to check on Tanner. She found him shivering on the bed, his teeth chattering.

She leaned over him. "Tanner, can you hear me? You're chilling. We need to get you out of your clothes and under the covers. You'll have to help me."

"Sorry it's not under more pleasurable circumstances," he muttered, fumbling with his belt buckle and buttons.

"Being sick's no excuse for that kind of talk!" Clara caught the legs of his jeans and jerked them down past his feet. His gray cotton underdrawers revealed barely a glimpse of what lay beneath. All the same, she averted her eyes as she pulled the covers out from under him and tucked them over his body. "We'll leave the shirt for now. I'll get you more quilts. By then your tea should be ready."

His eyes fluttered open. "What kind of tea? I'll be damned if I'm drinking more of that knockout potion your grandmother gave me last night."

"Stop fussing. It's just willow bark, for the fever." She hurried into Mary's room, stripped the quilt and coverlet off the bed and brought them back to lay over Tanner's chilling body. He had stretched out on his side, his profile starkly beautiful against the white pillowcase. Who was he, this man of secrets? Why had he risked his life to leave here this morning?

One tawny curl had tumbled over his forehead. Impulsively Clara brushed it back into place. Dear heaven, what if she couldn't save him? What if he was fated to die, right here in this bed?

By now the tea was brewed. As she stood by the open kitchen window, straining out the bark, a low rumble reached her ears. Leaning over the sink, she peered through the screen. Angry, black clouds were pouring over the mountains to spill across the sky.

Anxiety formed a knot in Clara's stomach. A heavy storm could keep her grandmother in town for the rest of the day, longer if the creek flooded the road. For Tanner, the delay could mean the difference between life and death.

Adding milk and sugar to the bitter tea, she carried the cup into the bedroom. Tanner was still shivering. Maybe the hot tea would help the chills. In any case, he was going to need plenty of fluids to fight the infection.

She touched his cheek. "Here's the tea. I sweetened it for you."

His bloodshot eyes blinked and focused on her. With effort, he raised his head, then fell back onto the pillow.

"Here." Sinking onto a bedside chair, she lifted his head, cradling it in the crook of her arm. His stubbled jaw rested against the curve of her breast. "Careful, it's hot." She held the rim of the cup to his lips.

He took a careful sip. "Hot and sweet," he mumbled. "Like you."

"You're out of your head. Just drink." Clara was acutely conscious of his heat through her shirt. Her nipples had contracted to aching nubs that showed through the thin fabric. She could only hope he wouldn't notice.

When he'd drained the cup, she lowered his head to the pillow and slipped her arm free. His fevered eyes burned into hers. Sick as he was, Tanner had a look of sharp-edged danger about him. He was like a wounded hawk, submitting to her care only because he had no choice.

As she rose and turned back toward the kitchen, the

storm struck. Chain lightning cracked across the sky, each flash followed by a cannonade of thunder. The clouds split open, sending a deluge of rain. Water pounded the roof and streamed down the windowpanes. Outside, the yard was fast becoming a sea of mud. Only then did Clara remember.

The horses!

Heaven help her, she'd left Tarboy tied to the corral. The mares were in the paddock, and Galahad was loose in the barn, still bridled and saddled. The animals would be terrified.

Without bothering to grab a slicker, Clara raced outside. The black gelding was snorting in fear, eyes rolling, nostrils flaring red. "It's all right, Tarboy. You'll be safe in a minute." Clara untied the reins and sprang into the wet saddle. Water fell in solid sheets as she drove Mary's horse into the barn and headed for the paddock to round up the mares.

Lightning struck close, splitting a huge cottonwood on the far side of the road. The sound of it crashed across the sky like the hammer of doom. By the time Clara reached the paddock, the two mares were wild with fright. But Tarboy, an experienced cow pony, knew his job. Galloping, shifting and pushing in response to Clara's touch, he soon had the mares galloping for the open corral. From there it was easy enough to close the gate and herd them into the barn.

With the horses safely inside, Clara closed the barn door behind her. There were only two stalls. She led the nervous Galahad into the first one, taking time to remove his saddle and bridle. Tanner's bedroll, lashed behind the saddle, seemed unnaturally heavy. Reaching inside she pulled out the .38 he'd used against the two robbers. She hesitated, then tucked the pistol into her belt. Having a gun in the house might not be a bad idea.

Tarboy went into the other stall. With much praise and petting, she lifted off the saddle and bridle and rubbed him down with a towel. By the time she'd finished doing the same for the two mares and Mary's gelding, her teeth were chattering. She was soaked to the skin. And she would get wet all over again going back to the house.

There was no use putting it off. Bracing herself for the downpour, she stepped out of the barn, sprinted through a quagmire of mud and manure in the corral and clambered over the fence. The yard was a spattering lake of rainwater. Clara ran toward the house, sloshing with every step. Her boots would be a mess, but that couldn't be helped.

Out of breath and dripping, she stumbled up the stairs and onto the porch. There she peeled off her wet boots and sluiced water out of her shirt, jeans and hair.

Even in the warmth of the house she was shivering. It was urgent that she get into some dry clothes. But first she needed to check on Tanner.

She found him sleeping so deeply that he barely stirred at her touch. He was still feverish but no longer chilling. Clara lingered a moment at his bedside, listening to the drone of the rain and the slow cadence of his breathing. Sleep was the best medicine for him, she told herself. Tanner was a powerful man. She could only hope that, with rest and fluids, his body would be strong enough to fight off the infection.

She couldn't let herself think of any other outcome.

Gathering up his pants and boots, she took them into Mary's room and shoved them under the bed. If he woke up and decided to leave again, it wouldn't do to have them close by. She would get the pistol out of sight, too. Then she'd look for dry clothes. Maybe she could put on something of her grandmother's. But what if she needed to rush outside again, or mount up and ride for help? Mary never wore pants, and Clara didn't want to brave the storm in one of her grandmother's housedresses. Hopefully there would be something more usable upstairs where the old clothes were stored.

After hiding the pistol behind the couch cushions, she climbed the narrow stairway to the upstairs bedrooms. Rarely used now, the rooms had housed Mary's growing brood of children. The smallest room had been converted for storage. Rough-hewn shelves held boxes of old books, canning jars, school papers, a guitar with broken strings, balls of used twine and a few worn-out toys. If Mary had saved her children's clothes—and the frugal woman rarely discarded anything—they would most likely be here.

A large, homemade pine wood chest stood against one wall. That would be the place to find clothes, Clara reasoned. The girls' dresses would be hopelessly out of style and a problem to ride in. But Mary had also raised three strapping sons. An outgrown pair of jeans or overalls and a warm shirt would do just fine.

The chest, which had no lock, did contain clothes. On top there were worn cotton dresses, petticoats, chemises and flannel nightgowns, all of them too small. Wet and shivering in the unheated room, Clara moved them aside and dug deeper. Now she found boys' clothes, as well. But the denim overalls and flannel shirts were child-size. One by one, Clara lifted them out and held them up. Nothing here would fit her. Maybe all the larger garments had been worn to rags by the time they were outgrown.

She had nearly reached the bottom of the chest when her fingers discovered a book-size object. Its solid shape yielded to her touch with a light crackle of paper. Curious, she reached in with both hands and lifted it to the light of the small window.

It was a packet of some sort, wrapped in brown paper and bound with knotted string. An address was written on it in faded ink. In the faint light, Clara could just make it out.

Miss Hannah Gustavson
General Delivery, Dutchman's Creek, Colorado

The return address was easier to read. The packet bore the official stamp of the U.S. Post Office in Skagway, Alaska Territory.

Wet clothes forgotten for the moment, Clara stared at the packet. It was addressed to her mother. But Hannah had been Mrs. Judd Seavers for twenty years. This piece of mail must have been sent to her a very long time ago.

Sitting on her heels, she examined the wrapping. One end appeared to have been opened, then tucked closed again. A probing finger revealed the contents. Inside the paper wrapping, Clara could detect a tightly compressed stack of letters.

Hastily now, she replaced the clothes in the trunk and closed the lid. The voice of discretion whispered that she should replace the packet as well. But curiosity was eating her alive. She had to know what was inside.

Rain drummed against the shingled roof overhead, cascading in torrents off the eaves. She couldn't stay here. The room was too chilly and too dim, and she needed to check on Tanner.

Holding the packet away from her wet shirt, she padded down the stairs and left it on the kitchen table. Tanner had flung off one of the quilts and was stirring feverishly, muttering as if in the grip of a bad dream. Clara straightened the covers and sponged his face with a damp sleeve. "Rest," she whispered. "It's all right. I'm here."

His eyes opened to stare into hers. He looked startled, almost as if he'd expected to see someone else. Then he drifted back to sleep, more peacefully this time.

Clara was shivering in her wet clothes. This was no time to be particular. If she needed to go out, she could put her damp things back on. Right now, she had to get warm.

Leaving Tanner, she went into her grandmother's room and found a thick flannel nightgown in the drawer. Stripping down, she pulled it over her head. The fabric was soft and warm, a comfort against her chilled skin. In the kitchen she hung her wet clothes over the backs of the chairs and lined them up in a half circle around the stove. Hopefully everything would be dry in an hour or two. Meanwhile, she could settle in the parlor, listen to the rain and explore the contents of the mysterious packet.

Curling up on the couch with a knitted afghan, she unfolded the crumpled end of the packet and let the letters drop into her lap. There were perhaps a dozen, none of them opened. They scattered as they fell.

Each envelope was rubber-stamped with the word *UNCLAIMED*. Evidently the postal clerk had decided to return them all together. Picking one up at random, Clara recognized her mother's neatly rounded school-girl handwriting. Her brows met in a puzzled scowl as she read the address.

Mr. Quinton Seavers
General Delivery, Skagway, Alaska

Strange, Clara thought. Uncle Quint had never mentioned being in Alaska. And why would her mother have written him so many letters? The two were close to the same age, so it was natural to assume they'd been friends. Still, it seemed odd.

With a prickle of foreboding, Clara worked her

finger beneath the flap of the envelope. Crumbly with age, the glue gave way easily. Unfolding the letter, she began to read.

May 19, 1899
Dear Quint,

There's no easy way to say this. We're going to have a baby, my dearest. It should be born in December. I know how much you want to find your fortune in Alaska. But we have to think of our child now. You need to come home so we can get married, the sooner the better...

Clara reread the first paragraph word by word, as if looking for some mistake. For the space of a long breath she sat in frozen silence, her eyes staring into space. Then her frantic hands began scrambling for other envelopes, ripping them open, pulling out the letters and arranging them by date. The earliest ones were simple declarations of love and longing. Most of the others were pleas for Quint to return, or at least to write back. Finally, one of the latter ones held the answer to the question screaming in her mind.

June 6, 1899
My Dearest Quint,

Judd has offered to marry me in your absence, to make our baby part of the Seavers family. With nowhere else to turn, I have accepted his offer. Please understand, the marriage is to be in name only. Your mother's lawyer will draw up divorce papers that need only be signed to become legal. When you return, we'll be free to wed. Please understand, my love, I'm only doing this for the sake of our child…

Hands stilled, Clara stared at the photographs on her grandmother's wall, at the faces she'd come to know as her family. Everything had changed in the light of one inescapable truth. Quint Seavers—her darling, dashing uncle Quint—was not her uncle at all.

He was her father.

Chapter Five

He was dreaming again, the nightmare as real as when he'd lived it. He could see Hollis's body sprawled half-naked on the bedroom floor, his blood soaking like spilled wine into the peacock-blue Persian carpet. He could see Ruby's bloodied cheek and purpled eye and feel the hot weight of the pistol as he slid it into his pocket.

His sister, clad in a torn mauve silk dressing gown, had been in shock. "Go to your girls, Ruby," he'd ordered her. "Make sure they don't see this. Give me a ten-minute head start. Then call the police. You know what to say."

The rest of the dream was always the same—running, running, down the long, curving stairway and out the front door and onto the porch, where he'd paused long enough to think about fleeing in his new green Packard. No good, he'd decided. The roads could be blocked, the flashy auto easily spotted. Decision made, he'd raced for the stable.

The irony of taking Hollis's prize Thoroughbred stud, worth a small fortune, hadn't escaped him. But he'd chosen the stallion for its power and speed, not for its pedigree. Ruby, he knew, would not report the horse missing.

"Where will you go, Jace? What will you do?" Her frantic questions had echoed in memory, lost in the scream of the train whistle as he raced through the night.

Where will you go? What will you do?

Lord help him, he had no answers.

Clara huddled on the wooden chair beside the bed. Beneath the loose flannel nightgown, her knees were drawn up against her chest. Her eyes watched Tanner's restless sleep, concentrating on him to distract herself from the shocking secret she'd uncovered. His legs twitched as if he were running in a murky dream. His lips moved forming words she couldn't make out. Only once had he spoken clearly—a name, Ruby.

Who was this Ruby? she wondered. A wife? A sweetheart? But why should she care? Until yesterday she hadn't even known the man existed. And as soon as he was well enough, assuming he survived, he'd be gone, taking the stallion with him. The only thing she knew about him for sure was that he couldn't be trusted. He was as mysterious as the wind.

But then, considering what she'd learned today, was anything what it appeared to be?

The clock in Mary's parlor chimed the hour of two.

Outside, the storm raged on, wind battering the house, rain turning the pastures to swamps and the yard to a sea of mud. A storm like this one would flood the road and probably wash out the bridge. Clara had already abandoned hope that Mary would make it home today. Her mother and Katy would likely be stranded as well and have to take a room for the night. The telephone lines were down—Clara had discovered that when she'd tried to call home. She was on her own here, with a man who could just as easily die as live.

This whole day had turned into a trip through the looking glass.

How many people had known that Quint was her father? Judd would have known, of course, as well as Mary and Aunt Annie and heaven knew who else. So when had they planned to let *her* in on the family secret?

Clara pressed her face to her knees, feeling the hardness of bone against her eye sockets. Questions flocked in her mind like the blackbirds she'd seen crossing the fields this morning.

Why hadn't Quint received her mother's letters? When had he learned he'd become a father? No doubt he'd at least found out when he returned home from wherever he'd gone. But the divorce had never happened. Quint had walked away, leaving Judd to raise his baby daughter. And six years later, after that terrible time in San Francisco, Quint had married Aunt Annie. Happy as the two of them appeared to be, they'd never been able to have children.

Clara stared down at her hands, at the square nails and the exaggerated webbing between her fourth and fifth fingers. Even her hands were a smaller version of his. She was Quint's child. His only child.

An image flashed through her mind—Quint's bruised and bleeding hands reaching toward her through the rubble of the San Francisco earthquake that had followed her kidnapping, the glimmer of tears in his eyes as he'd pulled her to safety. He had nearly lost his life rescuing her on that awful day. And he had known she was his. The whole time, he had known…

"Hello, there." Tanner's raspy voice startled Clara out of her reverie. She raised her head to see him gazing up at her sleepy eyed, his skin flushed and dry.

"How do you feel?" she asked him.

"Like hell," he muttered. "What time is it?"

"A little after two, and it's still raining outside. I fear my grandmother won't be back anytime soon." Clara rose from the chair. "I'll make you more tea and maybe some broth. You need all the fluids we can get down you, and the hot tea and broth will keep you warm."

"I have a better idea." He sounded drunk, although there was no way he could've had any alcohol.

"What's that?" She paused in the doorway.

"Since you're wearing your nightgown, why not just come to bed?"

Heat flashed in Clara's cheeks. She checked the impulse to lash out at him. The man wasn't in his right mind. Clearly he was even sicker than she'd feared.

His heavy-lidded eyes looked her up and down.

"Can't say much for the style. A little lace might improve it some, and maybe a nip in the waist…"

"Oh, for heaven's sake!" Clara exploded. "Having a fever's no excuse to act like a lout! Be still and rest. I'll be back in a few minutes with the tea!"

Slamming the door, she stalked into the kitchen, where she put the kettle on to boil and crumbled more willow bark. While the water was heating, she stood on a chair and searched Mary's supply of herbs for something else she could add. Yarrow…sage…creosote nodes… She put in pinches of the plants she knew to be safe. But she was still only guessing.

In the cool box, built into a shaded north wall, she found a pot of freshly made chicken soup. Silently blessing her grandmother, she put the soup on the stove to heat. While the tea was brewing, she carried the letters upstairs and replaced them in the trunk where she'd found them. She didn't have the time or energy to deal with her discovery now. She needed time to think. Maybe a long time.

When she came back downstairs a few minutes later, the tea was ready. Clara strained it into a white china cup and walked back toward what she'd begun to think of as Tanner's room. Opening the door, she gasped. Tanner was on his feet, moving unsteadily toward the doorway. Startled, she dropped the cup. It landed on the rug, not breaking, but spilling hot tea in all directions.

Her frayed nerves snapped. "What do you think you're doing?" she shrilled. "Get back into that bed, right now!"

He glared down at her as if she were a backward child. "*Miss* Clara, there are certain things a man likes to do standing up," he drawled. "Now if you'll excuse me—" He pushed past her, made his way toward the front door, stepped outside and turned toward the far end of the porch.

Clara retrieved the cup and found a rag to sop up the tea. Her cheeks were flaming. What was it about Tanner that made her want to fly at him with her fists and pummel him black and blue? The man was crude, arrogant, condescending and plain impossible. He had a way of making every word that came out of his mouth sound like an insult. Why, the ingrate hadn't even thanked her for taking care of him. Being sick was no excuse for being rude. It would serve him right if she rode away and left him here to rot!

Walking back toward the parlor, she flung the tea-soaked rag toward the kitchen sink. A tear welled in her eyes and made a salty trail down her cheek. Furiously she brushed it away. The last thing she wanted was for Tanner to see her cry. But more tears kept coming, like water spilling over a broken dam. It wasn't just Tanner. It was everything that had happened today—the whole blasted emotional bronco ride. The stress of dealing with Tanner had pushed her emotions to the brink. But what she'd learned about her parentage had carried her over the edge. She was exhausted and angry. Worse, her secure world had just shifted on its axis. Why hadn't they told her the truth? Who could she trust and depend on, if not her own family?

She had never felt so alone.

Tanner was gone for just a few moments. But by the time he came back inside, letting in the smell of rain, Clara's eyes were red and swollen from weeping.

"Rain's letting up, but the roof's blown off the damned hay shed," he said. "It'll take— What the—?" He broke off, staring at her. "Now what's the matter?"

"Nothing. Leave me alone." She turned her back so he wouldn't see how awful she looked.

"Oh, bloody—" He crossed the floor, laid his hands on her shoulders and turned her around, none too gently. "Listen, I know I've been a handful. If I'd had my way, I'd be long gone by now."

"And so would Galahad." She gave him a full view of her tear-ravaged face. "You were running out. It didn't matter that you'd likely fall off your horse and break your neck or drown in a puddle or die of the fever. You just wanted to get away—from *me!*"

"Not from you, Clara. There are other things, things you don't want to know. You and your grandmother would be better off with me gone."

His words triggered another surge of emotion. "It's not just you. It's...everything. This whole rotten day. If you only knew..." She gulped back a sob but she couldn't stop the tears. She ached to have him hold her, to melt into his arms and pour out her heart. But that would only make him uncomfortable, Clara told herself. Tanner didn't know her parents and he wouldn't care about her problems. All he wanted was to leave.

"Hellfire, I never could stand to see a woman cry!"

His hands cupped her face, hard and forceful, fingertips gripping the edge of her jaw. "I'd never hurt you if I could help it, girl. Don't you know that?"

Clara tried to answer him, but the only sound that emerged from her throat was a whimper of need.

"Oh, damn it all!"

With one swift, sure movement his mouth captured hers. His lips were fever hot, their power so compelling the Clara felt her knees go limp. She had wanted Tanner to kiss her, she realized, from the first moment she'd looked at him. And right now, kissing was exactly what she needed.

With a little whimper, she melted into his heat. Her arms slid around his neck. Her face tilted upward, lips softening against his. His own lips were chapped from fever, his jaw prickly with stubble. The roughness sent shivers of arousal all the way to her toes. She opened her mouth to welcome his probing tongue. More experienced girlfriends had told her that boys sometimes kissed this way, so she had some idea what to expect. She met each thrust with her own. The sensation was delicious and more than a little frightening—especially given Tanner's reaction.

A growl rumbled in his throat as he jerked her closer. Naked beneath the flannel nightgown, she could feel every subtle contour of his body against her skin—the muscled chest, the flat abdomen, the hard bulge pressing the length of her belly. The pulse between her legs had deepened to a savage throb. Instinctively she rose on tiptoe, straining upward to find him.

"Oh, damn it, don't do that, Clara..." he groaned in feeble protest. Then, as if to make lies of his words, his big hands groped for her buttocks through the worn fabric, found them and lifted her high and hard against him.

The contact triggered rocket bursts inside her. Clara's head reeled as she drank in the smell and feel and taste of him. She was spiraling out of control, and all she could think of was wanting more.

She wrapped one leg around him, curling her hips inward against that heavenly hardness. He rocked her, heightening the feeling until she wanted to scream. His breath had deepened to an urgent rasp. Her arms tightened around him as the sweet sensations swirled and peaked.

Lord, maybe it was the fever, Jace thought. Either that or he'd taken leave of his senses. Only two thin fabric layers separated his body from Clara's. She was pressed so close against his erection that he could feel the open cleft between her thighs. With a bit of imagination, he could feel the hard little bud inside it, rubbing against the sensitive underside of his shaft. Her hot young passion was driving him crazy. He wanted to rip away the nightgown, fling her on the bed and ram into her like a steam drill.

Do that, and he would hate himself forever.

Clara was all fire and innocence, trusting him to give her what she craved with no pain and no consequences. But that, Jace knew, wasn't possible. He was going to ride away, and he couldn't leave her soiled and hurting. Seconds more, and he'd be out of control. He had to put a stop to this madness. Now.

"No!" The word exploded out of him as he lowered her feet to the floor and shoved her away. "We're not doing this, Clara. I need to get out of here. Where are my clothes?"

Clara had stumbled against the back of the couch. Her lips were damp and swollen from his kiss. Eyes burning with humiliation, she faced him. "Don't be a fool. It's raining outside and you're too sick to ride."

He forced himself to stay distant, knowing he wouldn't have the strength to pull away if she touched him again. "If I'm well enough to make love to a woman, I'm well enough to ride a horse."

"We didn't make love, Tanner. It never happened. And if you try to ride out of here, you won't make it past the front gate."

"Maybe not. But that's not your problem. Whatever you might think of me, I have my own code of honor. The last thing I want is to repay a good woman's kindness by seducing her granddaughter. Now get my clothes."

"I'm not letting you leave. You're sick. You could die out there."

"That's not your choice to make," he said evenly.

"Isn't it?" Turning, Clara reached over the back of the couch and thrust her hand behind the cushions. At first Jace thought she was getting his clothes. Then she swung back toward him, and he saw the .38 Smith &

Wesson in her hand—the same weapon that had shot Hollis Rumford three times through the chest.

Eyes narrowed, she aimed the muzzle and thumbed back the hammer. Something told Jace the little sweetheart knew how to shoot.

"You're not going anywhere except back to bed."

Jace forced an easy grin. "Why, you little devil. You don't give a damn about me, do you? You just want to keep me here long enough for Galahad to do his manly duty."

"Believe me, if I pull this trigger you'll have no more worry about doing *your* manly duty," she snapped. "Now get back into that bed."

Her image swam before Jace's eyes. The past few minutes had drained what little strength he had. Now he was feeling light-headed again. It was all he could do to stay steady on his feet.

"You're not going to shoot me, Clara," he said. "That wouldn't make sense. Why would you shoot somebody you're trying so hard to save?"

He studied her from beneath one quirked eyebrow, struggling to appear as if he could stride out the door any minute. He sensed a slight hesitation, but she kept the pistol level, the hammer cocked.

"I'll grant you extra points for determination," Jace said. "Now put that gun down and find my boots and trousers, and I'll be on my way."

She shook her head. "Not on your life. You're ill. You're not thinking clearly."

"Then it seems we have what's known as a Mexican standoff."

"Call it whatever you want. Looking at you now, I'd lay odds you wouldn't even make it down the steps before you passed out." She lowered the pistol and released the hammer. "Try it if you don't believe me. Meanwhile, there's chicken soup heating on the stove and more tea left in the kettle. Stay until morning. If you're feeling better by sunup, I promise I won't try to stop you from leaving."

Bracing his hand on the door frame for support, Jace tried to ignore the hot chills creeping over his skin. His muscles ached; his eyes ached—and he was feeling worse by the minute. Like it or not, he knew he wasn't going anywhere. He would spend the coming hours here in this bed. Clara would tend him and fuss over him, but the outcome would hinge on whether his own body could fight off the infection. By morning the tale would likely be told. Either he would be past the crisis, or he would be dead.

Waves of red fog were sweeping over him, pulling him under. Jace made it into the room before his legs gave way. He heard Clara's voice as if from a great distance. Then he staggered, reeled and crashed onto the bed.

Outside, the rain had stopped. Trailed by a glimmer of stars, the moon rode the crest of the clearing sky. From the boggy ground along the creek, frogs piped a droning chorus. Crickets chirped in the drenched flower beds below the porch. Bats knifed through the darkness.

If Clara had taken time to check the clock, she would

have known it was past midnight. But for her, time had lost its meaning. Her attention was focused on the man who lay on the bed, muttering in half-conscious dreams.

Tanner was burning with fever. She felt the heat as she sponged his hot face, his closed eyelids, the hollow of his throat. Dipping and wringing the cloth again, she moved down to his chest and arms, his ribs and his flat belly. Hours ago she'd pulled off his flannel shirt and laid it aside. By now his torso was so familiar to her eyes and hands that she could have drawn it from memory—the broad shoulders and muscular chest, the wide-spaced nipples that shrank at her touch, the soft mat of light brown hair that spread over his chest, narrowing to a *V* that trailed off beneath the drawstring band of his cotton drawers.

Clara could not bring herself to wash him any lower. The memory of that jutting ridge pressing her cleft, driving her to a mindless frenzy, was too fresh, too painful. He'd been right to push her away. She'd made a fool of herself, and all she wanted now was to forget.

But what did her humiliation matter when the man could be dying? Early on, she'd spooned chicken soup into his mouth and dosed him with cup after cup of bark tea. But Tanner's condition had only worsened. Now, in his fevered half-sleep, she no longer dared give him fluids for fear he might choke on them.

Clara had tried everything she knew. Every hour she'd checked the telephone in the vain hope the line would be working. She'd wept. She'd prayed. She'd clasped Tanner's burning hands and railed at him to get well. Now, with nothing accomplished and nothing left to give, she was on the verge of collapse. She huddled on the chair beside the bed, listening to the shallow cadence of his breath. Her leaden eyelids drooped lower and lower. The damp cloth fell from her fingers and dropped to the floor…

The stallion was running at full gallop, flying against the wind over the rocky ground. Tanner strained forward in the saddle, lashing with the reins. Clara clung to his back, her arms locked around his ribs. Something, or someone, was chasing them, coming up hard behind, gaining fast. Galahad was giving his all, but he was carrying double. Only with a single rider could the great horse run fast enough to escape. There was just one way Clara could save Tanner.

Let go. Let go now.

There was no time to summon her courage. She leaned back and opened her arms wide. The wind sucked her off the back of the horse. She felt herself falling, spinning through space…

She woke to the sound of chattering teeth. Her eyes shot open. Tanner was shaking violently beneath the light blanket. Clara rose, gathered the quilts she'd tossed on the floor earlier and laid them one by one over his shivering body. Even then, he continued to shiver. There had to be something else she could do to get him warm.

Since you're wearing your nightgown, why not just come to bed? His fevered taunt surfaced in her memory. She hesitated. Her grandmother would never approve of what she was thinking. But a man's life was in peril, and desperate times called for desperate measures.

Lifting the covers, she squeezed into the narrow bed, stretched out on her side and pulled him close. He moaned as she molded to his solid body. His flesh was hot and dry, but he was trembling with cold. Surely the fever would break soon. If not, she realized, Tanner could die in her arms.

He nestled into her warmth, his heat burning into her. His head lay against her shoulder, shallow breath warming the hollow of her throat. Her leg lay across his thighs, keeping the contact close. Holding him, Clara felt a strange sweetness. Was this how it would feel being married, holding her husband in the night? The contact was more intimate than a kiss, more intimate, even, than the heady embrace that had ended in his thrusting her away. This was almost like loving.

Almost.

She felt him relax against her as the shaking quieted, heard the gradual easing of his breath. Dizzy with tenderness, she cradled him in her arms and slowly began to drift.

The parlor clock struck two, but in the hush of darkness no one heard.

She lay naked beneath him, the way he'd wanted her from the first time he saw her. Her chestnut curls, fragrant with the smell of summer grass, tumbled over the pillow. Her eyes were heavy lidded, drowsy with lust behind the dark veil of her lashes. Her lips were damp and swollen from the kisses he was now trailing down the hollow between her lush little breasts. Her skin was warm honey, so intoxicating that he could get drunk on the taste of her. His grazing lips found one puckered nipple, ripe and swollen. She arched upward as he took it in his mouth, teasing and tasting. Her hands raked his hair, pulling his head closer, driving his mouth against her breast. Hellfire, but she was sweet. He couldn't get enough of her. He wanted to taste more...everything.

His ravenous mouth moved down her belly, pausing to let his tongue explore the hollow of her navel. She whimpered as he touched the little knot of flesh. Her hands gripped his shoulders, urging him down between her parted legs. Drowning in her musky woman scent, he nuzzled lower. The soft curls of her pubic nest parted. She was hot and slick. His tongue found the satiny folds and the exquisitely sensitive little nub at their center. She moaned, hips arching upward against his mouth as he sucked her.

His own loins were pounding with need. He wanted to be inside her, pumping hard and deep into that tight, wet center. Rising on his arms, he shifted between her thighs and with one thrust...

He woke, drenched in sweat. Spent but clearheaded, Jace stared up into the fading darkness. The fever had broken. It appeared he was going to live after all.

Sensing a presence close by, he raised himself on one elbow. Clara lay beside him, fast asleep. Chastely clad in the oversize flannel nightgown, she looked as innocent as a child. Her dark lashes lay lush against her cheeks. Damp tendrils of hair clung to her forehead. A wave of tenderness swept over him. She had worn herself out working to save his life. And when she could do no more, she'd remained here, at his side.

Resisting the urge to touch her body, he brushed a light kiss across her forehead. She whimpered and settled back into sleep. Jace willed away the memory of his lascivious dream. Clara was little more than a girl, sweet and trusting. She had yet to know the misery that the wrong kind of man could wreak on her young life.

And he would not be the one to teach her, Jace vowed. Moving cautiously, he eased himself out of bed, leaving Clara asleep. For a moment he stood looking down at her, so beautiful in the dawn light that filtered through the curtains. It would be better this way, Jace told himself. She would awaken to find him gone. And if Mary returned later with the marshal, Clara would have nothing to tell them.

Caution whispered that he wasn't yet well enough to travel. Never mind that. If he could stand, he could walk. And if he could walk, he could ride. It was time he saddled up and hit the road.

Taking careful steps, he made it out of the room and

closed the door softly behind him. He was still light-headed. Some food in his belly should fix that. But first he would need to find his pistol, clothes and boots.

The .38 lay on the back of the couch where Clara had left it. But there was no sign of the other things he needed. Jace cursed silently, remembering that the little minx had hidden them. He had a clean shirt and pants folded into his bedroll. But he had only one pair of boots, and he couldn't go anywhere without them.

Muttering, he began his search. Every minute of time he wasted raised the odds that his pretty nurse and jailer would wake up. And knowing Clara, she would do anything to keep him and Galahad from leaving.

He started his search in the parlor, peering under the furniture and opening drawers and cabinets. Nothing. And the kitchen yielded no better. Jace checked the pantry and the cool box, growing more and more frustrated. Where would the little devil hide something as large as a pair of boots?

Only two of the downstairs rooms remained—Mary's bedroom and the smaller room where Clara now slept. Under Mary's bed, Jace found what he was looking for. The hiding place was so obvious that he cursed himself for not having looked there in the first place. Searching the house had cost him precious time.

Laying the pistol on the bed, he dressed hurriedly, pulling up the faded jeans and fastening the belt. He had tugged on one boot and was reaching for the second when he heard a floorboard creak behind him.

Clara stood in the doorway, looking angry enough

to spit hot nails. "I see you're feeling better, Tanner," she said in a taut voice. "Now suppose you tell me what you think you're doing."

Chapter Six

Jace yanked on his other boot as Clara challenged him from the doorway. She looked adorably tousled, her curls tumbling in her eyes, her swollen mouth ripe for kissing. Under different circumstances, he might have been tempted to sweep her up and carry her back to bed. But this was no time for games.

He rose to face her. "I'm leaving. And if you know what's good for you and your grandmother, you won't try to stop me."

She stood her ground, blocking the doorway. "What is it, Tanner? Have you done something? Are the police looking for you?"

Damn those wide, innocent eyes of hers. Jace had to look away. "You don't want to know the answers to those questions," he growled. "All I can say is it's time to call in that favor you promised me."

She bristled like a startled cat. "Promised? That's a joke! There's no promise unless you stay long enough for Galahad to breed my mares. And unless he's broken out of that stall where I put him and done the job in the night, I don't owe you a thing!"

Jace sighed. She had him there. "All right. But I still need your help. Let's just call it a favor, no promise attached."

"What kind of favor?" She eyed him suspiciously.

"All I'm asking for is your trust—and your silence."

"That's a pretty tall order. Why should I trust you, of all people?" She folded her arms, compressing her breasts until the nipples strained the worn pink flannel. Jace struggled to fix his eyes on her pretty face.

"Because I'd never harm you or your grandmother or any other innocent person."

"But you've done something. Why else would you be in such an all-fired hurry to leave?"

"Whatever I did, it needed doing, and that's all I'll say."

"So you're asking me not to tell anybody you're wanted by the law? Not even my grandmother?"

"Especially not your grandmother. She's been good to me. It would hurt her to know the truth."

"*I* don't know the truth. I don't even know your real name."

"And that's for the best." Damnation, he'd told her far too much. Those velvety doe eyes had a way of peering into his soul, probing out secrets he'd sworn never to tell anyone. He needed to get out of here before he put himself—and her—in even more danger.

"As far as you're concerned, I was gone when you

woke up, and I didn't tell you anything," he said. "I'm sorry about the stallion, but some things can't be helped. If you saved my life last night I want you to know I'm grateful."

"Right now I'm wondering why I bothered."

"That's the spirit." Jace forced a laugh. "I believe my shirt's in the other room. I'll get it and be on my way."

"Wait—please. I'll do as you asked, but I want to go out to the barn with you to check on the horses. While I'm getting dressed, you can help yourself in the kitchen. You shouldn't go away hungry."

"Fine." Her request made sense, Jace conceded. She probably wanted to make sure he didn't take anything from the barn. And he did need something to eat before he left.

Clara's dry garments were draped over the backs of the kitchen chairs. Snatching them up, she vanished into Mary's bedroom to change. Before donning his shirt, Jace checked the knife wound. The cut was clean and healing, already showing a healthy pink around the edges. Another day or two and he wouldn't need the dressing on it. One less thing to worry about. Maybe the fever had been a fluke, something unrelated to the wound. As long as he was getting better, it didn't matter.

In the kitchen he buttered some bread, sweetened it with a dollop of Mary's loganberry jam and poured himself a glass of cold milk. He would miss this place, Jace mused. He would miss the mountain peaks, the clean, fresh air and the sound of meadowlarks in the morning. He would miss the peaceful work, Mary's good meals and the friendly conversation that went along with them. And he would miss the chance to know Mary's fiery granddaughter.

Maybe that most of all.

It had been a long time since he'd thought much about Eileen. She belonged to that other world—the one he'd left behind and would never see again. She was a beautiful ornament whose presence on his arm would have opened the doors of power. But in the wake of his scandalous disappearance, Eileen would want nothing to do with him. Jace couldn't say he blamed her. Even if she'd loved him, she would have the good sense to turn her back and walk away.

Clara Seavers, on the other hand, was a girl who led with her heart. Passionate and impulsive, she had everything to learn about love and loss. But Jace cared too much to let himself be her teacher.

He hoped to heaven she wouldn't beg him to stay.

Clara's sudden reappearance broke into his reverie. She was fully dressed except for her boots. Her wrinkled shirt clung to her lush young body in a way that made his mouth go dry.

"I'll be on the porch knocking the mud off my boots," she said. "Come out when you're ready."

She swung the door all the way open, letting in a rush of rain-freshened air. The screen door snapped back into place. A moment later Jace heard her whacking her boots against the side of the steps. By the time he'd finished eating and brushed away the crumbs, the sound had ceased.

In the silence, Jace walked across the parlor and out through the screen door. Clara stood on the porch, holding her boots and gazing toward the distant road.

"What is it?" He squinted, eyes still adjusting to the glare of morning sunlight.

"There—through the trees. Somebody's coming."

Dread clenched a knot in Jace's stomach. Could he get to the barn and get away? Maybe he'd be better off hiding.

"I don't see—" he began. Then he realized where she was looking. A lone rider was approaching the gate at a trot. Skirts fluttered behind the saddle.

"It's Grandma!" Clara bent to yank on her boots. "The bridge must be out. Otherwise she'd have brought the buggy."

"I didn't know she could ride." Jace shaded his eyes, watching Mary approach.

"It bothers her rheumatism. But she can ride well enough if she has to." Clara bounded down the steps and raced across the yard, waving as Mary turned her gelding in the gate.

Jace remained on the porch, weighing his options. Mary's arrival complicated everything. At least it didn't appear that she'd brought the law with her. But there was no telling who she'd spoken to in town. He was caught in a dangerous trap. And now that she was here, he could hardly saddle up and gallop away. Not without rousing her suspicion.

The big question was could he trust Clara? She was a smart girl, and he'd revealed far too much. With nothing to hold her to her promise, she could betray him on a whim. But would she? Right now only one thing was certain.

Miss Clara Seavers held his fate in the palm of her pretty little hand.

By the time Clara met her grandmother, halfway down the drive, she was out of breath. Mary steadied the shotgun across the saddle and slowed the horse to a walk. Her sharp Nordic eyes took in her granddaughter's tousled hair and wrinkled clothes. "My stars, girl, what have you been up to? I didn't expect you'd be here at this hour!"

Clara chose to tell the truth. "Tanner got sick. I had to tend him all night."

Mary glanced toward the porch. "He looks well enough this morning."

"Last night he was burning up. The fever finally broke toward dawn. I got soaked putting the horses away and had to wear your nightgown till my clothes dried. I know how it looks, but honestly, nothing happened. Please don't tell Mama I was here alone with Tanner."

The older woman sighed. "It seems we have far too many secrets between us these days, my dear. But all right, just this once. Your mother and Katy were still at the hotel when I left, waiting for the bridge to be fixed. When they get home later today, you're to be there, cleaned up and looking like an angel. And no more secrets. Do we understand each other?"

"Yes, thank you, Grandma." Clara bit back the question that burned on the tip of her tongue. What about the biggest secret of all—the one contained in the letters she'd discovered upstairs? Mary might be the one to tell her the truth. But this wasn't the time to ask.

They were nearing the porch. Tanner came down the steps to help Mary out of the saddle. She gripped his hand, wincing at the pain in her stiff joints.

"Do you have a way to get the buggy home?" He took the shotgun from her and laid it on the porch.

"If you're offering, don't trouble yourself. I promised a boy at the livery stable a dollar to bring it when the bridge is open. He'll use his own horse to ride back." She hobbled up the porch steps and sank into the rocker. Her eyes surveyed the storm-battered yard and outbuildings. "What a mess! I hope you plan on staying awhile, Tanner. I'll need your help getting the place shipshape again."

Clara kept her eyes on Tanner. He shifted uncomfortably, saying nothing.

"By the way," Mary remarked as if by chance, "I saw our two friends in town."

Tanner looked ready to bolt. "What friends?" he asked in a casual manner that didn't fool Clara for an instant.

"The two no-accounts we chased out of here. They won't be bothering us or anybody else again." She paused to clear her throat. "Would one of you get me a glass of water?"

"I will." Clara flitted into the house, not wanting to

miss any of the story. She returned seconds later with a glass of cold water from the kitchen faucet.

"I saw them myself," Mary was saying. "Laid out like firewood on the back of the marshal's wagon, both of them deader than doornails. When I asked around, somebody told me that Ole Swenson had come outside with a shotgun and caught them stealing eggs from his chicken coop."

Clara handed her grandmother the glass. "He shot them? For stealing eggs?"

"They'd have done worse if they'd had the chance. Ole was protecting his property and his family. No law is going to fault him for that."

"Did you tell the marshal they'd been to your place?" Tanner asked.

"The marshal was busy. I didn't want to bother him. What difference would it have made? The men were dead. Nobody but the good Lord can judge them now." Mary shooed a horsefly off her skirt. "Besides that, my daughter would worry if she knew what had happened here. She and Judd would pluck me out of this house faster than you could say Jack Robinson."

Clara had kept her eyes on Tanner. She saw the tension ease in his face and body. Clearly he'd been expecting the marshal to show up. Maybe now he'd stay long enough to heal properly...and for Galahad to breed her mares.

"I'll take care of your horse and see to the others, Grandma," she said. "You sit here and rest awhile."

"I'll be getting to the chores." Tanner loped down the

steps and strode off in the direction of the milking shed. Clara watched him go as she led Mary's horse toward the barn. Maybe they'd get a chance to talk before her grandmother sent her packing for home. Then again, that might not be such a good idea. Talking with Tanner tended to strip away her defenses, leaving her raw and vulnerable. That was the last thing she needed today.

In the barn she found the horses safe but restless. The two mares were as demure as nuns, showing no signs of interest in the big stallion. Clara sighed as she turned them out to graze. "You ladies don't know what you're missing!" she scolded them as she closed the paddock gate. "A fine gentleman like Galahad doesn't happen along every day of the week!"

And a man like Tanner didn't happen along every day either, she mused. But what had put that thought into her head? By his own admission, Tanner was a fugitive, running from the law. If she had the sense of a plucked goose, she'd call the marshal and turn him in.

But something about him—call it pride, or even honor—made her hesitate. Tanner didn't strike her as a man who'd stoop to dishonesty or to harming innocent people. But then, who was she to judge? How many women had been taken in by a handsome face, only to end up with broken hearts and ruined reputations?

She'd be a fool to let that happen to her.

The stallion snorted when she opened his stall, but he allowed her to lead him out of the barn. After turning him loose in the paddock with her mares, she unsaddled Mary's horse and put the two geldings in the corral. Then she led Tarboy out of his stall to saddle him for the ride home.

She was bending to tighten the cinch, her hair tumbling over her face, when the east door opened. Sunlight spilled across the straw as Tanner stepped into the barn. His tall frame loomed over her, casting a shadow where she stood. Clara glanced up. Her pulse lurched at the sight of his stormy expression. Had he come to thank her or to threaten her?

Rather than wait to find out, she decided to make the first move. Rising, she swept her hair out of her face and met his gaze straight on.

"So, will you be staying awhile longer?" she asked him. "My grandmother could certainly use your help."

For a moment he stood silent, his narrowed eyes taking her measure. A chilly breeze from outside raised goose bumps on her skin. What if she'd been wrong about him? What if he was as cold as he appeared to her now? A man who could look like that might be capable of anything.

"That depends on you," he said. "Can I trust you to keep your word, Clara?"

"You can, as long as you stay until my mares are bred—and as long as you give me no reason to worry about my grandmother's safety."

"I'd never harm your grandmother, or you. You should know that by now."

She shook her head. "I don't really know anything about you, Tanner."

Except how I felt when you held me in your arms.

"You know enough to put me in danger. If I can't count on you to keep still, it's best that I leave right now. Your grandmother can hire somebody else."

"Tell me what you did."

His mouth tightened. "That's not part of the bargain. The less you know, the safer for both of us."

Clara took a breath to ponder his words. Tanner was right. Knowing about his crime could leave her open to arrest for aiding a fugitive. Not knowing was the only protection he could offer her. As for his own safety, what she didn't know, she couldn't repeat, even under threat.

"You'll stay until Galahad breeds my mares?"

"Only if I think it's safe."

"And if you don't, for whatever reason?"

"Then I'll ride out of here, and you'll never see me or the stallion again. Do we understand each other?"

"Yes. And don't worry, you have my word." Clara realized she was trembling. She put out her hand to seal the bargain. His big, leathery palm enfolded her fingers in a brief but firm handshake. Something like tenderness flickered in the blue depths of his eyes, then vanished.

"I'd better be getting back to work," he said. "I'll keep an eye on your mares and let you know what happens."

"Thank you. I guess I'll be going home now."

Neither of them moved. Clara stood gazing up at him, her feet rooted to the ground. What was she waiting for? Did she want the man to kiss her?

Yes, heaven save her, she did.

He leaned toward her, his face filling her vision. His lips parted. Driven by instinct, Clara strained upward. For the space of a heartbeat time froze. Then, without a word, he straightened, turned away and strode out of the barn.

Clara stood quivering in the straw, waiting for her pulse to resume its normal rhythm. Anger began a slow simmer in her belly, its heat rising to the roots of her hair. How could she have made such a fool of herself? She'd behaved like a silly schoolgirl. Tanner probably thought she didn't have a brain in her head.

Tarboy nickered, his nose butting her shoulder as if to remind her it was time to go. Willing herself to move, she led him out of the barn and swung into the saddle. A furtive glance around the farmyard confirmed that Tanner was nowhere to be seen.

Suddenly all Clara wanted was to go home. The past twenty-four hours had been like a runaway ride down the face of a mountain, leaving her physically and emotionally drained. She would swing by the porch for a quick goodbye to Mary. Then she'd head home for a hot bath and a nap under the pink eiderdown she'd kept on her bed since childhood.

She would rest, read and do her best not to think about the man who called himself Tanner.

Tanner stood in the shadow of the ruined hay shed watching Clara gallop away. On horseback she was so beautiful that she made his throat ache—her back straight and proud, her hair flying like a silk banner, her denim-clad buttocks bouncing in the saddle.

He stifled a groan at the memory of holding her against him, feeling the warm contours of her body, the ripe moons of her sweet little bum cupped in his hands. When she'd ground herself against his arousal, he'd damn near exploded on the spot. It had been all he could do to push her away. The flash of hurt in her eyes had cut him like a razor.

He'd seen that same hurt again moments ago when he'd resisted the temptation to kiss her plum silk lips. One day Clara would thank him for his restraint. But for now she was young and hot-blooded, driven by inner forces she could barely understand, let alone control. She was still discovering her power over men, still testing its limits. As an experienced male of twenty-nine, Jace shuddered to think where her curiosity might lead her next, especially with the wrong kind of man. Maybe he should speak to Mary about giving her granddaughter a firm talking-to.

Make that suggestion, and the good woman would likely run him off the place with a shotgun blast.

Jace watched Clara until she disappeared beyond the gap he'd left in the fence. Then he turned his attention to the ruined hay shed. By now, he was feeling all right. Whatever the cause of the fever, it had left him no worse than a little weak. Another day or so, and he'd be as good as new.

Meanwhile he had work to do. He would start with cleaning up the soggy hay and replacing the roof. That should keep him occupied through tomorrow. After that…

His gaze wandered to the grassy paddock beyond the barn, where Galahad was sniffing at the bay mare's haunch. Maybe the breeding would happen soon. Then, with the mares pregnant and Clara's wish satisfied, all he'd need would be an excuse to leave.

Maybe he'd head south this time—all the way to Mexico, where he'd be safe. He had never been to Mexico. Maybe he'd like it. Maybe he could even find a new life there.

But wherever he went, Jace knew that his dreams would be haunted by a pair of sunlit brown eyes—eyes he would never see again once he left Colorado behind.

By the time she neared home, Clara's spirits were sagging. She'd always felt so sure of herself, who she was and where she wanted to take her life. But the past twenty-four hours had shattered what she'd known as truth. She was adrift in a sea of uncertainty where nothing was solid or secure.

She'd never thought of herself as anyone but the daughter of Judd and Hannah Seavers. Now her whole identity had shifted. She was the illegitimate child of a charming, reckless man who'd fathered her in a moment of bad judgment.

Was it the heritage of Quint's hot blood that had caused her to catch fire in Tanner's arms? Or was it simply her own nature?

Her lips still burned when she thought about kissing

Tanner. She'd kissed a few boys at parties and dances. The one she'd kissed the most, redheaded Sam Perkins, had gone off to war and come home in a pine box. Even with Sam, though, the kisses had been tentative and awkward. She'd always pulled away when she'd sensed he wanted more.

This time Tanner had been the one to pull away.

As for the rest—Clara closed her eyes as a tiny aftershock of pleasure coursed through her body. Now she understood why some girls got in trouble. It was because they couldn't get enough of that wild honey sensation, that exquisite quivering that rose through the body to burst into flower like a tree of spring blossoms.

She'd always viewed herself as strong and sensible, one of the "good" girls. Now that perception had faded. She found herself thinking about Tanner, imagining herself in his arms, imagining the unspeakable things he could do to give her the pleasure she craved.

But what was she thinking? Everything about Tanner was wrong. What was more, he didn't even want her. When they'd kissed, he'd been half out of his head with fever. Even then he'd managed to shove her away when things got out of hand. This morning, in the barn, he hadn't laid a finger on her.

What in heaven's name was she going to do?

There was just one correct answer to that question— leave the man alone.

Crossing the last field, she rode into the yard and closed the gate behind her. The house was quiet, the

Model T still missing from its place in the shed. Clara sighed with relief as she swung out of the saddle. With luck, her mother would be in town for hours, waiting for the simple plank bridge to be rebuilt across the creek. By the time she returned, there'd be no reason to question where her errant daughter had spent the night.

She unsaddled Tarboy, gave him some oats and spent a moment fussing over Foxfire. The chestnut colt nuzzled her pocket, looking for the treat that wasn't there. Clara stroked the silky neck, her thoughts far away.

How would she feel, looking at her beautiful, perfect mother and knowing the truth?

How would she see her father—dear, kind Judd— who'd married his brother's sweetheart to raise and nurture a child who wasn't his?

How would she relate to Quint, who'd gone off adventuring and turned his back on a father's responsibility?

And how would she see herself? What would she feel when she looked into the mirror and saw Quint's hair, Quint's dimpled cheeks, Quint's eyes gazing back at her?

All this time. All the people who knew the secret. How could they not have told her? Should she confront her mother and demand to know why they'd kept the secret so long? Should she go to Mary and try to learn more?

Maybe it would be wiser to hold her tongue and wait for the right time.

As she came into the front hall, she heard Rosa, the family cook, rattling pans in the kitchen. Clara was hungry, but Rosa's sharp eyes were bound to see that something wasn't right and report it to her mother. Stomach growling, she hurried upstairs and ran a hot bath in the claw-footed porcelain tub. By the time she'd washed her hair and soaked away the tension in her muscles, her eyelids were drooping.

After toweling her hair dry, combing out the tangles and slipping into a clean white middy blouse and khaki knickers, she curled up under the eiderdown and closed her eyes for what she planned to be a short rest. Within minutes she was fast asleep.

The sound of an auto horn jarred her awake. Clara's muzzy gaze seized on the small dresser clock. It was almost one in the afternoon. Flinging aside the eiderdown, she bolted to the window.

The Model T was just pulling up to the house. Her mother and Katy were in the front seat. The back was piled with grocery sacks, shopping bags and two hat boxes. The tap on the horn was a clear call for anyone within hearing to come and help unload.

Shoving her bare feet into oxfords, Clara bow-knotted the laces and hurried downstairs. Rosa, a pretty, plump Mexican woman who'd ruled the Seavers kitchen for as long as Clara could remember, bustled out the front door ahead of her.

Clara's mother had climbed out of the car and was giving directions. "Katy, take the dresses and hat boxes upstairs. Clara, you can carry those feed bags to the granary while I help Rosa with the kitchen things. Then you can drive the auto into the shed." Hannah looked mussed and frazzled after spending an impromptu night in town on a saggy hotel bed. "Look at you, Clara," she fussed. "Your hair's a mess. And where are your stockings? I leave for one night and everything goes to ruin! Do you know whether your grandma made it home safely?"

Clara hesitated for a beat, not wanting to give herself away. "The last time I checked, the telephone was still out," she hedged.

"Well, never mind, then." Hannah brushed a stray lock out of her lovely cornflower-blue eyes. "Maybe after lunch you can ride over and make sure she's all right. Take Katy along if she wants to go."

"All right, Mama." Clara sighed as she hefted a bag of oats onto her shoulder and headed for the granary. There'd be no getting out of another ride to Mary's farm. Katy would want to go, and the girl was a notorious tattletale. Anything out of the ordinary would be duly noted and reported back to their mother—including the fact that Mary's hired man was tall and handsome with blue eyes to melt a woman's heart.

That description would be enough to send Hannah into a protective tailspin.

"Oh, wait, dear! There's something else."

Clara paused and turned at the sound of her mother's voice.

"I just wanted to share some good news!" Hannah

was smiling, holding up an envelope. "This was waiting at the post office. It's from your uncle Quint and aunt Annie."

Clara felt her heart plummet.

"They've been in France for the past month, you know," Hannah continued blithely. "Their boat just docked in New York. They'll be spending a few days there and then stopping here for a visit on their way home."

"When?" Clara forced the question from her tight throat.

"Let's see…" Hannah murmured, thinking out loud. "The letter says they'll be arriving June nineteenth. Why, that's just ten days off. Goodness, so much to do before then!"

Snatching up an armful of purchases, she hurried toward the porch. Clara stood for a moment looking after her mother. Then she turned away to hide an ambush of emotion.

Chapter Seven

They crossed the pastures in the blaze of afternoon sun, Clara astride Foxfire and Katy on Tarboy. Clara, whose golden skin never burned, was bareheaded. Katy, who'd inherited her mother's fairness, wore her brother's old straw fishing hat over her thistledown braids. She'd abandoned her town dress for the ticking-striped denim overalls she loved. At thirteen she was tall for her age, with gangly legs and features that had yet to come into balance. In a few years she'd doubtless be a pretty young woman. But she seemed determined to put off that time as long as she could.

In spite of the storm the previous night, the day was clear and warm, the distant fields bright gold with the bloom of wild mustard. Droning bees burrowed into patches of red clover. Where the horses walked, clouds of white butterflies rose out of the grass. Katy carried a basket packed with jam tarts from the town bakery and a batch of the fragrant cinnamon rolls that Rosa called *caracoles,* because of their shape, like the coiled shell of a snail. She shifted the basket from one arm to the other as she spoke.

"Why do I have to carry this? Why not you?"

"Because Foxfire might buck and make me spill the basket. Tarboy won't."

"I bet I could ride Foxfire. Can I ride him home?"

Clara shot her sister a stern look. "Don't even think about it. He's barely saddle broken."

"Please," Katy begged. "Just for a little way. I know I could ride him if you'd let me."

Clara shook her head. "Not yet, Katy. He could spook and throw you off. Maybe when you're older…"

"Maybe when I'm older. That's all I ever hear!" Katy pouted. "I hate being the youngest. I never get my way! You should see those dresses Mama and Miss Penny-worth picked out for me. Lace collars! Puffy sleeves! They're hideous. Why do I have to dress up anyway?"

"Maybe someday you'll *want* to dress up," Clara said. "In a few years you'll be old enough for dances—and boyfriends."

"Spare me." Katy rolled her eyes skyward, then lowered her gaze to her hands. "What's it like to kiss a boy, Clara?" she asked in a subdued voice.

A memory flashed through Clara's mind—Tanner's arms molding her against him, his mouth igniting a fire of need in the depths of her body.

"That depends on the boy," she said. "If you don't like him it can be gross, like biting into a rotten apple. If you do like him…" Clara paused, searching for the right words. "Then it's nice. So nice you'll want to do it again and again. But you shouldn't do it too much. Things can get out of control that way."

Clara glanced down at her hands. She knew how easily things could get out of control. She knew it all too well.

"You don't have to tell me about *that*," Katy said. "Beth Ann Ferguson had to get married last November, and she was only in the tenth grade. Now she's as big as a cow!"

"Katy!" Clara shook her head. Her sister could be a real terror when she put her mind to it. "Really, you're much too young to be thinking about such things."

"You sound just like Mama! I only asked about kissing. That doesn't mean I'm ever going to do it. Especially not with Henry Beecham."

"Oh?" Now, this was something new. "So you like Henry Beecham, do you?"

"That smart aleck?" Katy flushed. "I can't stand him! I wouldn't kiss him if he paid me a hundred dollars!"

"That's the spirit!" Clara teased. "You should hold out for at least a thousand!"

"I wouldn't kiss Henry Beecham for all the money in the world," Katy sniffed. "Hey, I see Grandma's house! Race you!"

"Whoa!" Clara moved in close to stop her sister from kicking the black gelding into a burst of speed. "You might drop the basket. Besides that, Grandma's new hired man fixed the fence a couple of days ago. You could ride Tarboy right into the new wire."

"Grandma's new hired man? The one with the stallion? Mama told me you were taking the mares over there to be bred."

"That's right." Clara headed for the open space where the new gate was to go.

"Is he handsome?"

"The stallion? Yes, he's a real beauty."

"No, the hired man, silly. What does he look like?"

"He's just a man," Clara lied. "Nothing special."

Nothing special at all. She would have to keep reminding herself of that. Any day now, Tanner would mount up and be gone like a passing whirlwind. The most she could hope for was signs of the stallion's bloodline in next summer's foals. By the time those foals arrived, Tanner's face would be nothing but a memory.

Why was the law after him? Clara wondered. What had he done? When she'd asked, he'd told her it had needed doing. But those words could be used to justify almost anything from petty theft to army desertion to murder.

It shouldn't matter, she told herself. Tanner would soon be out of her life. Bringing him to justice would be someone else's problem.

But he had kissed her until she ached. And he had lain in her arms, cradled against her body like a feverish, trusting child.

Whatever it took, she needed to know the truth about him.

"There's Grandma!" Katy's voice broke into her thoughts. "She's out by the clothesline."

Clara followed her sister's gaze. Damp sheets, towels and pillowcases drooped from the line where Mary was emptying the wash water. Clara's chest tightened with apprehension. What if her grandmother let it slip that she'd been here all night, alone with Tanner? The last thing she needed was for Katy to be carrying that juicy tale home.

The yard appeared strangely quiet. The unhitched buggy stood outside the barn where the boy from town would have left it. Timbers leaned against the side of the unfinished hay shed. In the paddock, under the big cottonwood tree, the two mares were sedately cropping grass.

There was no sign of Tanner or the stallion.

Clara rode into the yard, dismounted and looped Foxfire's reins over the corral fence. The sense of betrayal stung like lye in a fresh cut. So much for trusting the man! She'd thought they'd come to an understanding that morning—Tanner would stay and she wouldn't reveal what she knew about him. But he hadn't kept his word. For all she knew, he'd never meant to.

Anger simmering, she strode across the yard to where Mary was securing a dishcloth with a wooden clothespin. Katy slid off Tarboy and followed her with the basket.

"Hello, you two!" Mary turned away from the clothesline with a smile on her face. "What a nice surprise! I was about to sit down on the porch and rest my feet."

Clara exhaled with relief. So far, at least, her grandmother had remembered to keep her secret.

"We brought you a treat, Grandma." Katy held up the basket. "*Caracoles!* Rosa just made them this morning. And Mama put in some tarts from the bakery."

"Goodness, this calls for a celebration!" Mary said. "I bought some lemons in town yesterday, and they just arrived with the buggy. I'll go inside and make some lemonade."

"I can make the lemonade, Grandma." Clara hurried up the porch steps. "You sit down and rest."

"Thank you. The least I can do is come inside and keep you company. We can visit while you work." Mary glanced toward Katy. "Why don't you let your horses into the paddock, dear? That way they won't have to stand in the hot sun."

"Sure! Good idea!" Katy set the basket on the porch and trotted off toward the corral where Tarboy and Foxfire were tied. Clara opened the front door for her grandmother and followed her inside.

While Mary took a seat at the table, Clara washed the lemons and placed them on the cutting board. "I see that Tanner's moved on," she said, trying to sound disinterested. "Should I have Mama send somebody over to fix the hay shed?"

"No need for that. Tanner's still here."

Clara felt the leap of her pulse. "But I didn't see him or the stallion, and I thought—"

"You were mistaken, dear. Tanner started off fixing the shed, but I was worried about his lifting that heavy roof when he'd been so sick. So I ordered him off to ride the fence and check for any storm damage."

"Oh." Clara felt the telltale rise of color in her cheeks. She sliced a lemon in two and began squeezing juice into the glass pitcher.

Mary's eyes narrowed. "You aren't getting too attached to him, are you? You know that wouldn't be a good idea."

"Yes, I know." Clara's color deepened. "Has he told you much about himself?"

"Nothing I could put a finger on. But I've lived too long not to know when a man's got secrets. Not that I'm saying he's bad, mind you. I'd trust Tanner with my life. But he's a magnet for trouble. A girl would be foolish to give her heart to a man like that."

Clara sliced another lemon. "I hear you, Grandma. And believe me, you've nothing to worry about. I—" She broke off at a sound from outside. "What was that?"

"It sounded like a scream!" Mary was already on her feet. Clara rushed past her and burst out onto the porch.

Beyond the corral, she could see Foxfire bolting across the paddock. Katy was clinging frantically to the chestnut gelding's back.

Please, God, no! Clara raced for the paddock gate. Foxfire was headed for the far fence. If he jumped and failed to clear the barbed wire, horse and rider could go down in a horrific tangle of ripped flesh and broken bones. Katy could be killed or maimed for life.

The little fool! She just had to try it! Clara prayed with all her strength as the colt neared the fence, gathered his strength for the leap and soared over the top. For the space of a heartbeat his body seemed to hang in the air. Then his hind legs cleared the wire by a hairbreadth and he was down on the other side, staggering for balance. Righting himself, he wheeled and headed for the open fields with Katy hanging on to his back.

Tarboy was already saddled. Clara sprang onto his back and galloped him out of the gate. The black cow pony was smart and steady, but he was getting along in years and, even in his prime, he couldn't have matched Foxfire for speed. Clara's best hope was to keep the colt in sight and pray that Katy could hang on until he tired and slowed down.

Clara railed at herself as she raced Tarboy around the paddock fence. Why hadn't she realized her sister would try something like this? Katy was short on judgment and chafing to test her limits. If anything happened to her, Clara knew she would never forgive herself.

Foxfire was gaining distance. Clara could see him now, a hundred yards off, streaking through a field of blazing yellow mustard blooms. Katy, hatless now, had lost the reins and was clinging to the colt's neck. Her knees were awkwardly bent, feet out of the stirrups. With no control, she bounced dangerously at the slightest turn. The poor girl had to be wild with terror.

The colt was racing along the base of a low hill. Ahead lay a patch of bog. It was a treacherous, oozing spot of land, marked by sickly yellow grass, swarming gnats and unexpected sinkholes—a place where a horse could easily go down and break a leg. And Foxfire was flying straight toward it.

Clara pressed Tarboy harder, but the little black gelding was already giving his all. There was no way to stop Foxfire and save Katy from what lay ahead. Helpless and sick with dread she watched the colt carry her sister toward the bog and disaster.

It was only then that she saw the stallion. With Tanner in the saddle, Galahad came thundering across the flatland, long legs pumping, powerful body stretched in a blinding burst of speed. By now Foxfire was beginning to tire. In any case he was no match for the big stallion.

Clara eased the lathered Tarboy to a canter, watching from a distance as the stallion swooped in like a hawk on its prey. Foxfire was almost in the bog. Would Tanner be able to stop him, or was it already too late?

Heart in her throat, she watched Tanner bring his horse in hard alongside the racing colt. He could pull Foxfire to a halt by seizing his bridle. But the colt would almost certainly rear, flinging Katy hard to the ground under his trampling hooves.

Clara's breath caught as she realized what Tanner was trying to do. He had made a choice—the only choice he could make.

He moved Galahad in closer, pressing the colt's flanks. His hand flashed out to grip the back straps of Katy's overalls. "Let go!" he shouted. "Now!"

In a single motion he jerked her off the saddle and heaved her in against him. She dangled at his side, gasping as he swung the stallion, reined him to a halt and dropped her safely into the grass. As she collapsed in a sobbing heap, Foxfire rocketed into the bog.

Given the rain-filled holes and the colt's momentum, what happened next was almost to be expected. Clara heard the snap of bone and the scream as Foxfire pitched forward heels over head and went down. Seconds later she reached Katy, flung herself out of the saddle and gathered her close.

"I'm sorry, Clara," Katy sobbed. "I'm so sorry."

"Hush. You're all right. That's all that matters." Clara glanced up. Tanner had dismounted. She caught the gleam of the .38 in his hand. "Wait," she told him, then turned back to her sister.

"You're to get on Tarboy and ride him back to Grandma's," she said. "Not too fast, remember he's tired. Let Grandma know you're all right. Then take Tarboy to the barn and rub him down. You know what to do."

"But what about Foxfire? He's hurt." Katy's tear-swollen eyes were like red holes in her face. She'd grown up on a ranch. She had to know what needed to be done. But she was all innocence and denial.

"Tanner and I will take care of him," Clara said. "You go back to the house. Now, Katy."

Katy stumbled to her feet, climbed onto Tarboy's back and nudged the gelding to an easy trot. Clara watched as they moved off through the mustard field like a black boat in a sea of blazing yellow. Her eyes stung. Her throat was raw with emotion. She had come so close to losing her little sister. But there were other things to think about now.

Foxfire's front leg lay at a grotesque angle, the bone shattered. The colt's breathing was shallow. His eyes rolled with pain. Tanner cocked the pistol. "I'll put him out of his misery for you," he said.

Clara stopped him with a touch on the back of his hand. "No, give me the gun. He's my horse. I'll do it."

With a silent nod, Tanner passed her the .38. For the space of a breath Clara stood looking down at her colt, so swift and full of promise, like living flame when he ran. Then, placing the muzzle against his beautiful head, she closed her eyes and squeezed the trigger.

The shot rang out in the afternoon stillness. Nearby, a flock of mourning doves exploded into flight. In the far field, the black horse paused, then moved on. Katy would be crying, but that couldn't be helped.

Clara turned away. The pistol felt leaden in her hand, its weight dragging her down. Tanner eased it out of her clenched fingers and replaced it in the holster. Circling her shoulders lightly with his arm, he guided her out of the bog and back onto solid ground. By the time they reached the spot where the stallion waited, her whole body was shaking.

Without a word he gathered her into his arms and held her against him. Clara nestled into his warm strength, feeling the hardness of his chest, filling her senses with the rush of his breathing and the pungent aromas of sage and horse that clung to his clothes.

A little sob escaped her throat as his arms tightened around her. Part of her wanted to hear him say that everything was all right. But it wasn't all right. The colt she'd raised and nurtured had suffered an ugly, meaningless death at her own hand. And she was in love with a man who was all wrong for her. A man who could never be hers.

Jace inhaled the fragrance of her hair, breathing deeply as if he could take every molecule of her scent into his body. She was petal soft in his arms, as delicate as a rose. Yet she'd taken the gun from his hand and used it to shoot her beloved colt. Her strength was astounding. But right now, as she nestled against him like a little lost animal, what he sensed most of all was her need. He found himself wanting to cherish her, to protect her, to keep her in comfort and safety for the rest of their days.

Lord Almighty, what a mess he'd made of things!

She raised her face in open invitation for his kiss. He claimed her in one swift motion, his lips crushing hers, his arms lifting her off her feet. Her warm lips were salty with tears. Strong little hands seized the back of his head, wandering in his hair, pulling him down to her as the kiss deepened. Jace felt his body's response, the strain against the crotch of his jeans. Damn it, he was so ready he could take her right now, just fling her down in the soft grass, yank down her drawers and bury himself in the tight, wet silk between her legs.

But that wasn't going to happen. Not now, not ever. He would take Clara back to her grandmother's. Then he would get a pick and shovel, ride back here and dig a very large grave. It would break Clara's heart to think of her precious colt being left in the open for the buzzards and coyotes. He could do that much for her, at least.

Lowering her to the ground, Jace gentled his kisses, letting his lips graze her cheeks, her forehead, her damp eyelids. She whimpered as his arms released her, and it was all he could do to keep from pulling her close again.

"It's time to go," he said. "Don't worry about the colt. I'll come back and bury him for you."

She waited while he mounted the stallion, then gripped his hand and let him swing her up behind him. Jace willed himself not to respond to the press of her firm breasts against his back or clasp of her arms around his waist.

"I can shovel," she said. "Let me come back with you and help."

He nudged the stallion to a trot. "No," he said. "I'll do the job alone."

"But you've been sick," she argued. "Digging the grave could wear you out and cause a relapse. Give me one good reason why you won't let me help you."

Jace cursed silently. "Because I can't keep my hands off you, Clara," he growled. "We can't be alone anymore. It isn't a good idea."

She was silent for so long that Jace began to get uneasy. She took a breath—so deep that he felt it against his back. "I think I'm in love with you, Tanner," she said.

Jace stifled a groan. "Well, you can put that idea out of your silly little head right now!" he snapped. "If you want to be in love, find somebody else. Somebody who can stick around. Somebody who can make you happy. I can't do either."

He felt the sharp intake of her breath. He had hurt her, Jace knew. Well, fine. He'd damn well meant to. Hurting her with words was a kindness compared to other ways she could be hurt.

"What are you running away from, Tanner?" she asked. "What did you do?"

"Stop it. You know better than to ask."

"I've kept your secret so far," she persisted. "Don't I deserve to know the truth?"

"Let it go. I already told you, the less you know the better. Bring it up one more time, and I'll take Galahad and leave."

She'd gone rigid behind him. "Is that a threat?"

"Call it a warning. This isn't a game, Clara. I said I'd stay till your mares were bred. I know how much that means to you, especially since you just lost your colt. But I won't help you at the risk of my freedom. Do you understand?"

"Yes." Her answer was so subdued that Jace barely heard it.

"Good. Hang on!" He dug his boot heels into Galahad's flanks. The stallion burst into full gallop, legs pumping, hooves pounding, body straining forward in a thundering gait that seemed to devour the earth. Clara clung to Jace's back, her arms locked around his rib cage. They couldn't carry on a conversation while the horse was running so fast. That was what Jace wanted—that, and to get her back to the farmhouse before she pried out enough secrets to hold his soul for ransom. With her blend of curiosity, innocence and passion, Miss Clara Seavers could prove to be the most dangerous female he'd ever known.

Clara had been riding since she was old enough to perch on the back of a pony. She'd been breaking and training horses since her mid-teens. But she'd never experienced the thrill of galloping on a horse like Galahad. Even carrying double weight, he was flying over the ground with the grace and power of an animal born to run. What a shame she couldn't keep him around to enter the races at the August fair.

How had a man as poor as Tanner come by such a prize? The story of his having borrowed the stallion from his sister sounded too far-fetched to be true. The big Thoroughbred had to be worth a fortune. Yet it appeared that Tanner had made no effort to sell him. He'd even refused her offer of a stud fee, as if money didn't matter to him.

So many mysteries, and not one satisfactory answer.

Clara's arms clasped his body, holding on for dear life. Her head pressed his back so closely that she could feel each breath and hear his heart beating in counterpoint with Galahad's pounding hooves. The contact was almost intimate. But she might as well have been trying to reach him through a brick wall. Tanner was doing everything in his power to keep her at a distance.

What had she been thinking, telling him she loved him? How could she have been such a fool? Tanner had made it clear that he didn't love her. Oh, he'd given her kisses that burned all the way to her toes. But men kissed girls all the time, mostly because they could. She'd known all along it didn't mean anything. Hadn't she?

So why did his rejection of her continue to hurt every time? And deepening the sting was Foxfire's death—the senseless tragedy of it. It broke her heart. All of it did. And it was still sinking in.

Galahad's hooves pounded the earth. Each step quivered like a blow through Clara's body. The blazing sun turned her tears to stinging trails of salt. Every time she thought of Foxfire—his pain-filled eyes, the bullet smashing into his brain—the tears began all over again. She wanted to scream herself sick. She wanted to find Katy and shake her until her teeth rattled in her little head. All that beauty and promise, cut short by one reckless act.

But crying wouldn't get her colt back. Neither would taking her anger out on Katy. At least, thanks to Tanner, her sister was alive and unhurt. Whatever else the man might have done, she had to be grateful for that.

As Tanner slowed the stallion, Clara could see her grandmother's house across the pasture. Katy had just arrived. Clara watched as she halted Tarboy at the front of the porch, raced up the steps and flung herself into Mary's waiting arms.

Tanner slowed the stallion to a trot. "She'll be all right," he said. "Will you?"

"I'll have to be, won't I?" Clara loosened her grip on his waist as they rode into the yard. Tanner reined in the stallion outside the corral and waited for her to slide to the ground.

"There's a pick and shovel in the toolshed," he said. "Get them for me and I'll go on back. I could use a rope, too."

Trying not to think about the job he'd offered to do, Clara hurried to the shed and found what Tanner needed. Burying Foxfire would take him hours of miserable work. But it was the kindest thing he could do for her, and she was grateful. The least she could do was thank him.

Gathering up the tools and the rope, she walked back out to where Tanner waited, still mounted on the stallion. The blue eyes that looked down at her were veiled with caution, but she forced herself to meet their gaze and speak.

"I want to thank you for saving my sister. Who knows what might have happened if you hadn't been there."

"You can thank Galahad for that." His voice was cold, his manner distant.

"And thank you for burying Foxfire." She passed him the coiled rope and the pick and shovel. "That's going the extra mile. I want you to know I appreciate it."

"Since you saved me earlier, I'd say that makes us even." He looped the rope over the saddle horn and turned the horse to go.

Her searching eyes fixed on the canteen that hung from the saddle. "I can get you some fresh water. It's a hot day. You're going to need it."

"I've got plenty of water. And if you really want to thank me, Clara, stay away."

Holding the reins in one hand and the tools under his arm, he swung the stallion sharply and kicked him to a canter. Dried mud spattered under Galahad's hooves as they rounded the barn and headed back the way they'd come.

Fighting tears of humiliation, Clara watched them go. She'd done it again, made a silly fool of herself. But this was the last time, she vowed. If Tanner wanted nothing to do with her, she'd be only too happy to accommodate his wishes. She wouldn't give him the time of day. Not even if he begged her.

Glancing toward the porch, she saw that Katy was still sobbing with her head in Mary's lap. Tarboy stood by the steps, saddled and bridled, his coat rimed with sweat. His sweet brown eyes seemed to beg for her attention.

With a sigh Clara led the black gelding to the barn and found a bucket and towel to wipe him down. She knew she ought to make Katy do it, but rubbing the towel over the sleek, dark hide was pleasantly soothing. And when Tarboy turned and butted her with his nose, it was as if the little horse understood. Clara wrapped her arms around his damp neck, buried her face against his silky shoulder and gave full vent to her grief.

Chapter Eight

Jace paused to wipe his perspiring face with his bare arm. The afternoon was hot, and even in the soggy ground at the bog's edge, digging a grave for a horse was gut-busting work. Sweat beaded his face and dripped down his torso in stinging rivulets. His injured shoulder muscles throbbed with every move.

The vultures, with their razor-keen senses, had already caught the smell of death. Squinting into the sky, Jace counted three of them. They soared in lazy circles, their broad wings riding the updrafts like giant kites. At a distance they were majestic. Close up, they were hellish creatures with scaly pink heads, scrawny necks and hunched bodies cloaked in black.

As Jace watched, the trio of vultures was joined by a fourth, then a fifth bird. He swore, purpling the air with curses no one else could hear. If he didn't finish the grave soon, he'd be chasing them off the colt's body.

With renewed frenzy, he tore into the stubborn earth,

stabbing the pick into the packed soil and using the shovel to fling the dirt and rocks to one side of the grave. He was doing his best not to think about Clara, but the image of her warm velvet eyes, glimmering with tears, haunted him like a phantom. Her kiss whispered on his lips, the memory so vivid that if he closed his eyes he could almost imagine her there in his arms and hear that husky little voice of hers.

I think I'm in love with you, Tanner…

Lord, she didn't even know his real name. She didn't know him at all. And there was nothing he dared tell her except more lies. The truth was too dangerous to share.

It had taken all his strength of will to shove her away. Treating her with contempt had been even harder. She was so damnably honest, so open and genuine that the thought of her being hurt tore at his heart.

Falling in love with Clara would be as natural as breathing. But he couldn't let it happen. Not when one weak moment could ruin her promising young life.

The vultures were circling lower. The boldest one swooped in low, feet extended for a landing. Seizing a fist-sized rock, Jace flung it at the big bird and missed. Unhurt but warned, the creature flapped away. It would soon be back with all its feathered cohorts, hungering for a banquet. What a waste of a beautiful animal!

By now the grave was chest deep and as wide as he could reach with both arms. Another hour of digging should do the trick if he didn't have to spend too much time driving the birds off. When the hole was big enough, he would rig the rope to the colt's body, use the stallion to drag it over the edge and shovel in the dirt. After that he'd be ready for a cold dousing at the pump, a bowl of Mary's chicken soup and a long night's rest.

The sun crawled across the cloudless sky. By the time Jace had finished burying the colt, the vultures had gone and the light was beginning to fade. Exhausted, he stood beside the mound of raw earth, one hand rubbing the back of his neck. He ached in every bone and muscle, and he probably smelled worse than a Missouri hog farm. But at least the job was done. When Clara came back to visit the grave—and he imagined she would—she would find everything in order.

Wearily he coiled the rope and retrieved the shovel. The pick lay a few yards into the bog, where he'd flung it at one of the vultures. He walked toward the spot where he could see the handle sticking out of the yellow reeds. The flattened grass where he'd dragged the colt's body was streaked with an odd blackness that gleamed in the slanting light. Jace felt the hair prickle on the back of his neck as he bent to a crouch, dabbed a finger in the greasy substance and raised it to his nose.

Even before his senses caught the telltale chemical odor, he knew what it was. As a trained geologist and engineer, he'd made good money consulting for drilling companies, evaluating oil deposits and pinpointing the best places to sink a well. If there was one thing he knew about, it was oil. And this was oil, all right. The question was, what to do about it.

Walking deeper into the bog, he gripped the pick by its handle and twisted it out of the muck. Where the iron point had pierced the swampy ground, more black fluid was oozing into the hole.

Jace turned his gaze back toward Mary's place, studying the lay of the land. The bog lay beyond the boundaries of the farm. But it was just a low spot, where the earth was weak and prone to seepage. If there was oil here, there could be more under Mary's farm and under the Seavers Ranch as well.

His trained eyes measured the slight, rounding slope that rose from where he stood. There did seem to be an anticline here—an area where the rock layers formed a dome, leaving space for an oil deposit underneath. The anticline didn't appear to be large. Even so, there could be enough oil here to make Mary Gustavson a wealthy woman, and to make the Seavers family even wealthier.

Was that what they'd want? Even if it was, the situation wasn't his business, was it? He could hardly approach Judd Seavers with his real name and credentials—the name of a wanted man—and request a business meeting. No, maybe it would be best to do nothing at all.

The afternoon light was ebbing fast. Sunset edged the sky with watercolor tones of pink, mauve and gold. From the far side of the bog two egrets took wing, flashes of white against the deepening blue.

Weary beyond imagining, Jace shouldered his tools, trudged back to where he'd left Galahad and dragged his aching body into the saddle. If he had any sense, he'd pack up and hit the road at first light tomorrow. Every day he remained here gave rise to more complications. Sooner or later those complications could trap him.

True, he'd made a promise to Clara. Maybe if he broke his word, she'd be angry enough to forget him. That would be best for them both. But then again, she might be furious enough to go to the marshal with everything she knew. That was a risk he couldn't afford to take. In any case, how could he crush her hopes again, after the heartbreaking loss of her colt? Whether he liked it or not, he was stuck here until those blasted mares of hers were ready to breed.

They weren't ready today. Galahad's calm demeanor told him that much. If the mares had come into estrus, the stallion would have just one thing on his mind, and heaven help the poor fool who got in his way.

Jace rode back across the fields at an easy pace, sparing his tortured muscles and joints. The long grass whispered against the stallion's legs. Insects droned in the deepening twilight. Shadows lengthened and blurred into darkness.

In the distance, the lights had come on in Mary's house. Clara and her sister would be gone by now, he guessed. He imagined them plodding homeward, riding double on the black gelding, their shoulders sagging with grief and guilt.

He remembered Clara in his arms, trembling as he cradled her close. His tongue held the taste of her salty tears and the honey sweetness of her mouth. And even when he tried to block the memory, her words came back to him like a sigh on the wind.

I think I'm in love with you, Tanner…

Those words would remain, burned like a brand into Jace's memory, for as long as he lived.

Clara rarely drove the family's new Model T Touring Car. She preferred the intelligent company of a horse to a noisy, greasy machine that could break down or blow out a tire without warning. But never mind that. Today her mother had given her a list of items to pick up in town. To get everything home she would need the car.

She drove with the canvas top cranked back, her hair loose and flying in the breeze. The day was warm, the sunlit air hazy with cottonwood fluff. Two days had passed since she'd pulled the trigger and left Foxfire lying dead in the bog. Two days since she'd felt Tanner's arms around her, his kisses blotting out the nightmare of what had happened.

Two days of thinking about him, dreaming about him, wanting him.

The Model T swayed on its axles, wheels spitting gravel as she pulled around a flock of chickens in the road. After two days of moping around the ranch, it felt good to be out on her own. This trip to town had been the right idea. Her mother had told her to take her time, probably hoping she'd visit old friends. But most of Clara's school chums were either married or away at college. Only she was left in limbo, sure of her future plans one minute, racked with uncertainty the next. And her life seemed to grow more unsettled with each passing day.

She had vowed to keep her distance from Tanner. But it was high time she checked on her two mares. Surely her grandmother would have telephoned if they were bred and ready to bring home—unless Tanner had asked her to wait until after he'd left.

What if he was already gone? What if she'd set eyes on him for the last time?

It was all Clara could do to keep from turning around and driving back down the road to the farm. But she steeled herself against the impulse. Showing up at Mary's would only make her look foolish. If Tanner had wanted to see her, he'd have found a way. It was time she faced the painful truth. When he'd told her to leave him alone, he'd meant every word.

But she couldn't stay away from her grandmother's forever. She needed to see how the mares were doing. And she wanted to visit Foxfire's grave, to see the place at peace and leave a small remembrance of flowers. Maybe later today she would saddle Tarboy and ride across the pastureland. She wouldn't look for Tanner, but if she found him there…

Clara shoved his image from her mind as she passed the sign that marked the town limits. Where Tanner was concerned, there were no easy answers, and no way of knowing which would hurt more—seeing him at the farm or arriving to find him gone.

* * *

Dutchman's Creek was a prosperous town with a population of 2,500, not counting the families on outlying farms and ranches. Its thriving businesses included a bank, a saloon, a livery stable, several stores, a hotel and restaurant, a railroad station and a newly built garage that sold gasoline and repaired automobiles.

Today, the place was bustling. Buggies, wagons and occasional autos crowded the main street. Townsfolk and visitors strolled the sidewalks—farm wives stocking up on basics, mothers with children in tow, ranchers, businessmen and cowboys. At the curb, a well-dressed matron stepped daintily around a pile of horse manure. A scruffy white dog trotted behind his young master's bicycle.

Clara parked the auto and fumbled in her pocketbook for the list her mother had given her. There were nine items, each one numbered and written out in Hannah's precise schoolgirl handwriting—the same handwriting Clara had seen in those impassioned letters to Quint.

The discovery of the letters still haunted Clara. But she had yet to confront her mother, or even her grandmother, about what she'd learned. Doing so would open a Pandora's box, hurting the people she loved most. For now she would keep her secret. But she knew she couldn't wait forever. The truth would be there, worrying her mind, demanding to be heard until she gave it voice.

Shoving the thought aside, she turned her attention to her errands. Most of the items on the list were easy— fresh limes from the grocers, a two-pound slab of bacon from the butcher shop, medicine for an ailing milk cow and a salt block from the feed store, which a worshipful teenage boy carried to the auto for her. Katy's new frocks were ready at the dressmaker's. They were far prettier than Katy's complaints had led Clara to expect.

Katy was becoming a worry of late. When she wasn't brooding over Foxfire's death, she was babbling about Tanner and how he'd saved her. She seemed to have a schoolgirl crush on the man. It was probably harmless, but her mother had taken notice. Before long, Hannah would be making a visit to the farm to meet this knight in shining armor who'd rescued her daughter. Right now that was just one more complication in Clara's life.

Dressed in her khaki walking skirt, a simple middy blouse and low-heeled slippers, she trekked up one side of Main Street and down the other, carrying her paper-wrapped purchases. She greeted people she knew with a smile and a nod, but didn't stop to visit. She had too much on her mind to make small talk.

She had finished the last errand and was on her way back to the car when she passed the marshal's office. She gave the red brick building a glance, moved on, then paused and retreated a few steps to study the wanted posters in the front window.

None of the desperados looked familiar. But these posters were yellowed and faded from sun exposure.

They'd probably been in the window for months. The marshal would have newer posters in his office. To see them, she would need to go inside.

Fear brushed her senses like the touch of an icy hand. Clara willed herself to ignore the warning. If Tanner's face was on one of those posters, she needed to know. She needed to find the truth about what he'd done.

Dodging traffic, she dashed across the street to the car, laid her purchases on the backseat and cranked up the canvas bonnet to keep off the sun. For a moment she hesitated, torn by doubts. Tanner had insisted she was better off not knowing about him, and he could well be right. Curiosity would only stir up more misery—look what had happened when she'd opened the letters in her grandmother's trunk. Maybe she should just crank up the engine, get into the car and leave.

But she forced herself to keep moving, to stride back across the street and head for the marshal's office. If there was something to be learned here, she owed it to herself and her family to find out.

The door was standing ajar. When no one answered her tentative knock, she pushed the door open and stepped inside. The office was empty, the two cluttered desks both vacant, as if the marshal and his deputy had stepped out on the spur of the moment.

Maybe it would be best to leave, Clara thought. She could always come by the next time she was in town. But that would be taking the coward's way out. Besides, she'd known silver-haired Marshal Sam Farley all her life. Surely he wouldn't be upset to find her here alone.

Leaving the door the way she'd found it, she crossed the worn linoleum to stand in front of the bulletin board on the far wall. Announcements, newspaper articles and wanted posters were thumbtacked helter-skelter to its surface. Clara's eyes scanned the board from left to right. If it were here, Tanner's face would jump out at her like a flash of lightning, she thought. But to her relief, she didn't find him. Maybe his crime wasn't serious enough to warrant sending posters around the country.

To make certain she'd missed nothing, she studied the board in more detail, moving from right to left this time. She had worked most of the way across when a nasal voice startled her from behind.

"Well, now. If it isn't Miss Clara Seavers. Come to pay us a visit, have you?"

Even before she turned around, Clara knew who the speaker was. Something about Deputy Marshal Lyle McCabe had always made her skin crawl. He was handsome enough, tall and wiry, with bullet-sharp eyes and pomaded black hair. But he had a way of looking at her that made her stomach turn. Last winter, at the Christmas dance, he'd held her so tightly that she could feel his arousal through her skirt. He wore an air of sanctimony and attended church every week, but before the aging marshal had made him a deputy, McCabe had hung around with some of the meanest ne'er-do-wells in town. It was widely suspected that Sam Farley had deputized McCabe to help keep his unruly friends under control.

The last thing she wanted was to be alone with the man.

McCabe had emerged from the back of the building, where the prisoners were kept. Moving with an easy saunter, he positioned himself between Clara and the door. "Something I can do for you?"

"I was looking for the marshal," Clara said.

"Marshal's out sick for a couple of days. In the meantime, I'm the man in charge." McCabe's mouth spread in a lazy grin, showing the glint of a gold tooth. "If there's some way I can help, I'd consider it an honor."

Clara shrugged, trying to appear casual. "Don't worry about it. I just came in to look at these posters." She nodded toward the board. "I saw a man on the road today. Something about his looks made me wonder, but I don't see his picture here. He was probably just a harmless tramp."

"We can't be sure of that." McCabe leaned back against the edge of the marshal's desk. His long legs, ending in sharply pointed black boots, blocked her path to the door. "We got a new batch of posters in a couple of days ago," he said, picking up a brown manila packet. "Marshal hasn't got around to putting them up. Why don't you sit yourself down and have a look?" He walked around the desk and pulled out the marshal's big wooden swivel chair. "Here. Old Sam won't mind a pretty girl like you sitting in his seat."

Clara was becoming uncomfortable. But there was no way to leave without making things even more awkward. McCabe might make her skin crawl, but he was only doing his job. So far, he hadn't laid a finger on her or said anything inappropriate.

She settled into the chair while McCabe slid the posters out of the packet and laid them on the desk. There appeared to be no more than a dozen of them. At least this shouldn't take long.

McCabe took a seat on the corner of the desk, where he could see both the posters and Clara's face. His nearness made her squirm. "You needn't stay with me," she said. "I can thumb through these and let you know if any look familiar."

"It's my job to stay." He leaned over her, so close she could feel his breath on her hair. Clara picked up the thin sheaf of papers, wanting only to get this ordeal over with and leave.

She gave the first poster a glance. The tough-looking bank robber was no one she knew. Putting the poster aside, she studied the next one. The handsome, youthful fugitive had a face anyone would trust, but he was wanted for selling stock in fake oil wells. Clara didn't know him, nor did she recognize any of the next six posters she saw. Lyle McCabe was leaning so close that she could smell the pomade on his hair and the tobacco on his breath. The nauseating blend of odors made her stomach roil.

"This is a waste of time," she said, shoving the rest of the posters aside. "I glimpsed the man's face as I passed him in the car, and my overactive imagination did the rest. I'll go now, before I take up any more of your day."

"Might as well finish what we started." McCabe pushed the papers back in front of her. His position on the desk blocked her escape, and he showed no inclination to move.

With a sigh, Clara glanced at the topmost poster and put it aside to look at the next one.

Her breath caught in a silent gasp.

She had thought his features would flash at her like a lightning bolt. But seeing him on the poster was more like a bullet through the heart. Even with the well-trimmed hair and mustache and the immaculate suit he wore, there was no mistaking the man she knew as Tanner.

The blood had drained from her face. She knew McCabe was staring at her, but she couldn't tear her eyes away from the photograph, or from the bold lettering above and below.

WANTED DEAD OR ALIVE
JASON TANNER DENBY
For the Cold-blooded Murder of Mr. Hollis Rumford
Contact Sheriff John B. Clayton, Springfield, Missouri
$1,000 REWARD

There were more details in the fine print at the bottom of the page, but Clara was too shaken to read them.

McCabe had laid a hand on her shoulder, his palm too warm, his grip too possessive. "What's the matter?" he asked. "Is that him—the man you saw?"

Clara shook her head vehemently. "No. The man on the road was…older. And darker, more like…like a

Gypsy. I'm just feeling a bit nauseous, that's all. Maybe some fresh air—"

Rising, she pushed her way past the startled McCabe, fled out the front door and swung it shut behind her. She heard the click of the door opening again as she hurried up the sidewalk. Clara knew McCabe was watching her. She could feel his eyes following her every move as she crossed the busy street, reached the parked auto, switched on the starter and fumbled with the crank.

Had he believed her lie about the man on the road? McCabe might be a weasel, but he wasn't stupid. She could only hope he'd been paying more attention to her than to the face on the poster. At the very least she should warn Tanner not to go into town.

After cranking the Model T's engine to life, she climbed into the driver's seat, wove her way through the Main Street traffic and turned onto the road that led back to the ranch. Only as she drove did the gravity of what she'd learned begin to sink in. Tanner—she couldn't think of him by any other name—had admitted that he was a wanted man. And he'd told her that his crime had been a necessary one. But cold-blooded murder? How could she have feelings for someone who'd committed such an awful act? She'd promised to keep his secret. But now that she knew what he'd done, how could she justify protecting Tanner from the law?

Emotions churning, Clara drove faster and faster, flying over bumps and ruts, screeching around the familiar bends at more than forty miles an hour. The big cottonwoods that overhung the road blurred in her side vision. The wind clawed at her curls.

Where should she go with the truth? To Tanner? To her mother? To her grandmother?

What if she'd alerted Lyle McCabe to Tanner's presence? Heaven save her, what had she done?

Lost in frenetic thought, she didn't see the horse-drawn farm wagon, lumbering around the curve toward her, until it was too late to stop. The huge draft horses screamed and reared as she swerved under their very hooves. The auto lurched through the barrow pit and slammed into a tree. Pitched forward, Clara struck her head on something hard. There was a flash of crimson; then the world shattered into blackness.

Chapter Nine

Jace had spent the past two days rebuilding the roof on the hay shed. He'd cut new timbers to strengthen the old walls and tacked down each shingle before he hoisted the sections with a block and tackle and nailed each joint into place. At last it was finished. And he'd challenge any wind to blow it away again.

Filling the tin dipper with cold water from the pump, he swallowed long and deep while he took a moment's satisfaction in a job well done. It felt good to do meaningful work, even if it was only a shed. Mary would be pleased, and when her new hay crop came in it would be safe and dry.

A glance at the sun's angle told him it was mid-afternoon. If Mary didn't have anything else in mind, maybe he'd ride out to the bog where he'd seen the oil seepage. He hadn't made up his mind what to do about the discovery, but he was curious and wanted to look at the place in a better light. Maybe there was something he'd missed.

He found Mary bent over her ironing board, pressing the wrinkles out of a dampened pillowcase. She was mightily pleased about the finished shed and fine with his taking a ride on his own time. "Go on," she said. "You've been working way too hard. Take the rest of the day."

"No need for that. I'll be back in an hour to start on the gate for the pasture."

"And to have a fresh piece of gooseberry pie," Mary added with a laugh. "I was just about to take it out of the oven. It should be cooled by the time you get back."

"In that case, I won't waste any time."

Jace strode down the front steps and set off for the paddock to fetch Galahad. His gaze swept over the weathered outbuildings and outdated farm equipment, the laboriously tilled vegetable garden, the stark old house with its worn furniture, unmatched dishes and the barest of modern conveniences. Mary Gustavson was one of kindest, hardest-working women he'd ever known. She deserved a life of ease, in a comfortable home with a cook and housekeeper to wait on her needs. Maybe she'd enjoy visiting her distant children, or traveling back to her birthplace in Norway. Oil on her property could make all those things possible. But profiting from that oil would mean drilling noisy wells, bringing in work crews and triggering a stampede of money-hungry speculators. The peaceful landscape would be changed forever. From what he knew of Mary, Jace understood that she might not want that.

Either way, the least he could do was tell her about the oil and give her the name of a reliable firm to contact. Then, after he was gone, she could make her own decision.

After he was gone.

He would go. It would have to be soon. And he couldn't look back.

Making a clean break was the only decent thing he could do for Clara. She had offered him her trusting, vulnerable heart, and he had broken it. The longer he stayed, the more likely he was to hurt her again. Clara was a "for keeps" kind of girl, not a plaything to be romanced and left behind. She deserved someone solid and respectable—not a man doomed to spend the rest of his life looking over his shoulder.

Galahad came at his whistle. Jace saddled and bridled him in the corral. The two young mares were as coquettish as ever, frisking around the paddock and swishing their pretty tails like schoolgirls at a ball, but the stallion barely gave them a passing sniff. Pity there was no way to rush Mother Nature. But Jace had noticed that last night's moon was coming up on fullness. He'd heard that mares tended to come into estrus with the full moon. He could only hope it was true. Every day he remained here raised the odds that he might be recognized.

The bog was an easy ride from Mary's place. Jace could have walked the distance, but the idea of being on foot in open country made him nervous. If the worst happened and he had to make a run for it, he wanted the stallion close at hand. He'd strapped on the pistol for the same reason. Shooting at an innocent man was the last thing he wanted to do—let alone killing someone's husband, father, son or brother. But the very threat of the .38 could make the difference between his own freedom and his death at the end of a rope.

A meadowlark warbled from the top of a stump as he crossed the pasture. The whisper of grass against the stallion's legs brought back the memory of riding with Clara behind him, her arms wrapping his waist, her sweet fragrance stealing through his senses.

I think I'm in love with you, Tanner...

The words had broken his heart. He'd answered her harshly, called her foolish. But what he'd really wanted to do was sweep her off the horse, pull her down with him into the grass and bury himself in her ripe little body. Lord help him, if he could die that way, he would die with a smile on his face.

Blackbirds rose in a swirling cloud as he approached the bog. The colt's grave was much as he'd left it, with no sign of Clara's narrow boot prints in the fresh earth. So she hadn't come after all. Maybe that was for the best. There was something about this place, an evil miasma that set Jace's nerves on edge. If he spoke with her again, he would warn her against coming here alone.

Halting the stallion at a safe distance, Jace dismounted and walked into the bog. The high water from the storm had receded, leaving a morass of tangled roots and gaping holes. Flies swarmed over the drying mud.

The oil was where he remembered, its seductive

blackness oozing out of the earth. Jace took a folded handkerchief from his hip pocket and dropped to a crouch. Dabbing some oil onto a dry leaf, he laid the leaf between the folds of the handkerchief as proof of what he'd found.

Straightening, he slipped the handkerchief into his pocket. Out of habit, he scanned the country around him for any sign that he was being watched. The fields were silent except for the whisper of blowing grass. On the wooded hillside, nothing moved except a chicken hawk spiraling above the ridge. But Jace couldn't shake the feeling that something wasn't right. He'd been living by his instincts too long not to trust them.

Maybe it was time to move on.

Mounting up, he spurred the stallion to a canter. The big bay's powerful legs ate up the distance. He would finish the pasture gate and have it hung by day's end. Over supper, he would tell Mary about the oil. Later that night, under cover of darkness, he would pack his things and leave.

Mary would be hurt. Clara would be livid. But that couldn't be helped. His danger senses were prickling. If somebody was on to him, he couldn't wait around to be caught.

Minutes later Jace rode into the yard. Mary hurried off the porch to meet him. Even before she spoke, her ashen face and nervously clasping hands told him something terrible had happened.

"Thank goodness you're here, Tanner." Her work-worn fingers twisted her thin gold wedding band. "My daughter just called. Clara's been in an auto accident. The ambulance is bringing her home."

The shock slammed into Jace, followed by a rush of denial. Not Clara. Anybody but Clara. "How badly is she hurt?" he managed to ask.

"They say she's unconscious. I don't know about the rest. But I need you to hitch the buggy while I get my medicines. You never know what might help."

"I'll drive you." The words spilled out before Jace had time to think. It might not be safe going to the ranch with Mary. But right now nothing mattered except getting to Clara.

"Fine. Hurry." She rushed back into the house.

Jace had hitched the dun gelding to the buggy and was adjusting the harness when Mary came out carrying a black valise that resembled an oversize doctor's bag. She climbed into the buggy without waiting for Jace's help. He sprang onto the seat beside her, slapped the reins down hard and they were off, racing down the drive to the road.

Mary clutched her valise in silence, her thin gray brows knotted with worry. Jace kept the horse to a brisk trot, avoiding the worst of the ruts and potholes. The last thing they needed was a spill.

Only as they rounded the last bend and turned in the gate to the Seavers Ranch did Jace realize that he wouldn't be able to see Clara at all. He was a hired man, not a member of the family or even a friend. All he could do was drive Mary to the house and wait outside like a horse or a dog while fear gnawed at his gut.

Logically, he knew that was for the best. The fewer people who got a good look at him, the better. He should probably have stayed at the farm and let Mary drive the buggy herself. She certainly could have managed it. But even as the thought crossed his mind, Jace knew he couldn't have stayed away. The thought of Clara—the beautiful, passionate Clara he'd come to know—lying broken and unconscious was more than he could stand. If he couldn't be with her, at least he could be close by.

The ambulance, a sputtering relic of the war, had arrived ahead of them. Two men were lifting a stretcher out of the back. Jace glimpsed a spill of chestnut curls and a slight form beneath a flannel blanket. That was all he saw of Clara before they rushed her into the house. He gripped the edge of the seat to keep from charging after her. He had never felt so helpless in his life.

"Here's the doctor." Mary touched his arm as a dusty Model T chugged up to the house and stopped next to the ambulance. Forcing himself to move, Jace hurried around the buggy to help her out. Her face was colorless, her eyes sunk into creased pits of worry. "No sense in your waiting," she said. "I could be here a long time. You take the buggy and go on back to the farm. Somebody else can drive me home later."

Jace shook his head. "I'll stay until I know how Clara's doing. Will you come out and tell me?"

Mary gave him a jerky nod. He glimpsed tears in her eyes before she turned away and hurried after the doctor. Together they mounted the wide steps and vanished through the front door.

Jace drove the buggy to a shady spot on the east side of the barn. Pulling his hat brim low over his eyes, he settled back in the seat for what could be hours of hellish waiting. He had known Clara Seavers for less than a week. But he could no longer imagine a world—his world or any world—without her. Fearless, beautiful and so full of life, she was like air and sunlight and pure, clear water to him. Once, having her in his life might have made all the difference. Now there was nothing he could do.

From under the brim of his Stetson, he studied the Seavers home. A large, two-story frame with tall windows on both floors, it was surrounded by well-tended rosebushes and painted an elegant cream with dark green shutters. Compared to Hollis Rumford's marble-pillared Missouri mansion, the house was nothing. But for this part of the country it was grand enough. And from what he knew of the family, Jace sensed that within these walls there was love and respect. There'd been precious little of that in the twenty-one-room prison where Hollis Rumford had kept his wife and daughters.

He could only hope that Ruby and her little girls were doing all right. Maybe in a year or two they'd be able to exchange letters. For the time being, it was far too dangerous. The police were probably checking every piece of mail that came to the house. Even telephoning her would be too much of a risk.

His gaze followed the trail of a blooming honey-suckle vine up the side of the house to a second-floor window with white lace curtains. Through the glass, Jace caught a flicker of movement. Was that Clara's room? Were they moving her onto the bed, the doctor stepping in close to check her injuries?

Was she still unconscious? Was she even alive? Jace had never been much of a praying man, but he prayed now, his lips moving in a silent plea.

The two men from the ambulance came out the front door with the empty stretcher. Jace watched them climb into the front seat and drive away. Their faces told him nothing. Where was Mary? Why wasn't she bringing him some news?

He thought about getting out of the buggy and walking around to stretch his legs, but he'd glimpsed a couple of cowhands going in and out of the stable. They might get curious and want to talk to him. Better to stay here and keep to himself.

Resting his knees against the dash, Jace tried to settle back and doze. It was no good. All he could think of was Clara—racing the chestnut colt across the pasture on that first day, her sunlit curls flying in the breeze. Clara taking the pistol from his hand, aiming the muzzle and squeezing the trigger to put her beloved horse out of its misery. Clara in his arms, her mouth softening to his kiss, her hungry little hips rocking against his hardness, driving him to the brink of control.

Damn it, what was happening in that house?

Minutes stretched into what seemed like hours. The

sun was creeping toward the horizon when a rider on a lathered buckskin came thundering up the drive and reined to a halt in front of the house. Tall, lean and dressed in dusty trail clothes, he flung himself out of the saddle and pounded up the steps, leaving the two hired men to scramble after his horse. As he crossed the porch, Jace glimpsed graying hair and proud, hawkish features. Clara had mentioned that her father was on the mountain with the cattle. Someone must have gone to fetch him, for the newcomer could be none other than Judd Seavers, head of the family and owner of the ranch.

Judd opened the front door and nearly collided with Mary, who was just coming outside. With a cry, the old woman threw her arms around him. "Thank goodness you're here, Judd! Clara's awake and talking! She's going to be all right!"

Like a mountain stream trickling to life after a winter thaw, Jace felt his heart begin to beat again.

"Hello, sweetheart, how are you feeling?"

Clara looked up into the worried gray eyes of the man she'd known as her father—the man who'd taken in his brother's child, sheltered and protected her, disciplined her, schooled her and loved her as his own for the past nineteen years.

"Hello, Papa." She blinked back a rush of tears. The accident had brought her emotions perilously close to the surface. "I'm sorry about the car. Is it ruined?"

"I haven't seen it, but don't worry." His voice

cracked, the way Daniel's sometimes did. "Any machine can be replaced. The important thing is that you're all right."

"It was all my fault. I was going too fast and didn't see the wagon coming." Only as Clara spoke did she remember why she'd crashed. She'd been too upset about Tanner to pay attention to her driving.

What would her grandmother do if she knew her hired man was a murderer? Worse, what would her parents do?

Her mother appeared in the doorway with a silver tray. "I've brought you some chamomile tea, dear." She bustled into the bedroom, and set the tray on the nightstand. "The doctor says we need to sit you up and get some fluids down you. You've got a nasty bump on your head, most likely a concussion, so we mustn't let you go back to sleep for a while. Mercy, what a scare you gave us!"

"I'm sorry, Mama. And I feel terrible about the car." Clara allowed herself to be propped up with pillows before she took her first sip of the steamy, honey-flavored tea. She had a vague memory of the doctor peering at her, shining a light in her eyes.

"Does Grandma know what happened?" she asked.

"She came as soon as she heard. I believe that new hired man of hers drove her. I wanted to thank him for saving Katy, but they left before I had the chance."

Clara's pulse surged. So Tanner hadn't gone away after all. Maybe now she'd have a chance to talk with him again and learn the truth about what he'd allegedly done. She couldn't believe he'd commit cold-blooded murder.

"Your grandmother said she'd be back to see you tomorrow, after you'd had time to rest." Hannah shifted the pillow behind Clara's head. "She looked worn-out. I do wish she'd agree to move in with us. Maybe you can talk her into it, Judd. She won't listen to her own daughter. It's like talking to a wall!"

"I'll do my best, but your mother's a stubborn woman." Judd sighed wearily. "Now what's this about somebody saving our Katy?"

Clara's parents drifted toward the window, immersed in their own conversation. Judd would be more upset about Foxfire than about the Model T. The misuse of an animal always made him furious. Poor Katy would likely be in for a tongue-lashing, followed by loving forgiveness.

Clara cradled the teacup between her hands, grateful for a moment alone. There'd been way too much fussing over her. Except for the throbbing lump on her head, she felt fine. Tomorrow she was determined to be as good as new.

But what was she going to do about Tanner?

She'd given her word not to turn him in. But that was before she knew what he'd done. How could she justify protecting a cold-blooded murderer?

Closing her eyes, she let his image drift into her mind—the sharp lines of his face, the fathomless blue eyes that invited her trust, the firm, sensuous lips that fit so perfectly against her own. She remembered his gentleness, his tender regard for her grandmother and how he'd gone back to the bog to spend miserable hours digging a grave for Foxfire.

Cold-blooded? Those were the last words she'd have used to describe the man named Jason Tanner Denby. But then, how well did she really know him?

He'd told her that his crime had been necessary. So how could she judge him before she knew the whole story?

There was only one way to get his side. As soon as she was able, Clara resolved, she would go back to Mary's place, confront Tanner with what she'd learned and demand that he tell her everything.

The confrontation could be dangerous, Clara reminded herself. If Tanner was really the killer the poster claimed him to be, there was no telling what he might do. But that was a chance she had to take. Whatever the cost, she wouldn't be satisfied with anything less than the truth.

Clara's musings were cut short by the sound of voices from the downstairs hall. She couldn't make out words, but through the partly open door she recognized Rosa's shrill Spanish accent and a man's nasal voice—a voice that made Clara's stomach sink. They seemed to be arguing, but the voices abruptly ceased, followed by the sound of heavy footsteps coming up the stairs. Seconds later there was a light rap on the bedroom door.

Clara's parents had turned away from the window. Her father was striding across the floor.

"Don't—" Clara started to say, but it was too late. The door opened and Lyle McCabe stepped into the room clutching a bouquet of drooping yellow daisies.

"Deputy, if this is about the accident—" Judd began,

but then, seeing the flowers, he broke off and simply stared.

"I took the liberty of having your auto towed to the garage, Mr. Seavers," McCabe said. "The things in the back will be delivered here before nightfall. But what I really came for was to make sure your daughter's all right."

Judd stood like a wall between McCabe and the bed where Clara lay. "As you see, she's recovering. But she needs her rest. She won't be up to having visitors anytime soon."

"I see." McCabe slunk backward a half step. Not many men could face up to a protective Judd Seavers. "Well, in that case, I hope you'll give her these flowers and my best wishes. Tell her, when she's feeling better, I'd like to talk with her more about that man she saw on the road."

"What? What man?" Judd's response was fierce enough to make McCabe take another step backward. Clara cringed under the pink eiderdown. Why couldn't McCabe have stayed away?

"Ask your daughter. She can tell you. Now, if you'll excuse me—" McCabe thrust the flowers into Judd's hand and retreated down the stairs. Judd strode back to Clara's bed, holding out the flowers.

"Do you want these?" he asked.

"No, Papa. Take them away. And there was no man on the road. It was just something I said to get rid of Mr. McCabe this morning. I don't want anything to do with him."

Muttering something that sounded like "Thank goodness," Judd turned away from the bed and dropped the flowers into the wastebasket. Clara gulped the last of her tea and set the cup on the nightstand. What had she set in motion this morning—and what danger could it pose for Tanner? McCabe might not be long on courage, but he possessed a weasel's cunning. He'd noticed her reaction to the poster, and she'd lay odds that he hadn't believed her lie. If McCabe had his suspicions up, Tanner could be in trouble.

Clara knew Tanner was wanted for murder. But the thought of his being brought in by McCabe to be tried and hanged was more than she could stand. She had to warn him—even if that warning meant he'd leave and she'd never see him again.

Jace had told Mary about the oil on the way home from the Seavers Ranch. He'd shown her the oiled leaf he'd wrapped in his handkerchief, but by then, most of the oil had soaked into the cloth. Mary had declared that she wanted to see the oil in the ground for herself.

"Might as well take a look at it," she'd said. "But if you think I'd welcome a herd of strangers with noisy machines running around digging holes in my land, think again. Oil's like gold. It makes people crazy. Once word got out, this peaceful little valley would never be the same again."

Jace had turned the buggy up the drive. The setting sun cast streaks of purple shadow across the fields and tipped each grass blade with glowing amber. Mary's attitude hadn't surprised him. This was beautiful country, and oil had a way of turning things ugly—not only landscapes but people.

It had been too late in the day to get a good look at the oil, and Mary had planned another visit to Clara in the morning. "We'll go when I get back," she'd said. "No need to hurry. The oil isn't going anywhere."

They'd eaten a quiet supper of bread and milk, and Mary had retired early. Too restless to sleep, Jace had stood at the paddock fence, watching the moon rise above the craggy peaks. Tonight it was a whisker's breadth short of full. Tomorrow night it would be a perfect golden circle.

Beyond the fence, the stallion and the two young mares shifted in the darkness, the light breeze fluttering their manes and tails. He would give them one more night, Jace had resolved. Then, whether nature had taken its course or not, he would take Galahad and leave. He had stayed far too long. Long enough to put himself in danger. Long enough to fall in love.

Now it was mid-afternoon. Mary had taken the buggy and driven back to the Seavers Ranch. In her absence, Jace had finished the pasture gate, nailed down the loose floorboards in the granary and built a new corn crib in the barn. He'd done his best to wall Clara out of his thoughts, but she was there the whole time, flashing like a rainbow in the shadowed corners of his mind.

Would he ever see her again? But that didn't matter,

he told himself. She was safe and well, her future open to the happy life he would wish for her. And he would have her memory to hold on lonely nights—her luminous eyes, her ripe mouth and willing body; her intelligence, her fiery spirit, her tenderness.

The man he'd been before he walked away from Hollis Rumford's bleeding body would've had something to offer a girl like Clara. He could have courted her properly and gone to Judd Seavers to ask for her hand, knowing that he had ample means to provide for her and their children. But that man no longer existed. Jace had long since come to accept his new self—raw and running like a hunted animal, counting his survival by minutes, hours and days.

Clara would forget him in time. She would marry a good man, God willing, and with the passing years become as strong and wise as her grandmother. That was the best he could wish for her.

He could see Mary now, coming up the drive in the buggy. As she drove into the yard, Jace came forward to help her climb down. "How's Clara?" he couldn't resist asking.

"Much better. She wanted to ride over here and see her mares this morning, but her parents wouldn't hear of her leaving the house. Oh, I almost forgot—" Turning, Mary lifted a covered dish off the buggy seat. "My daughter wanted to thank you for saving Katy and burying the colt. She baked you this cherry pie." She lifted the corner of the clean towel to reveal a glimpse of flaky, golden crust.

"That's right nice of her." Jace managed an awkward smile. "You and I can share it."

"Judd wanted to thank you, too." Mary started toward the porch. "He says if you're looking for good, steady work, come over and talk to him."

Jace felt his chest tighten. "It's a generous offer. But I'm planning to leave tomorrow. I was going to tell you this afternoon."

Mary's step froze. She turned back around to face him. "But why not stay? Judd's more than fair with his hired hands, and I know for a fact you could use the money."

Jace shook his head. "It's time for me to move on. You've been a good friend, Mary, but I'm hoping you won't ask my reasons."

Sadness flickered in Mary's pale blue eyes. "I've never asked you about anything, Tanner, and I won't ask now. Just know that you'll be missed, and not just by me. Clara and Katy both asked about you."

"Then I hope you won't mind saying goodbye to them for me. Tell Clara I'm sorry about the mares. I waited as long as I could."

Jace turned away so she wouldn't see his expression. Against his better judgment, he'd let himself become attached to this place and these people. He was already paying the price.

"Are you ready to go for a ride?" he asked, changing the subject. There was no buggy trail to the bog. They would have to go on horseback.

Mary sighed. "Oh, I suppose so. I'll take this pie into

the kitchen and freshen up a bit while you put away the buggy. Remember to saddle me a slow horse."

Jace unhitched the buggy and wheeled it into the shed, then saddled both geldings. Because of Mary's rheumatism, they'd be taking the horses at a walk. It wasn't worth rounding up the stallion for such an easy outing.

By the time Mary emerged from the house, Jace was waiting with the horses. He helped her mount, pretending not to notice when she grimaced in pain. She would need to see the oil so she could show it to Judd later. The decision to exploit the oil or leave it alone was bound to be a family matter.

"The bog isn't on your land, is it?" he asked as the horses swayed along through the grass.

"No. The boundary line falls about fifty yards short of the bog. Everything beyond that line is government property. Is that a problem?"

"That depends. Judging from the lay of the land, I'd say most of the oil is under your property and the ranch. You might decide not to drill. But you'd have no control over the government land. Somebody else could lease the drilling rights, and you'd have all the things you don't want, right next door."

"Unless we leased it first. I'll talk it over with Judd." Mary shifted in the saddle to ease the pain in her arthritic hip. "How did you come to know so much about oil, Tanner?"

"Oh, I've worked on a couple of rigs," Jace answered, hating the half-truth. If he weren't masquerading as a drifter, he could do everything for them—read core samples, draw up cross sections, even negotiate the lease of the federal land. Repaying Mary's kindness would give him a lot of satisfaction. But why even think about it? He was a wanted fugitive, and he had no choice except to keep running. Run or hang.

They crossed the low fence that marked Mary's property line. From here they could see the mound of earth where Jace had buried the colt. Beyond it lay the bog with its sickly yellow grass, dank odor and clouds of swarming black gnats. Swallows dipped and darted, catching the insects in the air.

"We'll need to leave the horses and walk into the bog," Jace said. "Will you be all right?"

"I'd rather walk anywhere than spend another minute in this miserable saddle," Mary grumbled good-naturedly.

Jace laughed. "In that case, we'll dismount right here and walk the rest of the way." He swung off his horse and helped her ease to the ground. Stiff from riding, she tried a few tottering steps, then gladly accepted the arm he offered her.

"Getting old," she muttered, looking ahead. "So that's where you buried Clara's poor colt. My word, I can't believe you did that alone, right off your sick bed. That Katy! I only hope she learned her lesson! It broke Clara's heart, having to shoot the poor animal. She said you offered to do it for her."

"I did. She insisted on doing it herself." Jace steeled himself against the memory—Clara trembling in his arms, clinging to him, needing all the things he couldn't give her.

"She had such hopes for that horse, always said he had the makings of a champion. She—" Mary broke off. "What's the matter?"

Jace was staring at the soft ground at the edge of the colt's grave. The prints of his own round-toed English-style riding boots were there from his earlier visit. But there were other prints as well—long, narrow pointed boot prints, far too large to be Clara's—prints that followed his own, straight to the spot where oil was seeping into the bog.

Chapter Ten

Clara lay on her bed, covers flung aside, eyes gazing up into the darkness. The clock in the downstairs hallway had just struck eleven, a time when she would usually be asleep. But tonight sleep was the last thing on her mind. Every nerve in her body was alive and quivering.

Her parents had retired an hour ago, and there was no sound from their room across the hall. Katy and Daniel, who'd arrived home soon after his father, had gone to bed even earlier. Only the small settling sounds of an old house broke the nighttime stillness.

Shifting onto her side, Clara thought back on every detail of the family's after-supper conversation. Her grandmother had come in the buggy that evening bringing the news. Tanner had discovered oil seeping through the bog. He'd taken her to see it for herself, and he'd said there could be more oil under the farm and ranch. If they wanted to exploit their potential wealth, he'd given her the name of a reputable St. Louis firm they could contact.

"Who in blazes does this Tanner think he is?" Judd had demanded. "If he knows so much, why isn't he here in person? What's he getting out of this?"

"Nothing," Mary had replied calmly. "He seems to know a lot about oil, but he doesn't want any part of this. In fact, he's leaving first thing tomorrow morning."

Clara had suppressed a gasp.

"But that's not all," Mary had continued. "Whatever we decide to do about the oil, we'll need to do it right away. Tanner and I saw tracks out by the bog. Somebody else had been there, and it's likely they know about the oil."

"What kind of tracks?" A cold knot tightened in Clara's stomach. "What did they look like?"

"Boots," Mary had answered. "Long, skinny, cowboy boots. The toes were so pointed they looked like you could thread them through a darning needle."

"Lyle McCabe." Judd had looked as if he wanted to spit. "He wears boots like that, and the weasel showed up here yesterday with flowers for Clara. Maybe he figures the easiest way to get the oil is to marry into the family."

"Oh, please…" The memory of McCabe walking into her room had triggered a sick panic. Clara had barely listened to the rest of the discussion. All she remembered of it now was that the family had agreed to leave the oil in the ground. Tomorrow Judd would go to the nearest Bureau of Land Management office and arrange to lease the land around the bog to keep McCabe or anyone else from drilling there.

But Lyle McCabe was a dangerous man. Clara had known all along that he wanted her, and the oil discovery had just raised the stakes. Now McCabe would be doubly determined. And he was capable of destroying anyone who got in his way.

Clara sat up in bed. Moonlight shone through the lace-curtained window, casting a flower garden of patterns on the far wall. Maybe the full moon would work its magic on her mares. Tonight would be their last chance with Galahad—and her last chance to see Tanner.

Swinging her legs to the floor, she stripped off her nightgown, pulled on her jeans and shirt and picked up her boots. Her mother and father would be furious if they knew what she was up to. But she needed to warn Tanner about McCabe. And she needed to know the truth about the murder of Hollis Rumford.

Getting a horse could easily wake her parents. She would have to walk across the fields to her grandmother's farm. That would take twenty or thirty minutes. She could only hope that Tanner would still be there when she arrived.

Jace stood at the paddock fence, his eyes tracing the constellations in the night sky. Tonight the moon was a swollen sphere, hanging like a ripe peach against the velvety darkness. The wind was a musical murmur in the cottonwoods, carrying the scent of blooming honeysuckle from Mary's garden.

In the paddock, the stallion and the two mares

pranced and pirouetted in a dance as old as life itself. Their manes and tails flew as they frisked, nipped and swung their massive bodies.

A smile teased Jace's lips as he watched them. He'd witnessed the breeding process a number of times at the Rumford stables. A prize stud could be disabled by the kick of a mare's sharp hooves, so every precaution was taken to make sure this didn't happen. First a lesser stallion was brought into the corral to excite the mare. That done, the smaller horse was led away and the mare was confined in a narrow box, open at the back end. Only then was the stud horse allowed to approach her and finish the job, with handlers on all sides to make sure nothing went wrong. Jace had thought it a pitiful way to make love, even for horses.

Tonight, Galahad was entirely on his own, the way nature had intended. The big stallion seemed to know exactly what he was doing. Jace was grateful that he could leave Clara with this one parting gift. If all went as hoped, next spring's foals would carry the bay's bloodline into the future. Maybe as she watched those foals growing up, Clara would remember their time together.

But no—Jace brought himself up with a mental slap. That notion was pure romantic balderdash. The truth was, it would be better, and safer, for them both if she forgot they'd ever met.

Leaving the horses to their business, he walked up to the house and lowered himself to the front steps. The lights were out. Mary would be fast asleep. He'd be smart to get some sleep himself. He had a long road ahead of him tomorrow. But his bedroll and gear were already packed to go, and he was too restless to lie down and close his eyes.

Was Clara awake, too? Was she lying sleepless in her bed, her curls tumbling over the pillow, her night-gown tangled around her bare legs? Was she dreaming about how it would feel to let him make love to her, his flesh naked against hers, his body thrusting into her hot, wet sweetness?

Hellfire, thoughts like that could drive a man crazy!

Rising, he walked back across the moonlight-flooded yard toward the barn. The night was alive with sounds—the chirping of crickets, the swish of a nighthawk's wings, the ripple of wind across the hay-fields and the sounds of mating horses. Suddenly he became aware of another sound—footsteps rustling through the grass, coming closer.

Jace slipped into the shadows and stood motion-less, waiting. Why hadn't he strapped on the pistol? He should have known he might need it. He was cursing his carelessness when Clara stepped into the moonlight. She was moving at a graceful stride, her hair fluttering in the night breeze. An aching knot constricted in Jace's throat as he stepped into view. Seeing him, she stopped, turned and ran to him without a word.

He caught her close. Clara melted into his warm strength, clasping him tight against her, holding him as if her arms could bind him to her forever. "I was afraid I'd never see you again," she whispered.

His throat moved against her hair. "You won't see me after tonight. But come and look, Clara. You may be getting those foals you wanted after all."

Taking her hand, he led her to the paddock. Clara heard them first, the stamping hooves, the low snorts and nickers. Then, beyond the fence, she could see the horses moving like shadows. Moonlight flashed on their manes and flanks, on their exquisite faces and big, dark eyes.

"Oh!" she gasped, awestruck. "Oh, I can't believe it's finally happening!" She hugged him in her excitement. "Thank you, Tanner! Thank you for staying!"

"What do you say we give them some privacy?" He placed his hand at the small of her back and turned her away, guiding her along the path toward the blooming orchard. The night was so filled with wild magic that Clara was tempted to hold her tongue. But that wasn't why she'd come here. There were things that needed to be said, and no time to say them but now.

She groped for her courage, her mouth dry, her pulse racing.

"Are you all right?" Tanner asked, sensing her discomfort. "What is it?"

Clara cleared the tightness from her throat. "I was in town yesterday, before the accident," she said. "Something made me stop by the marshal's office. There were some new posters on his desk. One of them had your photograph on it." She took a sharp breath. "I know that your real name is Jason Denby and that you're wanted for killing a man."

His guiding hand dropped away. Clara could feel the tension in his silence. An eternity seemed to pass before he spoke.

"Are you afraid of me, Clara?"

"Would I have come here if I was afraid?" Her response came without hesitation. She knew he would never harm her. "I only want to know the truth," she said. "Who was Hollis Rumford? How did you come to kill him?"

They were standing under the oldest tree in the orchard, an ancient plum, heavy with blossoms. Pink petals shimmered in the moonlight. Even the wind seemed to hold its breath while Tanner hesitated. Seconds ticked by.

"Hollis Rumford was my brother-in-law," he said at last, "the husband of my only sister, Ruby. He was one of the richest men in Springfield, Missouri. Big house, powerful friends, a stable of the finest Thoroughbred racehorses in the state. The bastard cared more for those damned horses than he did for his wife and daughters."

He fell silent again. Clara touched his arm. "You once told me that what you did was necessary. But surely, killing a man—"

"You didn't know him." He stared past her into the darkness, as if seeing something far away. "Hollis and my sister were married ten years. He cheated on her from the beginning, and before long he was punching her, shoving her, choking her, damn near killing her."

Tanner's hands clenched into fists. "Ruby was—

is—a beautiful woman. You can't imagine how she looked after those beatings. I'd have thrashed the son of a bitch to a bloody pulp, but I knew he'd take it out on Ruby and the girls. When I threatened to have him arrested, Hollis just laughed. His family was hand in glove with every judge in the county. Besides, as he put it, didn't a man have the right to discipline his own wife?"

"Couldn't she have left him?" Clara asked softly.

Tanner shook his head. "He'd have taken their two little girls. That was the one thing Ruby wouldn't stand for."

Again he fell silent. Clara waited, sensing that whatever had happened, he was reliving it in his mind.

"Three months ago everything came to a head. I got a telephone call from her late one night. She was hysterical. She'd learned that once, when he was drunk, Hollis had tried to molest their nine-year-old daughter. When Ruby confronted him, he started beating her. She ran into the bedroom and called me—said he was pounding on the door, yelling that he was going to kill her. When I got to their place I could hear her screaming. I ran up the stairs—he'd broken down the door, and they were in the bedroom…"

"And so you shot him." Clara ended the story Tanner was too drained to finish. He was quivering like a horse at the end of a long race. Her arms went around him, holding him so tightly that she could feel his throbbing heartbeat. "I understand now. The man was a monster. You stopped him the only way you could. But why did you have to get away? You were defending your sister. No jury would have convicted you of murder."

Tanner exhaled, sagging against her. "I couldn't take that chance. Hollis's family is ruthless. Even the courts are afraid to cross them." His arms circled her, cradling her close. "All I could do was run, and I've been running ever since."

Blinking back tears, she gazed up at him—the tawny, wind-tousled hair, the weary lines that etched the corners of his shadowed eyes, the firm jaw and noble mouth. This man was anything but a cold-blooded killer. Jason Tanner Denby was an honorable man who had put his life and freedom on the line to protect others. More than that, he was the only man she'd ever loved—and she was about to lose him.

Stretching on tiptoe, she caught the back of his neck with one hand and pulled him down to her. For the barest instant he resisted. Then his mouth crushed hers in a kiss that burned through her body like flame through gunpowder. Clara melted against him, putting her heart, soul and body into that kiss. Her lips opened. She felt him gasp as her tongue invaded his mouth, seeking and finding. Her hips flattened against his hardness, pressing inward to recapture the heavenly sensations he'd awakened in her on that earlier night.

She could feel him fighting her still, but he was losing the battle. "Clara, please don't—" he muttered.

She clasped him close, never wanting to let him go. "Take me with you, Tanner," she whispered. "I'll go anywhere with you, sleep on the ground, run from the law—"

"Don't be crazy!" he growled, pushing her away from him. "That's no kind of life for any woman, especially for you. All you'd do is make it more likely for me to get caught. Let me go, and get on with your life, Clara. That's the only choice we have."

"Do you love me?" she asked, needing to know.

"Would it make any difference if I did?" His voice had chilled. "I need to go, and you need to forget me."

"You make it sound so simple." She knew he was trying to do the right thing; still his coldness stung her. She ought to leave now, and salvage the little pride she had left, Clara thought. But in the rush of seeing him again, she'd nearly forgotten her most urgent reason for coming here.

"Simple or not, it's the only way," he said. "I have to leave, and you have to let me."

"But you can't go now—not by the roads, at least. I told you I'd seen your photograph on a poster. At least one other person has seen it, too. That's why I came here tonight, to warn you."

His eyes flashed, then narrowed sharply. "Tell me everything," he said.

The story tumbled out of her in bursts—how Deputy Lyle McCabe had watched her go through the wanted posters, how he'd noticed her reaction and how she'd told him an unconvincing lie. "My grandmother's description of the prints at the bog matched the boots McCabe was wearing," she said. "If he's been nosing around here, chances are he's seen you, at least from a distance."

Tanner scowled, deepening the moon-shadows that masked his eyes. "So why doesn't he just ride in and arrest me?"

"Maybe he's not sure who you really are. You've changed since the picture was taken." Clara's knees went rubbery as a new possibility struck her. "You're wanted dead or alive. Maybe he's waiting to catch you alone, with no witnesses. That way he could just shoot you, and the town would call him a hero."

"What the hell kind of lawman would do that?"

"A sneaking coward like McCabe. And he's got some rough friends. He could have one of them bring your body in for the reward, then later they could split the money."

Tanner gazed up at the full moon, shaking his head. "Clara, you must've read too many dime novels growing up," he said. "That's the wildest scheme I've ever heard."

Clara clenched a fist in frustration. What was the matter with the man? Did he really believe he wasn't in danger, or was this his way of telling her not to worry about him?

She seized his upper arms, gripping hard. "You don't know McCabe—he's as treacherous as a two-legged rattlesnake! He wants the oil, and he sees me as the way to get it. He'd destroy anyone he thought was standing in his way."

Clara heard the sharp intake of breath and felt the sudden tension in his body.

"Has he been after you? Threatened you?"

"Hardly." She managed a bitter laugh. "He brought me some silly flowers after the accident. My father almost threw him out of the house."

"But he could get you alone—Lord, Clara, if the man is what you say he is, you need to be careful!" He was holding her now, protectively, almost possessively.

"Maybe you're the one who's read too many dime novels," she said.

"This isn't funny," he growled. "If the bastard tries anything I won't be here to stop him. I'm worried about you!"

"And I'm worried about you," she said. "By now, there's no telling who's seen that poster. If anybody recognizes you…" She let the words trail off, unable to voice what would happen. Her arms tightened around him as if, by holding him close enough, she could keep the whole world at bay. Shutting her eyes, she filled her senses with his clean, leathery scent. His skin was warm in the darkness, his heartbeat strong against her ear.

He cursed under his breath, his lips skimming her hair. "I'd give anything to have things different," he murmured. "You know I would, girl. But there's just no way for us. I've got to keep moving."

Clara forced herself to nod. Tanner was right; she had to let him go. It would be best to forget him and move on with her life. But how could she get through the days ahead, frantic for his safety, aching to see him and hear his voice?

"I just thought of something." She pushed back to look at him. "I know you can't stay here—this is one of the first places the law would look for you. And if that poster's gotten around, the roads could be watched as well. Even if you cut across open country, someone could spot you."

"Believe me, I've thought of that," Tanner said.

"Then listen to me. There's an old cabin in the mountains west of the bog. My grandfather built it for fishing—it still belongs to our family. We keep it locked, but I know where the key's hidden. You could stay there until it's safe to leave."

He hesitated, reflected moonlight flickering in his eyes. "How far is it? Can you draw me a map?"

She shook her head. "You'd never find it on your own. But I can take you there tonight—it's light enough to see the way. We could be there in about an hour—that is, if you can get Galahad to cooperate."

Tanner sighed. "I don't like involving you, Clara. Aiding a fugitive is against the law. Maybe I should just get away from here now, while it's dark."

"Word travels fast," she argued. "Unless McCabe wants to save you for himself, lawmen all over this part of the state could be on the lookout for you. Can you afford to take that chance?"

He shifted away from her, gazing toward the distant hills. Clara could sense the conflict in him as he weighed his choices. Had she done a reckless thing, offering him refuge in the cabin? Could she honestly say whether that offer had been prompted by concern for Tanner's safety or by the selfish desire to keep him near?

"The trail to the cabin is overgrown and hard to follow," she told him. "There's not much to eat there except for a few tins of sardines and some crackers, but you'll find good water in the stream and fishing tackle in the cabin. You'll be all right till I can bring up more supplies."

"No." He turned back to confront her, his expression a stubborn mask. "I won't bring you into this. Not in any way. Now that Galahad's done his duty, I'm going to saddle up and ride out of here."

"But it isn't safe!" she cried. "What if you're caught?"

"I'd rather take that chance than risk your coming to harm. Damn it, Clara, if I loved you any less—"

As if realizing what he'd just said, he broke off and strode back toward the shed where his gear and bedroll were stowed. Clara stood staring after him. He *loved* her. He'd just told her so. But what was love worth from a man who was leaving forever?

She fought back the urge to run after him, to fling her arms around him and beg him to stay. She loved him with all her heart and soul. But there was no arguing with reality. If she wanted Tanner to live and be free, she had no choice except to let him go.

Galahad stood resting under the big cottonwood, his energy spent for the moment. When Tanner opened the paddock gate and whistled, the stallion came willingly. Once he was bridled, Clara moved forward to hold the reins while Tanner positioned the saddle, tightened the cinch and tied on his gear. She noticed he was wearing his gun belt.

"Where do you plan to go?" She was fighting tears, determined that he not see her cry.

"You know better than to ask me that," he said. "Thank your grandmother and tell her—"

He broke off abruptly, listening.

"What is it?" Clara started to ask, but then she heard it, too—the clatter of shod hooves approaching up the drive. Riders. Three or four of them, at least. At this hour, that could only mean one thing.

"That's got to be McCabe and his friends. Go!" she urged him. "Hurry, before they get here!"

He shook his head. "I'm not leaving you and your grandmother alone with them. Come on."

Grabbing her arm, he led the stallion into the deepest part of the orchard. As they melted into the shadows, four riders, with Deputy McCabe in the lead, trotted their mounts into the farmyard and dismounted next to the corral. The men were laughing, talking, probably drunk on bootleg whiskey—and very dangerous.

"Spread out. Search the barn and the sheds. I'll talk to the old lady." McCabe, at least, sounded sober. Clara forgot to breathe as he stomped up the front steps, opened the screen and pounded on the front door.

"Deputy McCabe, ma'am," he shouted. "Open up in the name of the law!"

Seconds passed. Then a light flickered on. The bolt slid back with a click and the door opened. Mary stood on the threshold in her flannel wrapper, her long gray hair in braids, her shotgun cocked and aimed.

"I hope your business is important enough to justify

waking an old woman up in the middle of the night, Deputy," she snapped.

"We're looking for that hired man of yours," McCabe growled. "Where is he?"

"How should I know? I'm not his keeper." Mary held the shotgun steady. "He got paid today. Maybe he went into town to have some fun. Or maybe the footloose bum's packed up and gone. He did strike me as a flighty sort."

"We're going to have to search your house," McCabe said.

"A gentleman would take a lady's word. But seeing it's you…"

"I can't afford to take anybody's word," McCabe said. "The man's wanted for murder."

There was a beat of silence. "All right, but just you," Mary said. "The rest of those galoots stay outside. You've got one minute to look around and get off my property before I telephone the marshal. Sam Farley won't be happy to hear that you and your drunken friends are harassing me!"

Clara gripped Tanner's arm as lights flickered on and off in the bedroom windows of Mary's house. She could hear the other men throwing things around in the toolshed, whooping as they scared the chickens in the coop. Her heart hammered with terror. She envied her grandmother's spunk and courage.

After what seemed like hours, but couldn't have been more than a minute or two, McCabe emerged onto the front porch. Mary walked behind him, herding him with the shotgun. "See, I told you he wasn't here," she said. "Now take your friends and get off my property before I get nervous and start shooting. I can't see too well without my spectacles, but with so many bodies out there, I'm bound to hit something."

McCabe strode off the porch, stumbling slightly on the bottom step. "Mount up, boys!" he bawled, swinging onto his horse. "We'll spread out from the gate. If you see the murderin' bastard, shoot first and ask questions later!"

Clambering onto their horses, the impromptu posse thundered down the drive. Mary watched them from the porch until they disappeared, then turned and went back inside. Seconds later the lights went out.

Tanner's mouth flashed a grin. "What a spitfire! If I were forty years older I'd be tempted to propose to the woman!"

"Did you tell her you were wanted for murder?"

"No, but she didn't seem surprised. I'm guessing she figured it out. You can tell her the whole story after I'm gone."

"Should I let her know we're here?"

Tanner shook his head. "The less she knows, the better. But with that bunch of yahoos on the loose, I may need to take you up on that cabin offer after all."

"Fine. I'll saddle one of the geldings and come with you." Clara spun away. He caught her and jerked her back against him.

"No!" he growled. "McCabe's men might be out there watching. You'll need to come with me now on the stallion. Once I know how to find the cabin, I'll bring you down the back way and see that you're safely in the house. There's no way I'm letting you be out here alone."

The eyes that blazed down at her were as fierce as a cougar's. The night was electric with danger. Yet Clara had never felt more protected. "Let's go," she whispered.

They mounted stealthily, Tanner keeping low while he eased her up behind him. She clung to his back, spooning her knees behind his as they moved beneath the blossoming trees. Moonlit shadows danced in the wind.

In the stillness, Clara could hear the pounding of her own heart. Ever since that episode of terror in San Francisco, she'd played it safe, backing away from the unfamiliar, avoiding risk. But tonight she was risking everything for the sake of the man she loved. Anything could happen out there in the darkness. But she'd made her choice. She had crossed the line, and she had to be ready to take the consequences.

As they cleared the trees and moved into the open, a shout rang out from the direction of the gate. A single gunshot—a signal perhaps—echoed through the darkness. Had they been seen? There was no time to look back and find out.

Tanner dug his heels into Galahad's flanks. The big stallion exploded into a gallop, legs pounding, powerful body stretching, iron-shod hooves slicing the soft ground. From far behind came the sound of pistol fire as McCabe's gang took up the chase. But they were already outdistanced. Galahad was racing like the wind, a juggernaut of speed, power and beauty.

Clara felt a rush of exhilaration. She'd expected to be afraid. But she was strangely excited, almost euphoric. She'd heard both her parents say that Quint was addicted to adventure—that he was happiest when risking life and limb. Now, at last, Clara understood what that meant. Was this the heritage Quint had passed on to his daughter—this delicious stirring of the blood in the face of danger?

But there was no time to wonder. Tanner was leaning forward in the saddle, as the stallion shot across the level fields, clearing fences, jumping ditches. Wind shrilled in Clara's ears. She tightened her arms around Tanner's waist, pressing so close against his back that she felt as if the two of them and the horse were all one, like a statue forged in bronze.

She could no longer hear the shouts or the gunshots. She could feel nothing but Tanner's closeness and the pumping of the stallion's powerful body beneath her. They flew through the night as if they could run forever, to the ends of the earth.

If only they could.

Chapter Eleven

Within sight of the bog, Jace reined in the tiring stallion. Was anyone following them? He risked a backward glance at the moonlit fields—empty for now. Even if McCabe was still after them, no horse would have a chance of catching the stallion. But that wouldn't keep the posse from watching from a distance. And it wouldn't keep a decent tracker from picking up their trail. He could only hope McCabe's cohorts were as drunk and inept as they'd appeared to be.

"Go around the bog. The trail starts on the other side." Clara leaned forward to speak into his ear. Lord, what had he gotten her into? He should have left her safe with her family and taken his chances on his own. But with McCabe and his buddies combing the countryside, taking her with him to the cabin had seemed his only option.

Ahead of them lay the bog, its pale reeds gleaming white as bone in the moonlight. Swinging the stallion to the right, he gave the place a wide berth. It held bad memories and reeked of evil.

"There—just beyond those ragged junipers." Clara pointed past his shoulder. Sighting along her arm, Jace could make out a half-overgrown trail zigzagging through the scrubby foothills. Higher up, thickets of aspen and clumps of pine carpeted the slopes. They'd be safer once they reached the shelter of the trees. But the lower part of the trail would be exposed to anyone watching from below.

Clara's arms clasped his waist as they wound their way upward. Her body was warm against his back. The subtle wildflower fragrance of her hair crept over him, stealing through his senses. She was all innocence, all passion, his Clara—though he had no right to call her *his* Clara, especially when he could prove to be her ruin.

Tonight she was risking everything—her parents' anger, her reputation, her freedom, even her life—to help him. He had no right to do this to her. He should turn around, take her home and ride away, trusting Galahad's speed to carry him out of danger. But behind them was where the present danger lay. There was no telling what McCabe's men might do to Clara if they caught her with him. Turning back now was out of the question.

The stallion was climbing at a walk now, his gait slowed by the steepness of the trail. Glimpsed through the trees, the fields in the valley below spread like a patchwork quilt in night-muted shades of pale and dark.

Tanner couldn't have made it this far without her guidance, Clara knew. The mountainside was criss-crossed with a network of trails, some going to other cabins or fishing spots higher up, some going to farms or back toward town. It would be all too easy to take a wrong turn. She'd been coming up here all her life, but sometimes, in the dark, still she was uncertain.

Clouds were drifting in, veiling the moon in fleeting shadows. On the rising wind, she caught the scent of rain. Even here, Tanner continued to pause every few minutes to listen for signs of their pursuers. So far there were none. Only the rustle of aspen leaves and the steady plod of Galahad's hooves disturbed the stillness.

Tanner had been as silent as the night, lost in his own thoughts. Who was this man? Clara wondered. Some-times she felt as if they'd known each other all their lives. Other times, like now, it was as if he'd thrown up a wall between them. She understood that it was for her own protection. But that didn't mean she had to like it. She burned to know everything about Jason Tanner Denby—where he'd come from, his family and friends, what he'd done for a living, even little things like his favorite song and his favorite food. But aside from the story of the shooting, he'd told her nothing about himself. She had fallen in love with a stranger, a man as elusive and mysterious as a shadow.

Black clouds had moved in over the western peaks, spreading across the sky like spilled ink. Thunder quivered faintly on the air. A storm would hide their trail and hopefully send McCabe's men scurrying for home. But the open slope could be treacherous in a heavy downpour.

As the trail turned up the mouth of wooded canyon, Clara recognized the sound of a distant waterfall. They were headed the right way and would reach the cabin in fifteen or twenty minutes—none too soon with clouds blocking the moonlight and sheet lightning flickering in the west. The trail, at least, was more sheltered here, the slope of the land leveling off around them. Still cautious, Tanner nudged the stallion to a faster walk. His muscles were tense beneath her hands.

Unnerved at last by his silence, Clara cleared her throat and took a chance on getting answers.

"What was your old life like, before you left Missouri?" she asked.

The soft-spoken question caught Jace off guard. Clara had been quiet most of the way up the mountain. She must have been wondering about the man she was risking so much for.

"My old life's gone for good," he said. "What you see here, that's my life now."

She deserved a better answer, Jace thought. But the less she knew about him, the less she would have to forget.

"What did you do for a living?" she persisted. "You must've made good money. Those boots you're wearing look custom made."

His laugh was razor edged. "So you wouldn't believe me if I told you I stole them off a dead moonshiner?"

"No, I wouldn't. And stop insulting my intelligence. You're well educated, even well mannered—at least, when you choose to be. That doesn't come from nowhere." She shifted in the saddle, her shapely little body crowding his in a way that made his crotch ache. "You owe me some answers, Tanner."

Jace sighed. Clara was right. He did owe her some answers, or at least as many as he could safely give her. He paused, listening to the night. The trail here was overhung with aspen branches. White columbines and purple gentians bloomed in the shadows. From somewhere ahead came the whisper of rushing water.

"I'm a geologist, trained as an engineer," he said. "I used to hire out as a consultant for oil drilling companies. My job was figuring out where to sink the wells. If you'll excuse my bragging, I was damned good at it."

"So that's how you knew about the oil."

"It doesn't take a genius to recognize oil when it's oozing out of the ground. The tricky part is knowing where the oil is when you can't see it. Guess wrong, and the drilling company's out thousands of dollars."

Lightning cracked across the sky. Clara's arms tightened around him. Jace could feel her light breath on the back of his neck, her breasts pressing against his shoulder blades. The wind blew her hair against his cheek. He urged the horse forward on the narrow trail.

"From geologist to hired farm laborer," she said, making conversation. "That change can't have been easy for you."

"Honest work's nothing to be ashamed of. It's better than jail or hanging, for as long as it lasts."

For as long as it lasts. The words sent a quiver along Jace's nerves. Over the past three months, he'd tried not to wonder how it would feel, being captured, jailed, tried and hanged. But he'd never come this close to being caught. Knowing that his face was on a wanted poster, and that he'd been recognized, had brought reality crashing in on him.

He and his sister had never discussed what they'd do if he was captured. He'd fled Missouri with the idea that as long as he kept moving, he could run indefinitely and never be taken. It wouldn't be much of a life, but at least he could survive. Only now did the real possibility of capture sink home.

The trial would be swift, the evidence sure. Ruby might be called to testify, but Jace would plead guilty before he'd allow her to be put on the stand. However things went down, he had no doubt the prosecution would make the crime look like cold-blooded murder, and the judge would impose the maximum sentence.

What would it be like, being hanged—to climb the thirteen steps and wait for the drop of the trapdoor, to feel the tightening of the noose around his throat, the sudden snap?

But he mustn't think that way tonight—not while he was free. Not with Clara close beside him, so sweet and strong and unafraid. Right now one thing was certain. He couldn't let her suffer for what he'd done. Whatever happened, he had to make sure she'd be all right.

"Did you have a nice home in Missouri?" Clara asked him. "Did you leave a sweetheart behind?"

Thunder rolled across the horizon. Jace waited for the echoes to die away. "I had a nice bachelor flat in Springfield. And as for a sweetheart…"

He paused, trying to picture Eileen's sharply elegant face. The memory was colorless, like a black-and-white fashion photograph. "There was a woman I'd planned to marry," he said. "Somehow, the word *sweetheart* doesn't suit her."

"Did you love her?"

Had he loved Eileen? He'd admired her, coveted her, even liked her. But love? "I'm not sure I even knew what love was back then," he said. "I enjoyed showing her off and thought we might have a good life together. But when I had to leave, there was no time to tell her anything. Knowing how many beaux she had, I suspect she didn't waste much time pining over me."

Clara had fallen silent again, and Jace wondered if he should say more. Was it fair to tell her how much he loved her when he had no future to offer? Or would it be kinder to leave the words unsaid?

There was no time to ponder the question. Chain lightning cracked across the sky. With a shattering boom of thunder, the rain burst out of the clouds. Water poured down in gray streams, the drops so heavy that they stung like birdshot. There was no escaping the downpour. Within seconds they were both drenched to the skin.

On the mud-slicked trail, they had little choice

except to endure and keep moving. Clara clung to Jace's back. Through his rain-soaked shirt he could feel her shivering. The rain was misery. But for now, Jace reminded himself, it was also safety.

A few minutes later she nudged him, leaning forward to be heard. "The cabin should be right through those trees. Do you see it?"

Jace peered through the rain. The first thing he saw was a glimmer of reflected lightning on a glass windowpane. As they rode closer, the cabin took shape through the downpour. It was small and sturdy, with an exterior of oiled logs, a shingled roof and a covered porch. Screened by aspens, it blended with its surroundings.

Clara slid down the horse's flank and dropped to the ground. "You take care of Galahad," she said. "I'll get the key." Splashing down the trail ahead of him, she vanished into the rain. Acting out of caution, Jace drew his pistol as he rode in. But there was no need. The cabin was dark and quiet, with no sign that anyone had recently been there.

Dismounting, he unloaded his saddle and gear on the porch, then tethered the stallion behind the cabin, under the sloping eave that sheltered the woodpile. When he returned to the porch, Clara had found the key and was fumbling with the rusty padlock that hung from its hasp on the door. "I'll have this open in a j-jiffy!" She spoke through chattering teeth. Her shaking hands struggled to fit the key into the tiny opening on the lock.

"Here, I can do that." Clothes streaming water, Jace

stepped onto the porch. Curtains of rain cascaded off the eaves to fall around them. Clara handed him the key. Her wet fingers were quivering.

"You're cold," he muttered, reaching out to her. "So cold…" Without knowing quite how it happened, he was holding her close. She trembled against his wet flannel shirt, whimpering as his arms tightened around her. His mouth found her chilled lips in the darkness, their kiss softening, warming, becoming hungrier with each passing second. She strained upward, deepening the kiss, her head falling back, her body arching, her lips parting in unspoken invitation. Heat surged downward to his groin, igniting bonfires of need. Her hips rested against his straining erection. As she pressed tighter, he groaned.

Damnation! What were they thinking?

"We need to get you inside," he muttered, pushing away from her.

"Yes…" Clara's wet shirt clung to her body. Her aroused nipples strained the fabric with each breath as she moved aside for him.

Getting the lock open was harder than Jace had expected, but at last the hasp swung away and the door creaked open. As his eyes grew accustomed to the darkness, he could make out a table with two chairs, a potbellied stove and a counter with open shelves. Toward the back of the cabin was a double bed with a patchwork coverlet.

"There's dry wood in the stove. Dare we light a fire?" Clara was shivering again. Jace knew of one way to warm her, but that would be like touching a match to gunpowder. Once they started, it would be damned near impossible to stop. That kiss on the porch had already driven him to the brink of self-control. Her nearness in the dark, secluded cabin, with a bed close at hand, would be enough to send him over.

"Let's try the stove for now," he said. "Not much chance anybody will see the smoke in this storm. But we'd best keep the place dark. Lighted windows can be seen a long way off. As soon as the rain stops, we'll start back down." And it had damned well be soon, Jace thought. He couldn't keep his hands off Clara much longer.

"Matches." She handed him a miniature cardboard box she'd retrieved from a kitchen shelf. "Mind the damper. Make sure it's open. My father put a cap over the chimney to keep the birds from nesting there, so that should be all right."

Jace checked the damper, opened the front grate and lit a match. The distinct updraft told him the tall metal chimney was clear. Within minutes a blaze was crackling in the little iron stove. Blessing the person who'd laid the fire, he reminded himself to do the same when he left this place.

He couldn't remain here long, that much he knew. He was already imposing on Clara and risking her safety. The longer he stayed, the greater the danger of her being implicated.

Clara huddled close to the warmth, her backside turned toward the glowing stove. She was still shivering. If she didn't get warm and dry, she could get sick before he got her home.

Steeling his resolve, Jace spoke. "I shouldn't be the one to suggest this, but you need to get out of those wet clothes and wrap up in a blanket while they dry."

"You're as wet as I am." Her voice was husky in the darkness of the cabin.

"So I am. We'll both need to get warm." Striding to the bed, Jace pulled off the quilted coverlet and the soft woolen blanket underneath. Keeping the coverlet for himself, he tossed the blanket to Clara. "Here," he growled. "I'll turn my back."

And he would, Jace vowed. One look at Clara undressing and he'd be a lost soul. But even the mental picture of it, enhanced by the breathy little woman sounds she made, was driving him crazy.

Clara moved away from the stove and into the shadows. Her fingers fumbled with the buttonholes as she opened the front of her rain-soaked shirt. Somewhere behind her she could hear Tanner undressing— the scrape of his gun belt as he laid it on the chair, the thud of his boots on the floor. He seemed so distant now, as if that searing kiss on the porch had never happened.

She'd been secretly hoping for more once they were inside the cabin. But she knew him well enough to understand. He wanted her—maybe as much as she wanted him. But he was determined to make a clean break when he left her, with no ties, no false promises and no sordid memories to tarnish her future.

His intentions were noble enough. But didn't he realize what *she* wanted? Didn't the mule-headed man know she loved him with all her heart, body and soul? Couldn't he tell that she wanted more than the memory of a few brief kisses?

When the rain stopped he would saddle the stallion and take her home. Even if she came back to the cabin the next day, Clara sensed he would already be gone. Tanner was a tethered eagle, ready to fly at the first slip of the leash. If he couldn't leave by the road or the wooded fields, he would vanish into the mountains, living off the land until he could find a safe refuge. The only thing she knew for certain was that he would never come back.

Her hands were feeling warmer now. Slipping off her boots, she unfastened her jeans, pulled them down below her knees and stepped out of them. In her haste to dress tonight, she hadn't taken time to don her underwear. Beneath her wet shirt and pants, there was nothing but chilled skin.

With the blanket wrapped and tucked beneath her arms, she draped her clothes over one of the wooden chairs and placed them near the stove to dry. Tanner was standing with his bare back to her. He had taken off his shirt and peeled the top of his long johns down past the waist of his jeans, unbuttoned to hang low on his hips. The glow from the fire caressed his golden skin, casting the contours of rock-hard muscle into rippling light and shadow. His wet hair clung to the back of his neck in flattened curls, giving him the look of a statue cast in bronze.

The sight of him roused an ache in Clara's throat. Heart pounding, she walked across the rug to where he stood. Her hands touched his back, thumbs sliding up the muscled grooves along his spine. He quivered at her touch but didn't pull away.

Emboldened, she slid her hands around his rib cage. His breath hissed inward as her palms settled on his chest. His nipples shrank and hardened under her fingertips.

He groaned. "Clara, so help me, girl, if you don't want me to—"

"Hush." Her arms tightened around him, drawing him closer. Her lips nibbled a line of kisses from the back of his neck to the hollow between his shoulder blades. His breathing had quickened and deepened. Beneath her left hand she could feel the drumming of his heart. A startling sense of power rushed over her. *She* was causing those reactions in him, making him want her. For this short, precious time, she was in control. He was hers. And she was his.

Almost forgetting to breathe, she let her hands creep downward over the flat of his belly, past the hollow of his navel to where his long johns hung over the loosened belt band of his jeans. A shudder ran down his body as she moved a finger beneath the soft fabric, skimming his hip bones.

"Do you want to touch me, Clara?" His voice was thick and gravelly. Rain beat against the roof of the little cabin. Pitch wood snapped and crackled in the stove.

"Yes." The whisper trembled on her lips. "I want to touch all of you."

He muttered something under his breath—a curse, perhaps, or a final protest before surrender. "Here I am. And I'm not stopping you."

She gave the top of his jeans a slight downward push. His wet clothes slithered off his hips and down his thighs to bunch around his ankles. He stood with his back toward her, his body naked in the firelight.

Could she do this? Heart galloping, Clara placed her palms on his hip bones, slid them down and forward a few inches, then froze. "I want to," she gasped. "But I've never…"

"There's nothing to be afraid of." He took her hands and guided them down and forward, over the slope of his pelvis, down the hollow of his groin to touch—

"Oh!" she breathed. "You're so—so—"

Clara had seen enough of stallions and bulls to know what to expect. But she hadn't anticipated the size of him. She could never have imagined the petal softness of the skin that covered the hardness of his straining shaft or the heat waves that rushed through her body at the first brush of her fingers.

He moaned, his hips curving toward her hand as she clasped him. She moved her fingers up and down, exploring that amazing part of him—the exquisite swelling of the head, the bead of moisture at its tip. He was breathing hard, moving lightly against her hand. Heaven help her, she couldn't get enough of touching him, holding him.

She became aware that her own body was responding, flooding her loins with a moist, shimmering heat.

She could feel the subtle clenching, the flow of slickness between her thighs, and she knew that all this was to prepare her for him—to have him inside her.

Every womanly instinct told her that was what she wanted.

The blanket had come loose from around her body and fallen to the floor. Scarcely daring to breathe, she pressed herself against his back. His taut buttocks nested against the base of her belly. The contact sent a riffle of delicious quivers down into her thighs.

"Take me, Tanner," she whispered. "Whatever happens, I want to remember this as the night you made love to me."

A growl of frustration escaped his throat. "You know better than to ask that. You have your whole sweet life ahead of you. Don't throw it away on a man you'll never see again."

"But I need…" The throbbing in her loins had become an ache. She was drowning in sweet, urgent sensations. "How can you give me this much and not give me the rest, Tanner? If you leave me like this…I won't be able to stand it."

She kissed his shoulders, the back of his neck, loving the strength of him, the coolness of his skin. "Please," she whispered. "I'm begging you."

He was silent for a moment. When he spoke again, his tone had softened but his voice still carried an edge. "Come to bed, then. I won't take your virtue, but I can try to give you what you need."

Stepping away from her, he turned. Her gaze flickered downward, to his jutting arousal, then returned to his face. His eyes were fiercely gentle. "Is that what you want?" he asked.

She felt the hot color flood her cheeks. "Yes," she whispered.

He flung the blankets back on the bed, turned down the flannel sheet, then reached for her hand. Thunder shook the little cabin. Rain spattered the dark windows. "If things were different I'd stay, Clara," he said. "I'd court you properly and ask you to be my wife. But tonight, this is all I can offer you."

She slid between the cool sheets, gazing up at him as he stood over her. Firelight outlined his muscular shoulders and danced on his tawny hair. Cast in gold and flame, his aroused maleness took her breath away. In her wildest fantasies, how could she have imagined anyone so beautiful?

He stretched out next to her, pulling the covers over them. Turning, he rose onto his arms and leaned over her. "Don't be afraid, love," he murmured, bending down to brush a kiss on her lips. "Just lie still. If you move, I might not be able to control myself."

He kissed her mouth again, softly and tenderly, then trailed a line of kisses along her cheek. His tongue flicked the hollow of her ear. The light touch triggered a little spasm in the depths of her body. Her lips parted. Her hands reached up to clasp his shoulders.

"No, let me do this." He drew back, then bent to kiss her again, deepening the contact with his tongue, letting its tip tease the sensitive inner surfaces of her mouth.

She lay back on the pillow, letting the wild sensations sweep through her body. It was like hovering on the brink of heaven. Just when she thought she would topple into space, he gave her more, taking her higher.

As his lips nibbled their way down her throat to the hollow between her breasts, he shifted above her. Clara's gasp became a whimper, then a broken sigh as his mouth found her nipple and began a gentle laving—licking, sucking, nipping softly. The tugging sensations in her womb deepened. She could feel her wetness dripping onto the sheet. She ached to have him inside her, making her a woman at last. But she knew that wasn't Tanner's intent. Moments ago, she'd told herself she was the one in charge. Now she was at his mercy. He was her guide on a journey into a new and sensual world.

Her nipples had hardened into tingling nubs. Each touch of his tongue, each gentle nip of his mouth heightened her arousal. Every cell in her body seemed to burn with desire. Her body writhed with need. She wanted him. Oh, how she wanted him.

"Please, Tanner," she whispered. "Please—"

"Hush, love. I'll make it all right." His hand glided down her belly to splay over the soft tangle of hair that hid her sex. Her breath caught as he found the moist folds, and parted them to stroke the swollen bud at their center.

"Oh—" Her legs parted to open his way. Her hips arched upward, heightening the sensations that rippled through her body from that exquisite point of contact. Instinctively she began to move, thrusting against his hand, whimpering with need.

Gliding on her moistness, his finger entered her. Startled, she gasped.

"I won't hurt you, Clara." His voice was rough velvet. "Do you want me to stop?"

"No." She shook her head vehemently. "Don't…stop." Her senses were swimming in wild, animal heat. Her body clenched around his finger as he glided in and out of her. She quivered on the brink of sensual explosion. "I want you," she murmured. "I want—"

"You'll be all right, love." Withdrawing his fingers he bent and kissed her mouth. Then, brushing his lips in a line down her belly, he settled his head between her thighs.

The first brush of his tongue sent shock waves through her body. The feeling was so exquisite she almost wept. Drowning in sensation, she clasped his hair, opening to him, pulling him deeper as he licked and nuzzled. When his thrusting tongue slipped inside her, she gave a little cry. Hips bucking, she moved against him, pushing toward the brink. The tension built and built as she toppled over the edge, spiraling downward like a burning rocket until at last she lay still, spent and calm once more.

"I love you, Tanner," she whispered, cradling his head in her hands. "I'll never love anyone else like this as long as I live."

Tanner shifted forward, brushing tender kisses on her lips, her cheeks, her damp eyelids but saying nothing. The rain drummed on the roof of the cabin as she curled into his arms and began to drift.

Chapter Twelve

Jace lay with Clara in his arms, his body still aching with how he'd held back. It had taken every ounce of willpower he possessed not to thrust himself into that moist, inviting honey. But now, seeing the sweetness of her sleep, he knew it had been the right decision. Clara's innocence belonged to the man who would become her husband. He had no right to take it.

The rain had ebbed. Moonlight filtered through the thinning clouds. Water drizzled off the eaves. Outside, through the log wall, Jace could hear the stallion stirring. It was time to get up and take Clara home.

Rising on one elbow, he lingered for a few precious seconds, gazing down at her sleeping face. She was lying on her side, her body spooned against his. Her damp curls spilled over the pillow, framing the softness of her face. Her eyelashes lay like velvet fringe against her fair skin. Her ripe mouth wore the faintest hint of a smile, deepening the dimples in her cheeks.

The surge of love raised a lump in Jace's throat. He would do anything for this tender, passionate young woman—fight for her, even die for her. But the best thing he could do now was let her go.

He weighed the wisdom of waking her up while he was still in bed, then decided against it. Clara awakening in his arms, naked and warm and muzzy, would be too much temptation to resist.

Easing out from under the covers, Jace dressed quietly, then stole outside to relieve himself and check on Galahad. The rain had dissolved into mist, leaving a sky that was just beginning to pale in the east. The first morning birds were awakening to song.

Jace swore under his breath. He'd never intended for them to stay this long in the cabin. Not that they could have left much sooner. The trail would have been too dangerous in the rainy darkness. But now it would be light by the time they reached the valley. Getting Clara home without being seen could prove to be a real problem.

By the time he was ready to return to the cabin, Jace had thought of a solution. He couldn't say he liked it much, but it was the best guarantee of Clara's safety.

He stepped inside to find her sitting up in bed, looking deliciously rumpled, with the sheet clutched against her chest. "What time is it?" she whispered anxiously.

"It's morning. Time to get up," he said. "You're going to have to take Galahad down alone. I can't risk going with you by daylight."

"But what will you do?" Her eyes widened in puzzled dismay.

"I'll wait here for you. Tonight, when it's dark you can bring the stallion back, along with another horse to carry you home."

"But you'll be stranded up here until I get back," she argued. "Surely there's a better way. I could walk home in two or three hours."

He shook his head. "I won't hear of it. If McCabe and his bully boys are out there, you don't want to be on foot. Galahad can outrun anything on four legs. He's your best chance of getting home safely."

"But what if something happens and I don't make it back tonight?"

"Then I'll just have to wait for you." It was a calculated risk, Jace knew. Any number of things could go wrong, leaving him stranded on the mountain without his horse. But he'd made up his mind that Clara's safety had to come first.

"I'll leave the stallion in Grandma's barn," she said. "If something goes wrong and I don't show up, you can always walk down in the dark and get him."

"Fine. I'll saddle him while you get some clothes on." Jace went back outside to where he'd left his gear on the porch. Clara's backup plan was fraught with risk, but it was better than no plan at all. For all he knew, after this escapade, her parents might lock her in her room for a week, and he couldn't blame them. By the time she made it home, they'd undoubtedly be worried sick about her.

She came outside as he was tightening the cinch. Without a word, she ran to him and flung herself into his arms. Her kiss was wildly passionate, as if they were embracing for the last time. "I'll be back with the stallion," she vowed. "I promise."

"Just be careful, love. Don't take any chances." He kissed her hard, then thrust her away from him. "Get going now. I'll be all right here until you get back."

Clara swung into the saddle and nudged the stallion to a walk. She held her head high, staring straight ahead as if looking back at him might cause her to lose heart.

Jace stood watching her until she vanished through the trees.

Clara made the trip down the mountain in less than half the time it had taken to ride up in the dark. Except for some skittish moments on the trail, Galahad handled like a dream. Under different circumstances, riding the big stallion would have thrilled her. But this morning she had too much on her mind to think about the horse.

Every detail of last night was etched in her memory. Knowing she and Tanner could never have a life together had made their time bittersweet. Still, it had been wonderful. Her only regret was that they hadn't made love—not, at least, in the fullest sense.

She had wanted to give her first time to the only man she'd ever love. But Tanner's principles had denied her that. Oh, certainly he'd been concerned about getting her with child. But she would have welcomed even that—a little piece of him to hold and love forever. If only he'd understood…

But right now she had more urgent concerns. By the time she reached the farm, it would be full daylight. Her family would be looking for her, probably worried sick. She could only hope her plan to return Galahad to Jace would work.

By the time she passed the bog, the sun's blazing edge was rising above the peaks. Deciding against a dash through the open fields, she made for the woods, circling to emerge behind her grandmother's orchard. McCabe and his friends had seemed so drunk, they were probably sleeping off a hangover back in town this morning. Still, she couldn't be too careful.

In the orchard, she dismounted and led the stallion to the back door of the barn. The door opened with a creak, startling her grandmother, who was seated on a low stool milking the cow.

Mary jumped up, knocking the stool over and almost spilling the milk. "My stars, child, you scared the life out of me!" she gasped. "Where have you been? Your parents are fit to be tied!"

Clara had long since learned that her grandmother could see through any lie. "I took Tanner up to the fishing cabin last night, when McCabe's men came by," she said. "It was the only way I knew to protect him."

Mary righted the stool and sank onto it. "Protect him! Don't you know he's wanted for—"

"I know," Clara interrupted. "He explained everything to me. He's not a bad man, and he doesn't deserve what they'll do to him if he's caught."

"But you spent the night up there with him!" Mary's

glasses had tumbled askew. She made no effort to straighten them.

"It wasn't safe to come down the mountain in the rain. But Tanner's a gentleman. You said so yourself. I'm fine, Grandma, honestly." And that, Clara thought, was as much truth as she was going to reveal. "Look, he even lent me his stallion to ride home." She led the big bay into a stall, removed the saddle and bridle and poured some oats into the feed bucket.

"So Tanner's up there without a horse. What will he do if someone comes after him?" Mary demanded.

"He took that risk to make sure I got home safely," Clara said. "If I can't take the stallion back, Tanner will have to hike down here and get him."

"Well, you'd best keep the horse inside the barn for now," Mary snapped. "That weasel McCabe's still nosing around the place. If he sees the stallion, he's bound to get suspicious."

"Thank you, Grandma." Clara's knees buckled with relief. She'd hoped she could count on Mary but she hadn't been sure of it until now. "Let me go in the house and telephone Mama. I can tell her I'm bringing the mares home."

"And what else will you tell her?"

Clara's heart sank. "Please, Grandma," she begged. "I'll tell Mama and Papa everything in my own time. But until Tanner's safe, can't we keep it a secret?"

"I keep far too many secrets for you, young lady!" Mary turned back to her milking. The sharp spurts of milk in the tin pail expressed her thoughts far better than words. But Clara knew what her grandmother wasn't saying. For now, at least, Mary could be trusted not to betray her.

Clara trotted the mares home across the pasture, sitting bareback on Jemima while Belle followed behind on a lead rope. By now the sun had risen. Raindrops glistened on the long grass. A meadowlark caroled from one of Tanner's new fence posts. It was going to be a beautiful day. But Clara was too churned up to enjoy it.

So far she'd been lucky. Mary was already on her side. And even the telephone call to her mother hadn't gone as badly has she'd feared. Hannah had been upset, of course. And Clara's story that she'd gone to check on the mares hadn't been all that convincing. But her mother had been mercifully distracted. Twenty minutes ago they'd received a call from the railroad station that Quint and Annie had arrived days ahead of schedule, on the morning train. Judd had hitched the buggy and gone into town to fetch them. Meanwhile Hannah, Rosita and Katy were caught up in a whirlwind of cleaning and cooking. "We'll deal with your escapade later," Hannah had said. "Don't think we won't. But right now I need you here, helping us get ready."

Clara was grateful for the reprieve. But with so many other things on her mind, she'd put the issue of her parentage aside. Now the truth would be right in front of her, hidden in the depths of twinkling brown eyes that matched her own. What was she going to do? Heaven save her, she didn't know.

When she rode into the yard, the first person she saw was Katy, whaling the dust out of a Turkish carpet that hung over the clothesline. At the sight of her sister, Katy paused, rolling her pretty blue eyes. "You'd better change before Mama sees you looking like that," she warned. "She's fit to be tied. I don't see what all the fuss is about. Uncle Quint and Aunt Annie won't care what we're wearing. And they won't notice whether the windows have been washed, or if there's dust in this old carpet!"

Clara slid off the mare's back. "Mama will notice. That's what matters. And since she does so much for us, we shouldn't complain about making a little effort to please her."

Lecture delivered, she strode toward the barn, leading the mares. And while the words had been spoken for Katy's sake, Clara took them to heart for herself. Maybe it was time she stopped behaving like a rebellious teenager and joined the ranks of the grown-ups. At least it was time she viewed her mother with more understanding. Hannah Gustavson had grown up dirt-poor, the oldest of seven children. She'd been saved from the scandal of unwed motherhood only by Judd's offer to marry her. No wonder she seemed so overly concerned with appearances. It was her way of convincing herself she was worthy of respect.

But Clara was still plagued by questions. How had Judd felt about marrying the mother of Quint's child? Had he cared for Hannah or had he acted only out of duty? And why, in all these years, hadn't anyone told her the truth? Had there been an agreement to keep it from her, or had it been a simple matter of putting off the painful revelation, day after day, year after year, hoping it would be forgotten?

The one person Clara couldn't fathom was Quint. Why hadn't he answered Hannah's letters? Why hadn't he done the decent thing and married the mother of his child?

There was only one way to resolve that question— ask him. Meanwhile, it was urgent that she get the stallion back up the mountain to Tanner. Having Quint and Annie here could prove to be either a hindrance or a welcome distraction. Either way, one thing was certain. The next twenty-four hours would be as wrenching as any time in Clara's life.

By the time the buggy rolled through the gate and up the drive, it was late morning. The house was spotless, a pot roast simmering on the kitchen stove and fresh bread baking in the oven. Hannah and her daughters were dressed in pretty cotton frocks to welcome their visitors.

Energetic as ever, Quint sprang out of the buggy as soon as it pulled up to the house. At forty, he was still impossibly handsome, his thick chestnut hair barely touched with gray. Bounding up the porch steps, he enfolded Clara, Katy and Hannah in an exuberant bear hug.

"I swear you ladies get prettier every year!" he boomed.

Katy blushed and giggled. Hannah returned his hug with an affectionate squeeze. "It's good to see you, Quint," she said with a smile. "How was your trip?"

Clara stood back a little watching them together—her mother and the man she knew to be her father. Emotions welled in her, threatening to spill over—outrage, hurt and a strange sort of wounded love. How could these two greet each other as friends after what had happened between them? How had Judd managed to treat his brother with such kindness all these years? And again, for Clara, the most tormenting question of all—why hadn't anyone told her?

Quint turned back to help his slim, elegant wife out of the buggy. Annie was dressed in a mauve traveling suit and matching hat that set off her delicate coloring. She looked tired, Clara thought. But then, three days and nights on a train, even in a first-class sleeper, would exhaust anyone.

First Annie greeted her sister, kissing her warmly on the cheek. Then she turned to Katy. "My goodness, what happened to my little niece? She's all grown-up, and so pretty! I can hardly believe it!"

Katy blushed to the roots of her flaxen hair and muttered something under her breath. She wasn't used to compliments. But Clara had no reason to doubt her aunt's sincerity. Scrubbed, combed and wearing one of the new dresses she hated, Katy really did look pretty today.

Next, Daniel, his hair slicked with water and wearing a fresh chambray shirt, strode forward to shake his uncle's hand and give his aunt a manly hug. Both of them exclaimed over how tall he'd grown.

"And there's my darling girl!" Annie's embrace all

but undid Clara. The two of them had always been close, especially since their harrowing time in San Francisco. The awareness that Annie had known her secret, and loved her all the more for being Quint's daughter, brought a rush of tears to Clara's eyes. She blinked them away.

Stepping back, Annie looked her up and down. "You're as beautiful as ever, dear. But something…" Her thoughtful gray eyes narrowed slightly. "Something's different. Never mind, we'll talk later." She turned back to Hannah, who swept her into the house, chatting all the way. Quint and Daniel trailed behind with the bags while Judd drove the buggy back to the barn to unhitch the horses.

A little before lunchtime, Mary arrived to join them. More than a year had passed since she'd last seen her second daughter, and they had a world of catching up to do. But from time to time, as the two of them chatted on the parlor sofa, Mary's wise blue eyes flickered across the room to her granddaughter, and Clara knew she was thinking about the man in the cabin and the fearful secret they shared.

At Rosa's summons, everyone gathered in the dining room and took their seats. Judd sat at the head of the big family table with Hannah at the foot and the others arranged along the sides. As luck would have it, Clara found herself seated directly across from Quint. An unaccustomed shyness crept over her as she sensed the warmth in his gaze. She had adored him all her life— her laughing, loving, indulgent uncle Quint. He'd been her confidant, her comforter, her partner in fun and mischief. She'd always been aware that she held a special place in his heart, but until a few days ago, she hadn't understood why.

Now that she knew, she couldn't meet his eyes.

After a brief moment of grace, they began the ritual of food passing and small talk. Rosa had been cooking for the ranch for as long as Clara could remember. Her pot roast was tender enough to cut with a fork. The carrots, potatoes and gravy melted in the mouth, and the salad was crisp with freshly picked lettuce from the garden. Everyone was so hungry that conversation stilled for the first few minutes of the meal. Then Quint tapped his knife lightly on the side of his glass, bringing the family to attention.

"If you'll excuse the interruption, I have an announcement to make." He was beaming from ear to ear. A pink-cheeked Annie was staring down at her plate. "I know some of you thought this might never happen, but in about six more months, God willing, there's going to be a new little Seavers in the family!"

There was a hush of surprise, then everyone seemed to be talking at once, filling the room with sounds of laughter and congratulations. Hannah sprang out of her chair to rush around the table and hug her sister. Judd was raising his glass in an informal toast to his brother. Only Clara remained silent—thrilled, of course, but stunned as the realization struck her. She would be both a cousin and a half sister to Quint and Annie's child—

as closely related as she was to Daniel and Katy. That idea would take some getting used to.

"We didn't know about the baby till after we got off the boat in New York," Quint explained. "We thought Annie's queasy stomach was just seasickness. But when it hadn't gone away after three days on land we went to a doctor." He reached for his wife's hand. "What a surprise! We were bowled over!"

"That's why we decided to return to San Francisco," Annie said. "We both wanted to be where I could get good care and plenty of rest."

"And speaking of rest," Quint added, "this little mother-to-be is under orders to lie down and take a nap as soon as lunch is finished. When she's bright eyed again, we'll unpack and you can open the presents we brought you."

Only after the last crumb of apple pie had been finished, the dishes cleared away and Annie settled in the guest room did Clara get a chance to talk with Quint alone. She hadn't planned it that way. She'd stepped out onto the front porch for some air when he came outside to stand at the rail beside her, gazing across the yard.

"It always feels good, coming home," he said. "Your father's done a fine job with this place, better than I would've done if I'd stuck around."

"His whole life is here on this ranch, with his family," Clara said. "And now you'll have a family of your own. I'm so happy for you and Aunt Annie."

He took her arm, lightly guiding her down the steps. "Let's take a walk. When I tucked her in, Annie said she'd noticed something different about you. Maybe it's just that you've grown up. But if it's something you feel like sharing, here I am."

Now's the time, Clara thought. *Just say it. Five words—I know you're my father.*

But her throat choked around the words, and she couldn't make herself say them. Maybe later, but not yet.

Quint was angling their path toward the barn. "Why don't you show me your horses? That chestnut yearling I saw last time showed a lot of promise—what was it you named him?"

A lot of promise. Clara ached, remembering. "Foxfire. He was a beauty. But we lost him just a few days ago."

"Damn it, I'm sorry. Rotten luck."

Knowing Quint would want the whole story, she told him about Katy's escapade and the tragic accident in the bog.

"Poor, fool kid," he muttered. "I'm guessing she was pretty broken up."

"It could've been much worse, of course. Katy could have been hurt, even killed. But Grandma's hired man caught up with them and yanked her out of the saddle just before the colt went down."

Clara gave herself a mental slap. She hadn't planned on mentioning Tanner, but it was too late to bite her tongue. Now Quint would be curious. And being a reporter, he wouldn't back off until he knew all there was to know. The trouble was, there was so much she couldn't tell him.

"The hired man caught up with that colt?" Quint asked. "What the devil was he riding?"

"He had an amazing stallion, a Thoroughbred. I talked him into staying long enough for his horse to breed my mares. If it took, we should have some great foals next summer."

"I wouldn't mind meeting this fellow. Seems odd that a man doing menial work would own such a valuable horse."

"I'm afraid he's gone. He left last night." She was telling him too much, Clara knew. But Quint would likely ask Mary about the man she'd hired. It wouldn't do to get caught in a lie.

"Why would he just up and leave? Was he in some kind of trouble?"

Clara shrugged, feeling as if she'd just stepped into quicksand and was sinking deeper with every word. "He was a drifter. I don't think he ever meant to stay long."

"I see." Quint's handsome features were creased in a scowl. Groping for some distraction, Clara flung out the first question that came to mind.

"Uncle Quint, how do you know when you're in love?"

He stared at her, then burst into a chuckle. "So it's that old question, is it? Annie was right. There *is* something different about you! So, are you going to tell me about him?"

Clara shook her head. "Not yet. Not until I know what's going to happen."

Quint laid gentle hands on her shoulders, turning her

to face him. "But is he good for you? Because if he isn't I'll whip him within an inch of his life. You know what I'd do to anyone who tried to hurt you."

"He'd never hurt me."

"But do you love him, girl? Lord, you're so young."

"I'm almost twenty. And you haven't answered my question. How do you know when you're in love?"

"Why are you asking an old fogy like me?" Quint teased. "What makes you think I'd know?"

"You love Aunt Annie. I can tell by the way you look at her."

And you loved my mother once—at least, I hope you did. The words trembled on Clara's tongue but the courage to give them voice failed her again.

Quint studied her, his eyes narrowing. "I can tell you this much about love—when it's real, you won't feel the need to question it. And I can tell you something else. The heart's a tender thing, sweet girl. It's all too easily broken. But it can heal. Believe me, I know."

They resumed their walk, laughing as they parted to step around both sides of a big rain puddle. Clara was lost in thought. Had Quint's own heart been broken when Hannah chose to stay with Judd instead of marrying the man who'd sired her child? Was that what he was trying to tell her?

They had reached the shadows of the open barn. The two mares were dozing in their stalls, tired, perhaps, after last night's romp in the paddock. Clara thought of the stallion locked in Mary's barn and the dangerous errand she planned for tonight. Would she be able to get away without being seen? Would she find Tanner safe at the cabin?

How could she say goodbye to him, knowing it would be forever?

"What if I told you I *knew* I was in love? What sort of advice would you offer me then, wise Uncle Quint?" Clara spoke in a teasing tone, but her question was a serious one.

He was silent for a moment, thinking. "First, ask yourself if he's really the one. If the answer's yes, then give it your all. Fight for him, if you have to. Love him with all your heart. You may get that heart broken, but if you do, you'll be stronger and wiser for it, and ready for the next time." He quirked one eyebrow. "Not quite the advice you'd expect from your stodgy old uncle, is it?"

"Not what I'd expect from a different sort of uncle. But from you...somehow it fits."

"Just don't tell your parents what I said. They'd ride me out on a rail." He gave her a conspiratorial wink.

Clara felt a surge of warmth. Whatever had happened twenty years ago, she knew Quint cared deeply for her. Maybe if she told him everything he might help her, or at least cover for her while she took the stallion back up the mountain.

Weighing the idea for a moment, she decided against it. If she were to tell Quint about her secret plan, his desire to help her would come up against his need to keep her safe. In the end, his desire to protect her would most likely win out, and he would go to her parents. She didn't dare tell him. Until Tanner was safely gone, she didn't dare tell anyone but Mary. And even Mary didn't know all of it.

How was she going to manage tonight? So many things could go wrong. What if she couldn't find a safe time to slip away? What if her family discovered her missing and telephoned the marshal? What if her grandmother became concerned and spilled the whole story?

She'd told Quint she was in love. That much could work in her favor. If her absence was discovered, he'd likely assume she'd stolen out for a rendezvous. Hopefully he'd be able to reassure the family that she was safe—unless he got into a serious conversation with Mary and figured out where she'd really gone. Would he remember his advice then, how he'd told her to give herself over to love? Would he condemn her for following it?

"You're awfully quiet," Quint commented as they strolled back to the house. "What's going on inside that pretty head of yours?"

"Just thinking about your advice." Clara gave him a smile, imagining what Quint would say if he could read her jumbled thoughts.

A week ago her life had seemed so simple. Now she was drowning in a deluge of unanswered questions.

Chapter Thirteen

By the time Clara dared to leave the house, it was almost midnight. Mary had gone home after supper. Katy, Daniel and the women had retired by ten o'clock, but Judd and Quint had stayed up playing cards and visiting until the clock struck eleven. Lying awake, Clara had heard the familiar thud of their boots dropping to the floor. Even after that, she'd waited a very long hour before slipping into her clothes and stealing down the stairs.

By the time she returned, she was liable to be in a great deal of trouble. But as long as Tanner got away safely, nothing else mattered.

She'd left Tarboy loose in the paddock, but before she could ride him, she needed to get the saddle and bridle out of the tack room. Taking a route that couldn't be seen from the house, she circled the yard and entered the far end of the barn. Earlier she'd stuffed a flour sack with provisions from the kitchen and hidden it under the clean straw. Loading everything in her arms, she carried it out to the paddock.

The well-trained cow pony came at her whistle. A few minutes later she was in the saddle and headed across the fields to her grandmother's place.

Tonight, the moon was waning, its fullness marred by a razor-thin shadow along its west side. The stars were icy pinpoints in the clear black sky, the breeze erratic and gusty, like the breath of a wounded animal. Clara felt the tension as she rode—in the night, in her horse and in herself. Nothing she could see or hear seemed out of place. But her instincts told her some danger was afoot.

She tried to dismiss the feeling as she rode into the farmyard. Mary's house was dark and quiet, as was the barn. The two geldings drowsed in the corral, their breathing deep and even. Everything seemed fine.

Dismounting, she led Tarboy into the barn. Galahad nickered softly as they came inside. Clara had thought out this part of her plan carefully. She would saddle the stallion to ride up the mountain, with Tarboy on a lead rope. If trouble threatened, she could turn the black gelding loose and have the advantage of Galahad's speed. Tarboy knew the trail and could find his way home.

But nothing was going to happen, Clara reassured herself. She'd been careful. She'd checked again and again to make sure no one was following her. All she had to do was get the horse to Tanner, kiss him goodbye and ride home. What happened after that would be up to Tanner. He would be beyond her help, beyond her reach.

How could she learn to live with that—never hearing from him, not knowing whether he was safe, or even alive?

Still on foot, she led the two horses through the shadows, into the orchard. When they'd reached the far side and emerged in the open, Clara took a moment to scan the moonlit landscape. Seeing nothing, she mounted Galahad and headed toward the foothills at an easy lope.

Skirting the bog to where the trail began to climb, she slowed the pace to a walk. She was in a hurry to reach the cabin, but she couldn't arrive with exhausted horses or chance a slip on the muddy trail.

Uncertainty gnawed at Clara as she rode. She'd laid out her plan, taking every precaution. But she couldn't shake the feeling that something wasn't right. Maybe she should turn around and go back. She hesitated, then decided against it. If she didn't get to the cabin, she'd be leaving Tanner stranded. He'd be faced with the risk of hiking back to the farm to get his horse. She had little choice except to keep moving up the trail.

She could only pray he'd be there, safe and waiting for her when she arrived.

Jace stood in the shadow of the moonlit porch, ears straining to catch every sound. After three months of running for his life, he'd developed the instincts of a hunted animal. The swish of a branch, the nicker of a horse, anything out of place would be enough to set his nerves on edge. But tonight he wasn't listening for danger. He was listening for Clara.

With the whole day to wait, he'd spent far too much time thinking about her—remembering last night and the feel of her trembling against him, the baby softness of her skin, the smell of her, the taste of her juices as his tongue brought her to shattering climax.

Damn! He'd wanted her then. He wanted her now, under him in the bed, her legs clasping his hips, her breath coming in hot gasps as he slid into that wet sweetness, thrusting deep, again and again.

But he wanted more than that. He wanted a lifetime with her. He wanted to wake up to that beautiful face every morning for the rest of his days, to show her the world, to build a loving home together and fill it with their children.

He could have it all, Jace reminded himself. Everything he wanted was within his reach. But the price he would have to pay, even for a lifetime with Clara, was unthinkable.

Tonight, whatever happened, he would say goodbye to her and ride away. And no matter how he might want to, he wouldn't look back. This flicker of time together was all they would ever have.

Faint on the wind, he heard the snort of a horse, then another. His pulse leaped, but he suppressed the impulse to rush into the open. The cabin had been here a long time. People in the community, including

McCabe, would almost certainly know about it. Anybody could be coming up that trail.

The cabin was dark, the fire out. Jace slipped back into the trees and waited, scarcely daring to breathe as the horses approached. His pulse raced as they came closer. He was armed, but he had no desire to kill innocent people. And if he had to outrun mounted riders with guns, he wouldn't stand a chance of getting away.

The trees moved. Jace's knees buckled with relief as Clara appeared in the clearing, riding the stallion and leading her black pony. She reined up, staring at the darkened cabin. A sob broke from her throat. The sound of it tore at Jace's heart.

"Here I am, Clara." He stepped into sight, speaking softly.

She made a little broken sound. Then she was out of the saddle, plunging through the trees to fling herself into his arms.

He held her tightly for a moment, kissing her mouth, her cheeks, her eyes, knowing all the while what had to be done. "Are you sure you weren't followed?" he asked her.

"I didn't see or hear anyone. If I had I wouldn't have come."

"We don't have much time," he said. "I need to be well away from here before daylight, and you need to get home."

"I know," she murmured against the hollow of his throat. "I wish things could be different."

"So do I. But we have to accept reality. I can't stay."

Her arms tightened around him. "I love you, Tanner," she said. "I'll never love anyone else."

Jace swallowed the tightness in his throat. He felt the same way, but telling her would only make things harder. "Don't say that. Someday you'll meet someone else—the right someone, God willing. You'll get married, have a family and forget all about me."

"No—I'll never forget you." She was fighting sobs now. "I'll wait for you. You can send for me if you get to someplace safe, like Mexico or South America. Wherever you are, I'll come—"

"Stop it, Clara." The words sounded harsher than he'd meant them to. "That's no kind of life for you. I have to leave. I have to leave *now*, and you have to return home. That's all there is to it."

She drew back, looking as if he'd slapped her. Her jaw tightened. Her nostrils flared slightly as her temper rose. "Fine!" she snapped. "I'm not going to get on my knees and beg you. Go, if that's what you want to do. Just go!"

She spun away from him, her spine rigid with hurt pride. This was what he'd angled for, Jace reminded himself as he gathered his gear off the porch and carried it to the waiting Galahad. He'd been deliberately cold, knowing an angry parting would be easier for them both, even though he was bound to hurt like hell later on.

As he lashed his bedroll into place, he could feel the pain radiating from her like the heat of a fire. *Go!* he told himself. *Staying won't make it hurt any less. Just go!*

He put a boot in the stirrup, eased his leg over the horse's back and sank onto the saddle. When Clara didn't turn around, he swung the stallion toward an overgrown trail he'd scouted earlier, one that appeared to lead up the canyon and over the ridge. *Get it over with,* he told himself. *Let it end, once and for all.*

Lord help him, dying couldn't be much worse than this.

Clara turned her head in time to watch him start up the trail. Her heart felt as if she'd just taken a shotgun blast to the chest. How could she say goodbye this way, sending him off in anger? What if the words she'd just spoken were the last ones he ever heard from her lips?

Anguish welled in her, building until she could stand no more of it.

"Tanner!"

The cry ripped from her throat. He must have heard her. But would it make any difference? Would he stop and turn around or would he just keep riding until she lost sight of him?

Scarcely breathing, she stared at his proud shoulders. He'd halted the horse, but even at a distance, she could sense his inner struggle. Just when he'd finally managed to tear himself away, she'd called him back.

If he didn't turn around, she would wish herself dead.

Seconds crawled past before he moved, turning, his body and the horse in one motion. If he came back to her, she would have to let him go again, Clara knew. But this time it would be with her love and support.

He dismounted, leaving the horse next to the cabin. Only then, as he walked toward her did she see the torment in his eyes. She rushed toward him, stumbling as she flung herself into his arms.

He caught her and crushed her close, his mouth brutal with need. Her response flared like tinder, flaming downward into her belly, then downward further still. She returned his kiss, her hands furrowing his hair, her body melting into his. This time there would be no holding back. She was his woman, and there was nothing she wouldn't give him. She wouldn't let him leave until he'd claimed nothing less than all of her.

Scooping her up in his arms, he mounted the porch and carried her in through the front door. Clara heard the click of the bolt as the darkness closed around them. She clung to him in a fever of yearning, wanting his hands on her, his mouth on her, his flesh thrusting hard into her pulsing core.

Tonight there was no need for talk and no time for preliminaries. A button broke loose and bounced across the floor as she tore at the front of his shirt. By the time he'd laid her none too gently on the bed, he was already yanking her belt buckle open. The boots came next, thudding to the floor, with her jeans sliding down her legs to fly after them.

He took a moment to remove his gun belt and lay it on a nearby chair. Then, still dressed, he straddled her with his knees, leaned over her and worked her blouse open down the front.

Arching upward for his kiss, she pulled him down

to her. His mouth devoured her, lips grazing her breasts as his hand ranged downward to her belly, then to her dripping cleft. She bucked against his fingers, wanting that sweet sensation, wanting it all.

He muttered half-mouthed curses as he kissed the flat of her belly, then shifted to move downward. Seeing what he intended, she checked him with a touch. Her hands groped for his belt buckle and wrenched it undone. He groaned as she fumbled with the buttons, but he didn't stop her. There was no stopping either of them now.

"I want you inside me, Tanner," she whispered.

Without a word, he shifted off the bed long enough to shove his jeans and drawers off his hips and let them fall over his boots. Through the small, high window, a shaft of moonlight outlined his taut body and jutting arousal. He wouldn't undress all the way—with the chance of danger afoot, that wouldn't be smart. But to Clara that didn't matter. Nothing mattered except that she would be his.

Moving from the foot of the bed, he pushed forward. Ready and eager, her legs parted to welcome him. "I love you," she whispered into the darkness.

"And I love you, too, Clara. Wherever life takes you, remember that." He leaned forward and kissed her, lingeringly, tenderly. She could feel his drumming pulse, hear the low rasp of his breathing. His fingers stroked her, parting the moist folds and opening the way. She felt an intimate push, a pause; then, in one forceful stroke, he entered her.

She felt the slight tearing, but the pain was lost in the wonder of having him inside her. The sensation of fullness was exquisite. She moaned, raising her hips, deepening the penetration. "Yes..." she breathed.

Gently at first, he began to thrust, his shaft gliding in and out along the sensitive inner surfaces that sheathed him like a glove. The pressure triggered iridescent sparks that shimmered through her body like fiery little rainbows.

Her hips arched upward, pressing against him, matching her strokes to his. Her hands clawed his shoulders as the sensations mounted. He was breathing hard, rasping like a stallion as his loving carried her toward the brink of something she couldn't even imagine. She gasped—and then suddenly she was there, bursting like a rocket against a black sky. Again and again the tremors took her. Then Tanner shuddered in her arms. She felt the jerk of his body, the sudden spurt of wetness, and then they lay in a quiet embrace, spent and drifting.

"We have to go now, love."

His voice startled Clara as she snuggled against his chest. Her heart plummeted. It couldn't be time. Not already.

"You have to get home before daybreak. And I have to get out of here." Easing her from his arms, Tanner sat up and lowered his boots to the floor. Getting dressed again took him mere seconds.

Clara's hands fumbled with her shirt buttons. Her

eyes stared at him in dismay as he buckled on his gun belt. She'd promised herself she'd be brave, but their time together had been so short and so precious; and now it was almost over.

"What if I find out I'm with child?" she asked him. "Isn't there some way I can let you know?"

He shook his head. "I'm sorry, but there won't be any way to keep in touch. And if we do have a child, it'll be better if the poor little mite doesn't know his father. Make up some pretty story. Any story you want."

The words cut into her, as she knew he'd meant them to. His brusqueness was a show, calculated to make his leaving easier. And in truth, Clara was sure she wouldn't be having Tanner's baby. Her menses were due any day now, and she was always regular. But if by some chance it happened, she wouldn't be ashamed to have Tanner's child. And she would never regret having loved him.

"Hurry up now." He tossed her jeans and boots onto the foot of the bed. "I'll be outside checking around. Come out when you're dressed and we'll say goodbye." He paused in the doorway, his face a stoic mask. "Please don't make this any harder than it already is, Clara."

As the door swung shut behind him, she scrambled into her clothes. Tanner was right. For the sake of his life and his freedom, he had to leave—and she had to let him. There were some things that all the love in the world couldn't change.

Fighting tears, she came out onto the porch and

closed the door behind her. Tanner was standing by the stallion, waiting for her.

"You go first," he said. "I want to know you're on your way down the trail before I leave."

"What about you?"

"I'll take a few minutes to straighten up the cabin, lock the door and replace the key before I ride out. If you don't see me go, you can't be forced to tell anybody where I went."

"I'd never do that!" she exclaimed.

"I know. But I'm trying to protect you." He opened his arms. "Come here, girl. Let's say a proper goodbye."

She went to him and he gathered her close. His strong arms made her feel as if she'd come home. But Clara knew that without him, she would never truly come home again.

"Be happy," he murmured against her hair. "Know that wherever I am, you'll be my first thought when I wake up and my last thought before I go to sleep."

She suppressed a sob. "And you'll be in my prayers every night. Be safe, my love."

He kissed her gently, then eased her away and turned her toward the edge of the trees, where Tarboy stood waiting. "Go now," he said. "Don't look back. I won't be able to stand it if you do."

Squaring her shoulders and setting her chin, Clara strode toward the black horse and swung into the saddle. It took all her self-control to keep from looking back as they started down the trail. The time she'd dreaded with all her heart had finally come. She'd seen the last of Jason Tanner Denby.

She imagined him riding the mountain trails, looking for a safe place to rest. With the poster in circulation, no town would be safe for him. He'd have little choice except to stay out of sight and keep moving. Cold and wet and hungry, he'd be forced to run like a hunted animal, trusting no one. Even people who acted friendly might be planning to turn him in for the reward.

If he got hurt or became sick, he wouldn't dare see a doctor. With no one to help him, he could die alone and in pain. And even that would be better than what would happen if he was arrested.

But she couldn't bear to think of that now. She could only pray that Tanner would make it safely across the border into Mexico. Maybe he would find a new life there—a good one, with a family of his own. She would try to think of him that way, safe and happy, Clara promised herself. And she would try to be happy as well, here on the ranch with her family and her beloved horses. But she would never forget the man she'd known as Tanner. And whatever happened, she would never stop loving him.

The wind had freshened, cooling the tears that scalded her cheeks. Now that there was no need to hold them back, they flowed freely, trickling down the sides of her nose, leaving their salty taste on her lips. She remembered Tanner's loving, the thrill of feeling him move inside her. Never again in her life would anything be so perfect.

The sky was still dark, the light of the stars cold and comfortless. Aspen leaves fluttered in the wind, their sound like the patter of light rain. From a distant hilltop, a coyote yipped its mournful cry.

The surefooted gelding took the trail at a brisk walk. At this rate she'd be back at the ranch in an hour. She might even make it back into the house before anyone missed her. She no longer cared whether she was scolded or not. But her family didn't deserve the worry that finding her gone again would cause them.

Starting with the new day, Clara resolved, she would try to be less of a burden to her parents and more of a help. She would be a more obedient daughter, a more understanding sister, a more—

Her musings ended in a scream of terror. The scream became a gasp as the circle of rope that had landed on her shoulders jerked tight around her throat. She clutched at the rough hemp, fighting for breath as Tarboy reared and bolted away, flinging her hard onto the muddy trail.

For a few seconds Clara lay still, stunned by the impact. As her senses cleared she became aware of someone leaning over her. A sneering face emerged out of the darkness—a face that was all too familiar.

"Well, if it isn't the lovely Miss Clara Seavers. Fancy meeting you here," said Lyle McCabe.

Chapter Fourteen

Jace gave the cabin a final check, making sure the bed was smoothed, the mud tracks swept off the floor and fresh kindling laid in the stove. Caution and courtesy dictated that he leave things exactly as he'd found them. But there could be no undoing what he'd done to Clara.

A stern voice in his head lectured him that he should have left well enough alone, that she'd pay in anguish and regret for giving her innocence to a man who could never marry her. But what he and Clara had done had been an act of love, he argued with himself. To turn her away when she'd begged him to fulfill her would have been cruel.

Jace swore out loud, cursing himself in the darkness. He was rationalizing. He knew it and he hated it. The simple truth was, he'd wanted her—wanted her with all the hunger of his aroused male body. He'd wanted to take her, to possess her, to make her his the only way he could. Her need, and the fact that he loved her with his whole heart and soul, had only sweetened the temptation.

Clara was the one precious thing in his world. For what he'd done to her, he deserved to be tied to a post and horsewhipped.

But there was no time to dwell on what had happened. Right now he needed to make some fast tracks out of here. If anybody had recognized him from the poster, the whole damned county could be up in arms, looking for him.

The stallion was waiting outside, saddled, bridled and loaded with his gear. Jace had a web of trails to choose from, but the route he'd almost taken earlier, before Clara had called him back, showed the most promise of leading him away from the valley. He might have to rough it in the mountains, but the provisions Clara had brought him should last a few days, longer if he rationed them carefully. Once those were gone… But it was no use planning ahead. He could only take things as they came, one day at a time.

He was about to mount his horse when he heard Clara's scream.

In the awful silence that followed, he leaped onto the saddle and spurred the stallion down the trail. Had a cougar attacked the horse? Had some accident flung Clara out of the saddle? Scenes of horror flashed through his mind, each one worse than the last.

He didn't have far to go. He was less than a hundred yards below the cabin, zigzagging down the winding trail when a familiar voice stopped him cold.

"Hold it right there, Denby. I've got Miss Clara here, and she's going to get hurt if you don't do exactly as I say."

"First I need to know she's all right," Jace called back. "Unless I hear it from her, I'm coming after you!"

There was a scuffling sound. The next voice he heard was Clara's. "Run, Tanner!" she shouted. "Deputy McCabe won't hurt me! He wouldn't dare! My family would—"

A resounding slap cut off her words. "You'll keep quiet if you know what's good for you, missy!" McCabe growled. Then he raised his voice. "Throw your gun down the hill, Denby. Then get off your horse and walk down the trail with your hands up."

Jace was tempted to throw something else, like his canteen, down the hill. But he couldn't risk Clara's safety on the chance that McCabe wouldn't be fooled. Damn it, he should have known the bastard might show up. As a local, McCabe would have known about the cabin. All he'd needed to do was follow the tracks up the muddy trail.

Slipping the .38 out of its holster, Jace tossed it downhill. It crashed down the long, steep slope and into the heavy brush below the trail.

"That's it. Now get off your horse and walk down to where I can see you, hands in the air."

Jace eased out of the saddle, dropped to the ground and looped the reins around a sapling. Hands high, he began walking down the trail. There had to be a way out of this, but he wouldn't know what to do until he saw Clara.

"Make if snappy. No tricks now, or I won't be responsible for what happens to the lady here." McCabe sounded as if he relished being in charge. Lord knew what the bastard was capable of doing to Clara.

All thought fled from Jace's mind as he rounded the last bend and saw her. He bit back the moan that rose in his throat. Clara was standing in front of McCabe on a narrow section of trail, with a fifty-foot drop below. One end of a rope lashed her wrists behind her back. The other end was wrapped and knotted securely around an aspen trunk at the trail's edge. Between Clara and the tree lay about ten feet of slack rope.

Jace saw at once where the danger lay. The thought of what could happen made his gut clench. If anything went wrong, all McCabe needed to do was nudge Clara over the edge. The rope would jerk tight, saving her from a fifty-foot drop. McCabe would then have the choice of pulling her up or untying the rope and letting her fall to her death. But seeing the way Clara's hands were bound, Jace guessed that McCabe had failed to take one thing into account. The sudden upward stress on her arms would wrench the bones from their shoulder sockets. She wouldn't die, but the pain would be excruciating. Even worse, the injuries could cripple her arms for life.

Either way, McCabe would have a ready way to justify what he'd done. His story would be that he'd tied her up to keep her safe while he went after a wanted murderer, and in her struggles, she'd slipped off the trail. The story would be entirely believable. Clara had broken the law by aiding a fugitive. Even if she lived to talk, anything she said would be suspect. It would be her word against McCabe's.

Jace's eyes flickered from Clara's pale face to the cocked pistol in the deputy's hand. "Is this your idea of bravery, McCabe, using a woman for a shield?" he asked.

"Shut up!" McCabe snarled. "A murdering bastard like you doesn't deserve to be taken in fair fight! Down on your face, hands behind your back, before the little lady takes a tumble."

Jace lowered himself toward the ground. Moonlight glinted on the handcuffs that dangled from McCabe's belt. There had to be some way out of this mess. Maybe later, while the deputy was taking him to jail, he could make a break for it. Given what he was facing, he'd have nothing to lose—and he'd choose dying on the run over hanging any day. But right now nothing mattered except Clara's safety. Whatever the cost, he couldn't risk her coming to harm.

As his knees touched the ground his gaze met Clara's. In her eyes he saw terror, but he saw the flash of courage as well. She was a fighter, and she wasn't ready to give up.

Jace was proud of her defiant spirit. He loved her for it. But there was such a thing as too much bravery.

Clara was the most precious thing in his life. He was sick with fear for her.

Clara twisted against the rope that bound her hands behind her back. The prickly hemp chewed into her skin with every move, sliming her wrists with blood. If she could get loose while McCabe's attention was fixed on Tanner, she might be able to get the jump on him—crown him with a rock, push him off the trail or at least distract him long enough for Tanner to get away. But the knots had been skillfully tied. So far, she hadn't been able to budge them.

She was well aware of the danger. The trail in this spot was slick and narrow, the drop-off steep enough to cause a fatal fall. The rope that tethered her to the tree gave her room to maneuver, but if she slipped and fell...

Her thoughts were interrupted by the opening click of the handcuffs that hung on McCabe's belt. The man had a gun, she reminded herself. He could shoot Tanner on a whim.

She cursed under her breath—words that would have shocked her mother and grandmother. Why hadn't Tanner ridden off and left her to deal with McCabe? He could be far up the trail by now. Instead he'd ridden to her rescue and put his freedom, even his life, in peril. She had to do something.

McCabe had released his hold on her to walk over and clamp the handcuffs on Tanner. Still tethered to the tree, with her hands behind her back, Clara had just a few feet of slack, and less than a second to make up her mind.

With one desperate leap, she flung herself against McCabe's departing back and sank her teeth into the side of his neck, just above the collar.

"You little bitch! I'll kill you!" With a yowl of pain he swung around to get her, but Clara held on like a bulldog, biting so hard she feared her jaw would crack. She could taste the warm saltiness of his blood.

Tanner charged, springing to his feet and smashing into McCabe's gut. McCabe grunted as the breath whooshed out of him, but he kept his grip on the pistol. His finger was tightening on the trigger when Tanner seized his wrist, using his strength to twist the muzzle upward. The gun fired into the air, the report echoing down the canyon as the two men grappled for the weapon.

Clara struggled to hang on to McCabe but she was stretching the limit of the rope that tethered her to the tree. As the rope tightened, the tension yanked her loose. She reeled backward toward the edge of the trail.

Fighting for balance, she teetered on the edge of the drop-off. Only by flinging herself facedown on the earth did she manage to keep herself from tumbling over. But she still wasn't safe. With no arms to counterbalance her weight and no hands to grip for purchase, her legs began sliding over the slippery edge. She couldn't stop herself. She was going to fall.

"Tanner!" she screamed. "Tanner!"

Tanner was still grappling with McCabe for the pistol. At Clara's cry he wrenched himself away. In a flash he was beside her, clasping her shoulders and pulling her up onto solid ground. She scrambled to her feet, standing beside him. He had saved her, but he'd lost any other advantage he might have gained. McCabe had the gun, cocked and trained on them both.

"That's more like it," he snarled, dabbing at his neck with his free hand. "I'll be taking the both of you to town and turning you over to the marshal for murder, Denby, and you, Miss Clara, for aiding a fugitive." His eyes narrowed. "Down on the ground, Denby, till I get the cuffs on you. No more foolishness, now, or you know what will happen to the lady."

This time Tanner submitted, eyes blazing with suppressed fury. It broke her heart to see him sprawled on the ground while McCabe manacled his wrists behind his back.

"Where are your friends, McCabe?" Tanner taunted. "I'm impressed that you'd have the balls to come up here alone."

"I don't need those drunken clowns," McCabe snapped. "And I don't need that old goat, Sam Farley, either. I can do this job by myself."

"You still have to get me down the mountain. A lot can happen between now and then." Tanner had regained his feet, but Clara knew he wouldn't try to get away. Not while McCabe had her at his mercy.

"I can handle it. The plan is, I'll ride your horse and walk the two of you ahead of me on lead ropes, like a couple of hound dogs." McCabe grinned, showing the sliver of meat that had stuck between his teeth. "We can pick up my horse on the way down. Once you're turned in, I'll collect that fat reward that's on your head and hightail it out of this flea-bitten town."

"You can't collect the reward," Clara pointed out. "You're an officer of the law."

"Is that so?" McCabe grinned, and Clara noticed for the first time that the silver deputy badge was missing from his vest. "For your information, I've resigned from hauling drunks to jail and found myself a new line of work—one that'll pay a lot better than that piddling deputy job." He gave her a mocking bow. "Meet Lyle McCabe, professional bounty hunter."

In the shocked silence that followed, Clara measured the impact of McCabe's announcement. A peace officer was bound by rules of ethical conduct. A bounty hunter was bound by no rules at all, including those of common decency. Jason Tanner Denby was wanted dead or alive. Rather than take a chance on his prisoner escaping, McCabe would likely kill him on the way down the trail. It would be easy enough to fake the evidence, making Tanner's death look like an accident.

And it would be just as easy for him to do the same to her—not only easy but probable, since she'd be a witness to what he'd done.

Her eyes met Tanner's in a flicker of understanding. He knew the danger, too. If they couldn't get away, odds were that they would both be dead by morning.

Tanner was the first one to speak. "If you're in this for the reward, McCabe, you've got no reason to hold Clara. She's not worth anything to you. Let her go, and I promise not to give you any trouble. I'll go with you peaceably and you can turn me in for the money."

"You're asking me to let that little hellcat go?" McCabe's free hand fingered the still-bleeding side of his neck. Something akin to madness glinted in his eyes. "Not on your worthless life! She's my insurance policy. Long as I've got her, you'll behave—because you know what'll happen to her if you don't. Now let's get moving." He motioned to Tanner with the pistol. "Your horse should be up there, around that bend in the trail. We'll leave the little lady here while we get it. Then it'll be time to head for town."

McCabe motioned again with the gun, indicating that Tanner was to come with him. Watching him, Clara sensed a subtle change in the man. His eyes had narrowed. His gestures had become jerkier, more nervous. The tip of his tongue slid uneasily across his upper lip.

Her heart lurched as she realized what McCabe was planning to do.

The section of trail where Tanner had left the stallion was wider and more level than here. But it ran along the top of a sheer cliff with jagged rocks at the bottom. A fall onto those rocks would be fatal.

Once the two men rounded the bend in the trail, Clara would no longer be able to see them. There would be no witnesses when McCabe forced the handcuffed Tanner over the edge of the cliff. And no one in town could question McCabe's claim that Tanner had fallen while trying to escape.

Tanner was already walking away from her to follow McCabe up the trail. As long as she was in danger, Clara knew he wouldn't make any trouble. Somehow she had to stop him.

And she knew of only one way.

"Wait!" she shouted. "Wait, both of you!"

Both men turned to look at her, McCabe's eyes narrow and suspicious, Tanner's reflecting her own desperation.

"I have an offer for you, Mr. McCabe," she said. "I want you to listen and think it over before you walk up that trail."

"I'm listening." McCabe had stopped. His eyes flickered toward Clara, but he kept his pistol trained on Tanner. "This better be good, you little bitch," he muttered.

Clara ignored the epithet. "Think about this," she said. "A thousand dollars isn't that much money. A big spender could go through it in no time at all."

"So?" McCade's voice dripped contempt. "I'd say that'd be my problem."

"My horse is worth ten times that," Tanner interrupted. "Take him and let us go."

McCade grinned. "I'd pretty much figured that stallion into the deal already. Unless you can come up with a bill of sale, I'd say he's stolen property, and I have as much right to him as you do."

"Listen to me!" Clara raised her voice. "This isn't about the reward or the stallion. This is about the oil."

That got their attention. Both men were staring at her. Without giving them time to speak, Clara plunged ahead.

"I know you've seen it, McCabe. Your tracks were in the bog. And you know that if it's there, it's likely under Seavers and Gustavson land as well. Why else would you have shown up at the ranch with flowers that day, after my accident, if you weren't trying to court me?"

McCabe looked startled, but the pistol didn't waver in his hand. "You mentioned something about an offer," he said coldly.

Clara's chest felt so tight she could scarcely breathe, let alone talk. She willed herself to speak the words.

"Let Tanner go, and I'll marry you," she said. "We can find the preacher first thing tomorrow. My share of the land, and the oil, will be yours. You'll have all the money a man could ever want. But without me, my father won't let you anywhere near it."

"Clara, for God's sake—" Tanner took a step toward her, but McCabe held him at bay with the pistol.

"Sounds interesting," he drawled. "But for all I know, soon as this yellow bastard's gone over the hill you'll change your mind. How do I know you'll keep your word?"

Clara was trembling. "I swear it," she said. "I swear it on Tanner's life."

"No!" Tanner lunged toward her, ignoring the pistol. "I'm not leaving you, Clara! McCabe can have me. He can kill me—hellfire, I'll probably die anyway before long, but you can't do this. I—"

The butt of McCabe's pistol crashed into the side of Tanner's head. The words trailed off as he crumpled to the ground.

"Now…" McCabe turned back to Clara. "Where were we? As I recall, you'd just sworn to become my wife."

"Only after I know Tanner's safe." Clara was trembling.

"Hmm…" McCabe frowned thoughtfully, playing her. "If I were buying an auto, I'd certainly ask for a demonstration ride before I put down the cash. Makes sense to do the same for a woman, don't you think?"

"What are you saying?" Clara edged back against the tree where he'd tied her, mindful of the trail's slippery edge.

McCabe walked toward her, using his free hand to unbuckle his belt. His fingers fumbled with the fly of his trousers. "Before I accept your terms, I'd like a little demonstration of what I'll be getting. Get down on your knees, Miss Clara, and open that pretty mouth. I'm guessing you've done this sort of business before."

"No…" But despite her protest, Clara sank to her knees. Her whole being wanted to shrink away from him, but there was no place to go and he was right there in front of her, fully exposed. She wanted to be sick.

He laughed at her hesitation. "Come on, honey, have a taste. It's no worse than a lollipop. You might even get to like it."

"No…please…" Clara begged. But she'd do anything to save Tanner, even this, she reminded herself. She closed her eyes, just wanting this awful nightmare to be over.

McCabe laughed. He was still laughing when Tanner slammed into him from the side, knocking him off balance. The pistol flew out of his hand as he reeled sideways and toppled over the edge of the trail. His scream echoed through the darkness as he hit the brushy slope below and crashed through the trees.

Startled, a flock of sage grouse exploded out of the scrub. As their cries died into silence, Tanner inched his way back from the rim and managed to sit up. Blood smeared the side of his head where McCabe's pistol butt had struck. His breath came in gasps.

"Are you all right?" Clara stood and braced herself against the trunk of the aspen where she was tied. Her voice shook.

"As well as could be expected." Tanner managed a raw laugh. "But I'm afraid McCabe went over the edge with the key to these handcuffs on him. Can you get loose?"

"I've been trying the whole time, without much luck. Last year in Denver I saw a Tom Mix movie where his horse chewed through the rope and helped him get away."

"I don't think Galahad's trained to do that. Anyway, he's up the trail, tied to a tree." Tanner exhaled raggedly. "Would you really have married that snake?"

"I'd have done anything to save you." Clara felt herself beginning to crumble. A sob jerked her chest. "I love you so much," she whispered.

"And I love you, my brave little Clara. But this isn't a movie. The only happy ending we can hope for is to get you safely home."

"I won't leave you like this!" she declared passionately.

He ignored her words. "I've got a knife in my boot.

I can't reach it by myself, but if we work together we should be able to cut through your ropes. Move back over here, away from the edge, and we'll try it."

Clara moved carefully to the spot he'd indicated, her back to his. This wasn't going to be easy, but at least, if she got loose, she could take him back to the cabin while she took the stallion and went for tools to break the handcuffs apart. Even with McCabe gone, Tanner wouldn't be safe in the open. There were cougars, bears and wolves in these mountains. Mostly they kept out of sight, but a helpless human could be vulnerable prey.

Maneuvering Jace's boot within reach of Clara's bound hands was more awkward than either of them expected. Minutes passed as Clara fumbled for the knife.

"This is all so unfair!" she sighed. "You only shot the man to save your—" She broke off as a faint sound reached her ears. "Listen! I hear horses! Somebody's coming up the trail!"

"Let's hope the hell they're friendly," Tanner muttered, rising and shifting his position to protect her as best he could.

They waited in breathless silence as the riders wound their way closer. Judging from the sound of hooves on the trail, there were at least two horses, maybe three. Whoever was out there at this hour, it wasn't likely they were up to anything good.

Now Clara could hear the murmur of voices—men's voices, blessedly familiar. Her heart leaped. "Papa!" she shouted. "Uncle Quint! We're up here!"

Tanner moved behind her. She heard him mutter something under his breath. It sounded like, "Thank God!"

Moments later, two tall riders came around the bend, trailing Clara's black gelding. Jace recognized Judd Seavers in the lead. The man behind him was a stranger with dark eyes and thick chestnut hair. His features bore a striking resemblance to Clara's. Uncle Quint, she had called him.

They were an imposing pair—noble in bearing, fearless in the way they sat their horses, like two knights from the storybooks Jace had loved as a child. He knew instinctively that he could trust them.

He knew, as well, what had to be done. When he'd left Missouri, he'd hoped to keep running indefinitely. But the choices he'd made had finally caught up with him. By accepting Clara's help, he had placed her in terrible danger. As long as he remained at large, she and her family would be compromised.

For her sake, he had to end this.

Over the past months, Jace had been haunted by the dread of confinement and hanging. All he could do now was face what lay ahead with courage and dignity.

Judd had his knife out before his boots touched the ground. In a matter of seconds he had sliced through the ropes that bound Clara's hands. She stumbled into his arms. "Oh, Papa, thank heaven you're here!" she murmured against his shirt.

Quint stood looking on, his face a study in naked

emotion. Jace caught the glimmer of a tear in his eye. It was evident that he cared deeply for his niece.

Clara had pulled away from her father. "How did you know where to look for us?" she asked.

It was Quint who answered. "When we discovered you were gone, and that you'd taken Tarboy, we pieced together what we knew. Your grandmother told us the rest. She didn't want to break your confidence, but she was worried about you. We all were."

"It's my fault." Jace stepped forward to face the two men. "I was the one who got Clara into this mess. She's done nothing wrong. She was only trying to help me."

"No!" Clara moved to his side. "Tanner didn't want my help, but I insisted on coming up here to bring his horse. He saved my life tonight. McCabe would have killed us both."

"We found McCabe's body lower down, not far from the trail." Judd's stormy expression confirmed that he'd noticed McCabe's unfastened trousers. "We'll be asking you some questions about what happened."

"No need for questions. I'll tell you everything." Jace felt Clara's fingers tighten around his arm as he spoke. "I'm wanted for killing my sister's husband back in Missouri. His friends put out a one-thousand-dollar reward for me, dead or alive, and McCabe was trying to collect it. Clara got caught where she never should have been, and he used her as bait to draw me into a trap."

"You killed your brother-in-law?" It was Quint asking the question. "There are two sides to every story. I'd like to hear yours."

"Clara knows the story. She can tell you later." Jace felt an unaccustomed sense of peace. He'd been running long enough. It was time to come clean and face the consequences before he brought any more grief to this good family.

"I'll tell you now!" Clara exclaimed. "The man was an abusive monster. Tanner shot him to save his sister's life! You've got to help me get these cuffs off him so he can get away from here."

"No." Jace spoke with icy calm but his heart was aching for her. "I love you, Clara, but I won't implicate your father and uncle in my trouble. I've done you and your family enough harm already. It's time I face up to what happened and let a judge decide whether it was right or wrong."

"No!" she gasped. "What if they hang you? You told me yourself you couldn't get a fair trial in Missouri! This can't be right!"

He continued as if she hadn't spoken. "Take Galahad home and keep him, Clara. He's yours. As for me—" He turned to face Quint and Judd. "Gentlemen, I'd consider it an honor to have the two of you escort me to jail."

Chapter Fifteen

❧◆❧

Clara took the stallion at a careful pace down the mountain trail. By the time she reached the foothills, pewter light was streaking the eastern sky. In an hour's time the sun would rise on a bleak and anxious day.

By now, Judd, Quint and Tanner would be reaching the outskirts of town. Tanner would be mounted on Tarboy, his hands still cuffed behind his back. She imagined them stopping by Sam Farley's place to turn over the prisoner and let Sam know about McCabe. Once the marshal had grumbled himself awake, the four men would proceed to the jail, where the handcuffs would be removed and Tanner would be led to a cell. Clara had imagined the closing of that iron-barred door a hundred times on her way down the hill—a cold, metallic clang, as final as a death knell. She would hear it in her sleep.

Not that she'd given up—that would be unthinkable. She was already preparing to fight for the man she loved. The first thing she planned to do was contact the one person who might be able to help him.

Emerging from the foothills, Clara spurred the stallion to a gallop. The big bay was hers now, the most splendid gift she'd ever received—but under the worst of circumstances. It wasn't joy she felt as they flew across the open pastures. It was a pulse-pounding urgency. Time was her enemy—and every minute she lost was a minute of Tanner's life.

The lights were on at the farmhouse. Mary had probably been up all night, worrying and waiting. By the time Clara loped the stallion into the yard, her grandmother had come out onto the porch, clad in a rumpled housedress and an old sweater. She rushed down the steps, her braids frizzy, her face haggard in the wan light.

"Thank the good Lord you're safe!" she exclaimed. "I've been praying for hours! But where are the others? What's happened?"

Clara slid out of the saddle and looped the reins over the hitching rail. "Please phone my mother and let her know everybody's all right. I'll tell you the rest as soon as I've caught my breath. But before that, I need to make one telephone call."

"Coffee's on the stove." Mary didn't waste time scolding. "Pour yourself a cup while I call your mother. Don't you want to talk to her yourself?"

Clara shook her head. "She'll be upset, and I need some time. Tell her I'll be home soon."

Mary bustled back into the house. Clara followed more slowly, stretching her tired limbs as she walked. The twinge of soreness between her thighs brought back the memory of Tanner's loving. No regrets, she vowed. No regrets ever, no matter what the days ahead might bring.

From the kitchen, Clara could hear Mary's voice on the telephone. Leaning against the counter, she poured a mug of coffee and took a sip. The strong black brew jolted her to full alertness. Outside the kitchen window, the birds had begun their awakening calls. Leaden gray clouds hung heavy in the morning sky.

"You said you need to make a call." Mary had come back into the kitchen. "Go ahead. I'll fix you some breakfast."

Clara moved out into the shadowed parlor where the phone was mounted on a wall near the door. Her hand shook as she picked up the receiver and waited for the local operator's voice.

"This is long-distance," she said. "I don't have the number, but I need to speak with Mrs. Hollis Rumford in Springfield, Missouri. It's an emergency."

An eternity seemed to pass while she waited, fiddling with a strand of her hair while she listened to the buzzes and clicks on the line and the muffled exchanges between operators. At last, so faintly she had to strain to hear it, she heard the ringing on the far end of the connection.

"Hello?" The female voice was low and throaty through the static.

"I need to speak with Mrs. Rumford, please."

"This is Mrs. Rumford. But I can barely hear you. What is it you want?" Her tone was chilly.

Clara shouted into the receiver. "My name is Clara Seavers. I'm a friend of your brother's. He's been arrested."

"Jace? What happened? Where is he?" The voice had become breathy, almost frantic. "You can't let them take him away till I can get there!"

"We'll try. He's in jail in Dutchman's Creek, Colorado."

"Dutchman's Creek? How do I—?"

"You can change trains in Denver. There's a station here. Tell the stationmaster to call the Seavers Ranch. We'll pick you up. We can talk then."

The static on the line was getting worse. Clara could barely hear. "I'll be on the next train west!" Ruby Rumford shouted. "And I'll be bringing my lawyer!"

"You'll be bringing *what?*"

Clara waited for an answer, but the line had gone dead. Hanging up the receiver, she turned to find Mary standing at the entrance to the kitchen, her hands on her hips.

"There's bacon and eggs in the skillet," she said. "Come sit down at the table, girl. You've got a lot of talking to do."

By the time Clara had ridden home, let the stallion loose to graze and calmed her frantic mother, it was midmorning. By the time she'd bathed and changed for the day, Quint and Judd were just returning from town.

They came through the gate and up the drive on their tired horses. Tarboy trailed behind on a lead, his saddle empty. Watching from the porch, with Annie and a devastated Katy beside her, Clara felt an ache rise in her throat.

She ran to meet them by the barn. She arrived as they were climbing out of their saddles. "Don't worry about the horses," she said. "I'll take care of them. That's the least I can do."

Judd's eyes were bloodshot with weariness. "Fine," he said. "Is your mother all right?"

"Yes, I told her everything."

Well, not quite everything, Clara amended silently. She was still pondering her mother's response to this latest misadventure. "You're a grown woman, Clara," she'd said. "Whatever you've done, you're responsible for your choices and their consequences." It was almost as if she knew and understood what had happened.

But it was Tanner Clara was most concerned about. Quint answered her unspoken question. "Tanner's in jail. Sam Farley locked him up this morning. There was no trouble."

"Did he say anything—anything for me?"

"Only that you weren't to come and visit him. He didn't want you to be seen coming and going from the jail. He strikes me as a proud man, a decent man. And your grandmother seemed to think the world of him. He didn't say much on the way to town, but I believe what you told me about him. I'd be interested in hearing the whole story."

"I'll tell you after you've had a chance to rest," Clara said. "This morning, as soon as I got to Grandma's, I telephoned his sister in Missouri. She'll be on her way here by train. I think she said she was bringing a lawyer."

"Good idea," Judd commented.

"She wants Tanner kept in Dutchman's Creek until she can get here. Will that be a problem?"

"Shouldn't be," Judd said. "Between the paperwork for the extradition and the inquest into McCabe's death he'll likely be here for at least a week."

"The inquest?" Clara felt a jab of fear.

Judd gave her a stern look. "You broke the law by helping Tanner, Clara. But Sam's willing to keep you out of it if he can. Quint and I will testify that we found McCabe below the slope with his neck broken and his pants undone. Sam says, as far as he's concerned, the man was pissing off the side of the trail and stumbled over the edge. Let's hope that'll be the end of it."

"But the marshal knows what really happened? He knows I was there?" Clara asked.

"He does. But he says a young girl in love is entitled to a few mistakes. And I judge him to be a wise old man."

Clara stood with the horses as her two fathers walked toward the house. Only as they went inside did her knees begin to shake. She sagged against Tarboy, pressing her face into his warm, satiny neck.

Never in her life had she known Judd Seavers to bend the rules. But he had allowed the rules to be bent for his daughter. And her mother had not only forgiven her but set her free. To be surrounded by so much love was almost more than she could stand. It would have been easier if they'd railed at her, lectured her, sent her to bed without supper for what she'd done. Clara had never imagined that growing up could be so complicated.

A young girl in love is entitled to a few mistakes.

Maybe she was finally beginning to understand her parents.

For the next three days, time crawled. Clara's menstrual period started the day after her return, dashing her meager hope that she might be carrying Tanner's baby. She'd imagined how it might be, having a child with his blazing blue eyes and quick mind. But she'd known it wasn't likely, and she'd been right. An unaccustomed sadness crept over her, deepening with each day. She ached for the sight of him, yearned for his touch. But he'd left strict orders that she wasn't to visit him in jail. To try, and have him turn her away, would crush her.

The inquest into the death of Lyle McCabe went off without a hitch. As Judd had predicted, McCabe's death was ruled an accident. His body was released by the coroner and buried, without ceremony, in the city graveyard. By the time the hole was filled in, most of McCabe's wild cronies had left town.

Judd and Quint had ridden into Dutchman's Creek to testify at the inquest. On the way home, Judd had picked up his newly repaired Model T at the garage. He also planned to visit the land office to apply for mineral rights to the bog. Quint had gone home ahead of him with the horses.

Clara had been watching the drive all morning. She

trailed Quint into the barn and began unsaddling Judd's tall buckskin. "Did you see Tanner?" she asked him. "Did you talk to him?"

"He wasn't at the inquest." Quint hefted the saddle off Tarboy and laid it over the side of a stall. "But we did stop by the jail to see if he needed anything. He said to tell you he's doing fine."

"He would say that. He'd say it even if he was miserable, as I'm sure he is." Clara toweled the damp sweat off the horse's back. "Did you tell him his sister was coming?"

Quint took a moment to answer. "We did. And his reaction was a bit surprising. He said he didn't want her involved—practically demanded that we stop her any way we could."

"It's too late for that—and if my first impression counts for much, Ruby Rumford is one unstoppable woman." Clara sighed. "Why on earth wouldn't he want her to come, especially if she's bringing a lawyer for him?"

"I was wondering the same thing. Maybe the man's too proud to accept any kind of help. Or maybe…" Quint paused to brush a horsefly off his cheek. "Maybe she knows something—some secret he wants kept quiet. After all, if his story is true, and there's no reason to doubt it, she was the only eyewitness to the shooting."

"Maybe if I went to the jail and tried to talk to him—"

Quint laid his hands on her shoulders. His deep brown eyes seemed to wrap her in warmth. This man was her father and he knew it, Clara reminded herself. Whatever had happened in the past, this blood tie would always be a bond between them.

"Don't do it, sweet girl," he said. "You'll only get your heart broken."

"You're the one who told me that broken hearts can heal."

"I know. But Tanner doesn't want you to see him behind bars. And he doesn't want anyone interfering. I've never seen a man so determined to meet fate on his own terms."

"But if they send him back to Missouri he'll be hanged!"

"I know. And he knows it, too. His best hope is to get the trial moved somewhere else. Not much chance of it, but maybe that's what his sister's attorney will try to do."

Clara's spirit lightened. "Do you really think—?"

Quint shook his head. "Don't get your hopes up. Even if he isn't sentenced to hang, he could still go to prison for the rest of his life. It's clear that he loves you, but he doesn't want you hurt. Letting him see your pain would be the cruelest thing you could do to him."

Clara closed her eyes, her legs unsteady beneath her. Maybe it was time she faced the truth—no matter how much she might want to save Tanner, there was nothing she could do.

But love didn't work that way. She couldn't allow Tanner to give up and go like a lamb to the slaughter. She would fight at his side until there was nothing left to fight for.

She looked up at Quint. "I need to see him again. Will you drive me to town tomorrow? Maybe if you're with me it will ease things a little."

"You're sure you want to do this?" Quint's gaze probed hers. "You might be sorry."

Clara knew what he meant. Tanner was capable of saying cruel things just to push her away. He'd done it before, but she'd seen through him and understood. Whatever he said or did, she would understand again. But that didn't mean he was going to get away with it.

"I'm sure," she insisted. "And after I've seen him, I'll want to stop by the train station. If his sister caught an early train out of Springfield, she could be arriving as soon as tomorrow afternoon."

Quint pondered the idea for a moment, then nodded. "Do you think Judd will trust me with his precious Model T?" he asked.

Clara managed a halfhearted laugh. "Maybe, but only if you promise not to let me drive."

They left the next day, after a lunch that Clara was too anxiety-ridden to eat. Annie had been wanting to visit a friend in town, so she went along as well, sitting in the front seat of the auto with Quint while Clara sat in the back. Her lively patter eased the long, bumpy ride. Quint had almost certainly told his wife about Clara's relationship with Tanner, but Annie was the soul of discretion. She would never betray a confidence.

Unfortunately, the Model T was less of a pleasure.

Twice in the course of the trip its engine sputtered asthmatically, coughed, and coasted to a stop at the side of the road. Between them, Quint and Clara were able to tinker with the car and get it going, but by the time they reached the outskirts of town they were both spattered with grease and had wasted an extra forty-five minutes.

Clara's stomach had clenched into an ugly knot. Maybe this was a mistake. Tanner had said he didn't want to see her and hadn't wanted her to call his sister. Now she could be making yet another mistake. What if he simply turned his back and refused to hear her?

But she couldn't let him refuse. Jason Tanner Denby was the proudest, most stubborn man she had ever known. But she knew how to be stubborn, too. She would get through to him if she had to stand outside his cell all day.

After dropping Annie off at her friend's house, Quint and Clara drove up Main Street and parked the auto in front of the marshal's office, which fronted the city jail. Sam Farley was at his desk. He rose to greet them. "Your friend's back there in his cell," he said. "But he won't be here for long. Just got a telegram from Missouri. The folks back there aren't wasting any time with this. They've already sent a U.S. Deputy Marshal from Springfield with the extradition papers. He'll be arriving today on the three-fifteen, with just enough time to pick up his prisoner and get him on the east-bound train at four."

Clara felt the blood drain from her face. Her knees were wilting beneath her. She clutched Quint's arm and forced herself to stand ramrod straight. "I want to see him," she said.

The marshal frowned, looking more uncomfortable than stern. "Don't know if I can do that, Clara. He gave me a specific request that you weren't to be allowed back there."

Quint stepped forward, blocking the marshal's view of the hallway that led to the cells. "Well, how about this? What if you and I were talking, and you took your eyes off her for a few seconds, long enough for her to slip out of sight? You couldn't be blamed for that, now, could you?"

"Well, I don't know…"

Quint grinned. "Say, who are you picking to win the pennant this year, Sam? Don't know about you, but I've got my money on the Red Sox."

"The Red Sox? Those bums? You've gotta be kidding. Let me tell you…"

Clara couldn't be sure if the marshal was going along with the ruse or if Quint had sucked him into it, but there was no time to wonder. While the men continued their good-natured argument, she ducked behind Quint and made for the hallway.

As she stepped into the shadows, a distant sound chilled her to the marrow of her bones.

It was the mournful whistle of an approaching train.

Slumped on the edge of his metal bunk, Jace had heard the whistle, too. Sam Farley, who'd shown him nothing but kindness, had informed him that the U.S.

Deputy Marshal would be coming to take him back to Springfield. Jace could only pray he'd be gone before his sister arrived. Whatever the cost, he had to keep her out of this mess. All Ruby needed to do was open her pretty mouth, and everything he'd endured over the past three months would be for nothing.

Rising, he stretched his cramped limbs. For a man used to an active life, confinement was hell. Being hanged couldn't be much worse than this. In a way, it would set him free.

Since his arrest he'd had plenty of time to think—too much time. Needless to say, most of his thoughts were of Clara. Memories of their loving haunted his dreams and tormented his days. There'd been moments when he would have bargained away his soul just to hold her one more time. But Jace had willed those moments to pass. His soul was the one thing of value he had left. Throw that away and he would no longer be a man.

But that didn't keep him from wanting what he couldn't have. Impossible fantasies plagued his mind— Clara as his wife, wearing his ring, sharing his home and his bed, mothering his children. Even worse was the mocking voice in his head, the voice that taunted him by the hour, reminding him that he could have everything he wanted for the price of a few words—words he'd vowed to carry in silence to his grave.

"Hello, Tanner." Clara's voice was barely a whisper but Jace would have known it anywhere. She stood in the shadowed hallway outside the row of cells, looking small and sad. Jace stifled a groan.

He'd asked the marshal to keep her away. Not because of pride, but because he'd feared her presence would be the one thing that could push him over the edge. And he'd been right. Just seeing her was torture.

"I didn't want you to come, Clara," he said.

"I know." She moved forward to press against the bars of his cell. "I'm sorry but I had to see you."

The urge to reach through the bars and clasp her close was eating him alive, but he forced himself to stay back. Wanting her could break him. He couldn't let it happen. "We already said goodbye. Is this the way you want to remember me, as a criminal behind bars?"

"You're not a criminal! You killed a man defending someone you loved! Any fair judge and jury would see that. If your sister's lawyer can get the trial moved, and if she tells her story—"

"Leave my sister out of this! There's nothing she can do except make things worse. No thanks to you, she's going to be wasting a long train trip. Go home to your horses and forget me, Clara. That's the kindest thing you can do."

He expected her to back away or burst into tears. Clara did neither. "I love you, and I'm not giving up on you, Tanner," she said. "So you mustn't give up on yourself."

Her hands stretched through the bars—those small, callused, work-stained hands he'd fallen in love with the first time he'd met her. They reached out to him, silently begging for his touch.

Jace felt himself beginning to weaken. He seized

her fingers and pressed them to his lips. "I love you, too," he murmured. "I'll always love you. But you have to go. Please, before I do something I'll regret to the end of my days."

"I don't want to leave you," she whispered. "Not till it's time."

They were still clasping hands when Clara heard the rising sound of voices in the office out front. The wooden floor in the hallway creaked under the weight of approaching footsteps.

There was no mistaking the U.S. Deputy Marshal. He was a big man with a jowly face and a middle-aged paunch that overhung his belt. His silver badge was pinned to his vest, half hidden by the jacket of his brown suit. His narrow eyes were steely gray beneath the brim of his Stetson.

"Let's go, Denby. We've just got time to make that train."

Tanner had released Clara's hands. She felt the pressure on her arm as Quint drew her back against the wall. The lawman waited while Sam Farley opened the cell and handcuffed the prisoner. Tanner made no effort to resist.

Their eyes met one last time. Clara fought back a surge of tears. She didn't want him to remember the sight of her crying.

In a loose procession they filed back through the corridor. Sam Farley led the way, followed by the U.S. Marshal and his prisoner. Clara and Quint brought up the rear.

Emerging from the hallway, Sam halted abruptly. The people behind him almost collided before they moved forward again and spread out into the office.

Standing in the doorway was a stunning woman. She looked to be in her early thirties, strikingly tall, with a wealth of red-gold hair spilling from its pins. Her dove-gray traveling suit was wrinkled. Her cobalt eyes—the same blazing hue as Tanner's—were bloodshot with weariness. Beside her, the bespectacled man clutching a briefcase seemed a mere shadow.

Clara heard a subtle groan from Tanner.

Ruby Denby Rumford had arrived.

Her first words were for the U.S. Marshal. "Where," she demanded in a throaty, imperious voice, "do you think you're taking my brother?"

The federal lawman was not intimidated. "He'll be going back to Springfield for trial, ma'am. I'm escorting him to the train now."

"I can't allow you do that."

The man shot her a contemptuous glare. "You don't say? Step aside, ma'am. We've got a train to catch."

Ruby stood her ground. "I said you can't take him. My brother is innocent."

"Ruby, for God's sake—" Tanner blurted, but she cut him off.

"No. It's all right, Jace. I can't let you do this anymore." She turned back to the federal marshal. "He's innocent. My lawyer has proof, a signed confession right here in this briefcase."

All eyes were on her as she squared her shoulders and lifted her chin. "Jace didn't kill Hollis Rumford," she said. "I did."

It took time for the full story to emerge. Jace—whose real name Clara was still getting used to—was freed from his handcuffs. Sam Farley ordered coffee for himself and the four people sitting around his desk, as well as for Clara and Quint, who'd been allowed to stay and listen. The four-o'clock train arrived and departed with two empty seats.

When all was said, it came down to this. On the night in question, Hollis Rumford had been pounding on the bedroom door, threatening to kill his wife. She'd had seconds to place a frantic call to her brother before Hollis smashed his way into the room and began beating her. To save her own life, Ruby had seized her husband's loaded pistol from the drawer of the nightstand and shot him dead.

Soon after that, Jace had arrived in response to her call. Knowing that murder charges would destroy Ruby's future and leave her two little girls without a mother, he'd convinced her to let him take the blame for the shooting. Still in shock, Ruby had agreed, and Jace had fled into the night.

Weeks later, a conscience-stricken Ruby had gone to her lawyer and told him the truth. The lawyer had been confident of winning an acquittal on a plea of self-defense, but he'd advised her to wait until Jace could be located to serve as a witness. With Jace missing and out of touch, the matter had hung unresolved until Clara's frantic telephone call.

Clara listened in amazement as the story unfolded. Emotions surged, clashed and faded—relief, dismay, admiration, anger. Had Jace lied to her? As she recalled, he'd never really admitted to killing Hollis Rumford. But he'd implied it and let her draw her own conclusions. Wasn't that the same as lying?

He could have trusted her with the truth. But how could he? In her desperation to save him, Clara would almost certainly have betrayed his secret. Jace had been prepared to give his life for his sister and her little girls. His loyalty and courage astounded her. How could she not love such a man?

By the time the interview was finished and a decision made, shadows were long in the room. Jace would go back to Springfield with Ruby and do whatever was necessary to wipe the slate clean. They'd be leaving on the early morning train, in the company of the federal marshal and Ruby's lawyer. The case could take weeks or months. But neither Jace nor his sister could move on until everything was resolved.

"I'll come back, Clara," Jace promised as he kissed her goodbye. "And when I do, it will be to lay everything I own on the table and ask your father for the honor of your hand in marriage."

"You already have my answer," she whispered.

"And you have mine," he said, holding her tight. "All I ask is that you trust me and wait."

Epilogue

Clara and Jace were married on the last day of August under a sky as blue as the groom's eyes. The aspens below the peaks were just turning gold, and the late-summer roses were still blooming around the ranch house. It was as perfect as any day could be.

Quint and Annie had come from San Francisco for the wedding. A glowingly pregnant Annie had brought Clara's finished gown with her, a fantasy creation of the white Indian silk shot with silver threads, now crowned by a veil of floating tulle. Ruby, exhausted after the trial that had acquitted her of her husband's murder, had taken her daughters on an extended trip to Europe. But in her absence she had left a gift—Galahad's pedigree tucked between the folds of an exquisite Irish linen tablecloth.

The couple planned to live near the ranch on a section of land Judd had given them as a wedding present. Their house was already under construction and would be finished by the time they returned from their honeymoon. Clara would pursue her dream of raising fine horses. Jace, who could work from anywhere, would carry on with his consulting business.

As time for the ceremony approached, the house and yard bustled with activity. On the lawn, Daniel was busy arranging rows of chairs for the arriving guests. Katy, in peach organdy, was draping a garland of ivy and fresh flowers over the archway where the ceremony would take place. Mouthwatering aromas drifted from the barbecue pit in the backyard, where long tables had been set up on the grass.

Upstairs, in the master bedroom, Mary, Hannah and Annie were dressing Clara for the ceremony. It was a happy scene, replete with jokes, hugs and laughter as they buttoned her into her gown, pinned up her hair and added the sheer veil to her tiny pearl tiara.

Clara studied them—the three strong women who'd shaped her life. Mary, who'd pioneered a new land with her husband, given him seven children and carried on alone after his death. Hannah, who'd married to give her unborn baby a name, then fallen in love with her husband. And Annie, who'd loved and wed the father of her sister's child. What magnificent examples they'd been to her. How lucky she was to have them here today.

Clara's questions about her parentage remained unasked. But the answers no longer mattered. Hannah belonged with Judd. Quint belonged with Annie. And she belonged to all of them. That was enough to know.

"It's time!" Katy came pounding up the stairs, her face flushed, her hair ribbon askew. Clara straightened the ribbon, then waited for her grandmother, mother and aunt to go outside and take their seats. Katy would walk behind to look after her train and veil.

Judd waited for her at the bottom of the stairs, his eyes bright with pride. He was the only father Clara had ever known, and he'd more than earned the right to walk beside her today. Smiling, she took his arm. Together they moved out through the open doorway into the sunlit afternoon.

Every face turned toward her, but Clara saw only one. Jace stood at the end of the aisle, with the preacher on his right and Quint, his best man, on his left.

Jace's eyes warmed at the sight of her. A tender smile lit his face as she took her place beside him and waited for the words that would make them husband and wife.

Everything was as it should be. They stood together on the threshold of a new life, surrounded by love.

* * * * *

Aella closed her eyes and sensed a distinct shift, like movement from the world around her to the unseen world.

She opened her eyes. And had a slight shock at the man standing ten feet away. He wasn't just any man. Her heart leaped and pounded. He reminded her of a fierce warrior from an ancient civilization. Incan? She wasn't sure but she felt his deep power and masculinity.

I'm Aella. Are you the guardian of this sacred site? she asked, hoping her telepathy was strong.

Fox's entire body soared with joy. Fox struggled to put his personal pleasure aside.

Greetings, Aella. I'm the assistant guardian to this sacred area. You may call me Fox. How can I be of service to you, Aella? he asked.

I'm searching for a green sphere. A legend says that the Emperor Pachacuti had seven emerald spheres created for the Emerald Key necklace. He had seven of his priestesses and priests travel the world to hide these spheres from evil forces. It is said that when all seven spheres are found, restrung and worn, that Light will return to the Earth. The fourth sphere is here, at your sacred site. Are you aware of it? Aella held her breath. She loved looking at him, especially his sensual mouth. The desire to kiss him came out of nowhere.

Fox was stunned by the request. *I know of the Emerald Key necklace because I served the emperor at the time it was created. However, I did not realize that one of the spheres is here.*

Aella felt sad. Why? Every time she looked at Fox, her heart felt as if it would tear out of her chest. *May I stay in touch with you as I work with this site?* she asked.

Of course. Fox wanted nothing more than to be here with her. To absorb her ephemeral beauty and hear her speak once more.

Aella's spirit lifted. What *was* this strange connection between them? Her curiosity was strong, but she had more pressing matters. In the next few days, Aella knew her life would change forever. How, she had no idea....

Look for REUNION
by USA TODAY *bestselling author*
Lindsay McKenna,
available April 2010,
only from Silhouette® Nocturne™.

ROMANCE, RIVALRY
AND A FAMILY REUNITED

THE BRIDES
of
BELLA ROSA

William Valentine and his beloved wife, Lucia, live
a beautiful life together, but when his former love Rosa
and the secret family they had together resurface,
an instant rivalry is formed. Can these families
get through the past and come together as one?

―――――――――――――

Step into the world of Bella Rosa
beginning this April with

Beauty and the Reclusive Prince
by

RAYE MORGAN

Eight volumes to collect and treasure!

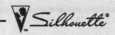

SPECIAL EDITION

INTRODUCING A BRAND-NEW MINISERIES FROM *USA TODAY* BESTSELLING AUTHOR

KASEY MICHAELS

SECOND-CHANCE BRIDAL

At twenty-eight, widowed single mother Elizabeth Carstairs thinks she's left love behind forever....until she meets Will Hollingsbrook. Her sons' new baseball coach is the handsomest man she's ever seen—and the more time they spend together, the more undeniable the connection between them. But can Elizabeth leave the past behind and open her heart to a second chance at love?

FIND OUT IN

SUDDENLY A BRIDE

*Available in April
wherever books are sold.*

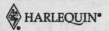

REQUEST YOUR FREE BOOKS!

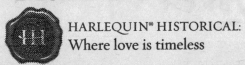

HARLEQUIN® HISTORICAL:
Where love is timeless

2 FREE NOVELS PLUS 2 **FREE GIFTS!**

YES! Please send me 2 FREE Harlequin® Historical novels and my 2 FREE gifts (gifts are worth about $10). After receiving them, if I don't wish to receive any more books, I can return the shipping statement marked "cancel." If I don't cancel, I will receive 6 brand-new novels every month and be billed just $4.94 per book in the U.S. or $5.49 per book in Canada. That's a saving of 20% off the cover price! It's quite a bargain! Shipping and handling is just 50¢ per book in the U.S. and 75¢ per book in Canada.* I understand that accepting the 2 free books and gifts places me under no obligation to buy anything. I can always return a shipment and cancel at any time. Even if I never buy another book from Harlequin, the two free books and gifts are mine to keep forever.

246 HDN E4DN   349 HDN E4DY

Name _____ (PLEASE PRINT) _____

Address _____ Apt. # _____

City _____ State/Prov. _____ Zip/Postal Code _____

Signature (if under 18, a parent or guardian must sign) _____

Mail to the **Harlequin Reader Service:**
IN U.S.A.: P.O. Box 1867, Buffalo, NY 14240-1867
IN CANADA: P.O. Box 609, Fort Erie, Ontario L2A 5X3

Not valid for current subscribers to Harlequin Historical books.

Want to try two free books from another line?
Call 1-800-873-8635 or visit www.morefreebooks.com.

* Terms and prices subject to change without notice. Prices do not include applicable taxes. N.Y. residents add applicable sales tax. Canadian residents will be charged applicable provincial taxes and GST. Offer not valid in Quebec. This offer is limited to one order per household. All orders subject to approval. Credit or debit balances in a customer's account(s) may be offset by any other outstanding balance owed by or to the customer. Please allow 4 to 6 weeks for delivery. Offer available while quantities last.

Your Privacy: Harlequin Books is committed to protecting your privacy. Our Privacy Policy is available online at www.eHarlequin.com or upon request from the Reader Service. From time to time we make our lists of customers available to reputable third parties who may have a product or service of interest to you. If you would prefer we not share your name and address, please check here. ☐

Help us get it right—We strive for accurate, respectful and relevant communications. To clarify or modify your communication preferences, visit us at www.ReaderService.com/consumerschoice.

HH10

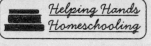